INKODED

INKOUNTER SERIES #1

Inkoded

Inkounter #1

Decorated detective Gibson Shaw must work an AI mutilation case that's beneath him. The claw-like wounds of the AI mimic its ownership tattoo of a cat, but he dismisses that as coincidence. When more AI bodies litter Nova City with the same modus operandi, Shaw must bring the world's first serial killer of AI to justice before the killer targets humans, all without falling for his rookie partner.

Tattoo artist Nate Dough has always sensed the sorrow in others. By using drug-laced ink to alter his clients' moods, he creates happiness one tatt at a time. Except, it's the clients' AI showing emotion. When he discovers the mutilated AI are ones he tatted, he's dragged into an investigation that reveals more about himself than he ever imagined.

It's only when Shaw and Dough's worlds collide that the clues point to the real culprit.

This is a work of fiction. The characters, incidents, and dialogues in this book are of the author's imagination and are not to be construed as real. Any resemblance to actual events or persons, living or dead, is completely coincidental.

Published by Sevannah Storm.

First Edition 2025

Copyright © 2025 - 2095 Sevannah Storm All rights reserved.

Cover Art by Sevannah Storm

This eBook is licensed for your personal enjoyment only. This eBook may not be re-sold or given away to other people. If you would like to share this book with another person, please purchase an additional copy for each recipient. If you're reading this book and did not purchase it, or it was not purchased for your enjoyment only, then please return to Smashwords.com or your favorite retailer and purchase your own copy. Thank you for respecting the hard work of this author.

https://sevannahstorm.com

Version_1

Also by Sevannah Storm

The Blood of Legends Series

The Huntress

The Healer

*

The Gifting Series

Soul Forged

Fate Forged

Sun Forged

War Forged

Star Forged

Shadow Forged

Earth Forged

Lust Forged

Fire Forged

Time Forged (Coming soon)

*

The Qaldreth Warriors

Sol Survivor

Dark Survivor (Coming soon)

*

The Space Hunter Chronicles

The Shikari

The Justisaar

*

Standalones

Xiaxan Fox

Ire of Silver

The Crucible of the Eternal

*

Plump Playwright Series

Plump Jane

Seducing Amelia

Loving Finley

Keeping Tessa

Kissing Navy

1

0/\/3

Date: 2170.10.10
Several kilometers below Nova City.

THE STENCH—SATURATED WITH DECAY, a miasma of rotting foods, and the dustiness of shifting smog—burned Gibs's throat the second he climbed out of the air-sterilized chaser. Grimacing at the mildew taste infesting his mouth, he flipped the mask in place. While rolling his shoulder in an erratic shrug, he activated his enhanced left eye, hoping to pierce the gray air blanketing the crime scene.

Standing amid a vortex of pollution was Martin Davis, hunched as he studied something in his hands. The dampened light glimmered off his receding hairline. His glasses flickered as he read information from the precinct's databases off the lenses.

Gibs tightened his coat around his crumpled uniform despite the wet heat dewing sweat on his brow. Stomping toward Davis, he scanned the eroded buildings, searching for unfriendlies. The Dead-zone denizens were unworthy of life above the pollution layers. Poor air, a rat diet, and dodging law enforcement meant a good life was impossible for them. They scavenged what fell from the upper levels, arming themselves with discarded weapons of various ages. Gibs had recharged the blaster strapped to his thigh, and if that didn't work as new tech was known to do, he kept an antique Glock holstered to his side.

"Detective Gibson Shaw, what the frack?" Davis spat something onto the sponge-like ground covered in decades of rotting litter.

Gibs gritted his teeth. He would have to incinerate his boots after this. Who knew what disease still lingered in the moist mass beneath him?

Davis deactivated his lenses and peered through the clear glass at him. "Didn't expect to see you here."

"Who reported this?" Gibs stiffened then slid his fingers around the grip of the blaster.

In the shadows surrounding the crime scene, faces appeared then faded. He wasn't up for a shoot-out today, not when they surrounded him with unknown firepower.

"Anonymous." Davis pursed his lips, flicking a glance at the shadows. "Relax, they won't touch this no matter how much they can sell it for."

Gibs released his grip and exhaled, easing the tension in his shoulders. "What do you have?"

He tugged on sterilized gloves as he approached the demarcated area. Neon lights scanned and verified his credentials when he stepped through the holographic bands. If the precinct hadn't granted him access, the bands would have tasered him.

"I've never seen the like." Davis was the dinosaur of the forensics department, preferring a solo existence in the abandoned bowels of Nova. His knowledge was invaluable hence his delayed retirement, and for that, the Force showed him respect. "It, or she, is missing an eye and its recordings." He tapped his left eye, his bushy gray eyebrow twitching. "Whoever took their frustrations out on the inkjob didn't want us to identify them."

Sprawled in an unnatural pose, as if it had plummeted from above, lay the remnants of an AI in the guise of a young woman. It was nude except for the various encoded ownership tatts covering its limbs. The 'wounds' were serrated as if a wild animal had raked its claws across the eternally youthful skin, and its inner mechanical workings were spewed out in a tangled mess.

Its hair splayed out like it was underwater. Images flashed in Gibs's mind: a young boy, swirling hair, lifeless eyes.

Shaking his head, he crouched beside the tattooed synthetic known as an inkjob. "Destruction of private property still applies."

Green lubricant oozed from the tubes spilling from its abdomen. No expression crossed its face, not in life nor death, and neither did he expect emotion from a machine. There was something artistic about the pose, though, as if someone had taken the time to arrange the limbs with care. This wasn't a crime of passion—this was premeditated, but for what purpose? Perhaps the vandal killer practiced before he targeted humans?

Gibs frowned, tempted to rub his jaw in deep thought as he worked through the possibilities. He stiffened his fingers, pulling his gloves tight. After he sterilized himself, he would ponder the whys and hows.

"The owner reported it missing hours ago. If it wasn't for its older encoded tatts, I wouldn't have identified it." Davis flipped his stylus to gesture to the shredded, palm-sized tatt of a cat. "That's the current owner's stamp. The embedded data is unreadable."

"Personal vendetta?" Gibs mused aloud, not veering his focus from the tatt. It was familiar though he couldn't place it. "It would explain the removed video footage and the crime itself. The inkjob didn't fight back, which meant its owner wasn't present or in danger."

"Or they commanded it not to defend itself." Davis shrugged.

"Frack. Summoned here for this?" Gibs huffed and rose to his full height, stretching his old knees. "I don't do mutilations or anything to do with synthetics." He hadn't pissed off any gods or politicians, just one woman, who had shacked up with his boss—his now ex-wife, Tamara. "Any clues?"

Whatever Davis gave him, he would start there. Whoever had attacked and mutilated a defenseless synthetic had to hate the owner.

"Thomas Walker, son of Senator Walker," Davis said, his tone dismissive as if who the inkjob belonged to didn't matter.

"Frack," Gibs muttered, now placing the cat-like tatt.

The Walkers had more than the usual number of enemies. And he would have to change his clothes. No way would their butler let him in with the stench of Deadzone Nova clinging to him.

Dealing with the rich worsened his mood. Notorious for their disrespect of the law, their disregard for possessions, and their political clout twitched pain behind his left eye. That little shit Thomas must have given permission for someone to ravage his inkjob out of boredom or an artistic display of overindulgence. Gibs shook his head. Both sounded unlikely. Thomas wouldn't report it missing unless for the insurance.

"There was a partial footprint in its lube which I managed to scan before the litter absorbed it. I've got no fingerprints, and I can't see for shit to find hair or skin flakes, not even with my upgraded bionics.

There is evidence of sexual activity. I took a sample for DNA analysis." Davis dropped to his haunches to snap his tool kit shut. "I got the drones doing a multi-dimensional scan. I'm hoping for residual heat signatures, and there's an abandoned yet active sec-cam. I'll send you the vids of that. I tasked the department's inkjobs to search for the murder weapon." Davis chuckled. "I sure as hell don't think we have a wild animal roaming these streets."

He shuffled closer, and in the humidity of the fog, Gibs fought to remain immobile. With Davis's body heat and potent odor consuming what oxygen remained, claustrophobia pressed down on him. Squeezing his eyes shut, he drew in slow, calming breaths and circled the inkjob, hoping to gain some distance and a pocket of untainted air.

"Tech's on the way. They'll check the inkjob further before sending it to Renovare for incineration." Davis crouched to brush a blonde curl off the inkjob's temple. "It's a pity. It's a beaut—one of the deluxe entertainment models."

"The Walkers can afford to splurge." Gibs tugged off his biodegradable gloves and tossed them onto the littered ground. "Let me know if you find anything else." He strode to his chaser hovering twenty meters away. As he approached, the door opened. He climbed in and ripped off his mask to suck in gulps of purified air.

"Welcome, Detective Gibson Shaw," the automated driver said in a calm feminine voice.

"Deep cleanse and home." He deactivated his enhanced eye and rubbed it.

Air gushed around him, cooling the sweat on his brow and stripping some of the stench saturating his coat. The doors sealed, and the chaser climbed the kilometers to the present surface. Old neon signs and flickering three-dimensional faces appeared through the swirling fog, as abandoned as the streets below. Light pollution dimmed the night sky, but he didn't care that the view wasn't perfect. The sight eased his tension, and he released the death grip he had on his knees.

Other vehicles sped past, using designated, well-lit pathways. His chaser slipped into traffic and headed for his small apartment border-ing the shitty side of Nova. He couldn't afford anything else after the divorce. At least, a bottle of cheap vodka waited for him. Just thinking about it had him salivating.

Bile pooled at the back of his throat, and he coughed, tasting fresh mildew. Frack, he hated the Deadzone and rookie cases. His furious glare reflected off the panoramic windows. For a moment, he didn't recognize himself. A week-old stubble darkened his jaw. Shadows un-der his eyes screamed his insomnia. He ran a hand over his face as if it would alter the years wrinkling his eyes and mouth.

"Call ahead and schedule an appointment with Thomas K. Walk-er."

A few seconds later, the auto-driver said, "Appointment scheduled for 1800 hours."

Gibs grunted and shifted in the seat, searching for a comfortable position. He didn't need to command his chaser to wake him. It would do so out of protocol. Folding his arms across his chest, he closed his eyes, hoping the circulating air would lull him to sleep.

He rubbed his neck, hoping to massage away the headache forming and ease the tick in his eye. Questions swirled, blurred, reformed until he drew in a long breath. Perhaps this case was just what he needed.

Date: 2170.10.10
Nova's Blue Sector AKA "The Holies"
Nate

NATE CLIMBED OUT OF the taxi, swiping his wrist to pay. He stepped onto the metallic platform jutting out from The Skin Canvas, his small tattoo parlor. Wind whipped his hair across his face, and he sighed as the warmth burned his temple. Whining chasers darted past, their anti-gravitational engines whirring as they dropped off their fares.

A glance at the level below showed various shops opening for the day, and beneath that, thick fog swirled in a haunting pattern. Despite the railings, people still fell off as if they offered their idiotic selves to a faceless god. Nova's mayor gave his assurances that there were safety nets to catch the unlucky. No one had traveled below to confirm this.

The front door chimed as Nate entered. He readied a smile for his receptionist, Lissa. Two owners and their modelesque inkjobs waited for him. One was a housewife who stroked the inkjob's angular jaw and broad shoulders, her lustful gaze implying the poor synthetic would be used for more than housework. Almost humanlike, Nate could see the appeal. Loneliness drove people to do desperate things, and in this case, fucking a synthetic. He'd never been tempted, but then again, he'd never been lonely enough to consider it.

Fighting to keep the smile in place, he nodded a greeting without meeting his clients' curious stares and slipped into the back room. How he longed for a job where he could test his artistic mettle.

After he draped his jacket over the back of his chair, he pulled the synthetic identification kiosk closer. He couldn't complain. He shouldn't. Tatting inkjobs with their ownerships kept The Skin Canvas afloat, and it *was* Half-Price Wednesday, so he was bound to be overwhelmed by midday.

"We have a lovely couple wanting joint tatts." Lissa giggled, placing a fresh cup of coffee-flavored sludge on his side table—she made it strong enough to resurrect the dead. Brown curls bobbed, echoing her merriment as did the swaying of bright-yellow hoop earrings and a matching summer dress.

Nate shook his head and smirked at her words. "Married?" He pinned his hair into a bun, tugged up his sleeves, exposing his ink-stained forearms, and gestured to her to escort them in.

"Just this morning," she said before skipping from the room to usher them in.

Nate had known Lissa for years, but what mattered the most was her bubbly personality. He had never seen her sorrowful. No shadows lingered around her, with nothing triggering his unusual gift.

Last night, he had *seen* Kylie's mood the moment he stepped through his front door. As much as he adored his wife, he hated it when she was sad, with darkness engulfing her figure and blurring her sweet smile.

As a Rights-4-Synthetics advocate, what she dealt with daily would scare the hell out of him. Inkjob abuse formed a large portion of her struggles since no laws prevented the destruction of one's own property. Thankfully, the government had denied Renovare permission to manufacture child synthetics. His home life would have been in constant darkness, with her mood swinging from light thunderstorms to full-on hurricane-mode.

"Nate, Mr. and Mrs. Collins," Lissa said, a bright smile breaking across her plump features. She was a romantic at heart, and her enthusiasm spilled over anyone in her vicinity. He loved that about her.

The diminutive man escorted his *wife* with a courteous hand on her back. Pale hair fell across his face and glasses, and an unavoidable smile warped his cheeks. He was happy now, but regrets had a way of sneaking in. His entertainment-model wife had various tatts screaming her history. She was well-*loved,* having known many owners.

Mr. Collins guided her into the chair and scanned his wrist across the kiosk. A stylized woodpecker appeared. Each client chose from the available tatts when they purchased the rights to own a synthetic. Exchanging or selling models without tatting and notifying Renovare was a chargeable offense and included the possibility of a lifetime synthetic ban. That law kept Nate in business.

"Where would you like the tatt placed, Mr. Collins?" Nate gestured to the inkjob, who sat stiff as a board, staring at the wall behind him.

"On Viv's left wrist, please," he said, turning the AI's arm with a gentle touch.

Within moments, Nate had the encoded tatt printed and branded into *Viv's* skin. With Mr. Collins, he traced the pattern and inked it on the corresponding spot to his wife's, but he used The Skin Canvas's patented drug-laced ink. His client would experience a gentle euphoria for two days, keeping buyer's remorse and thoughts of divorce at bay for a little while longer.

"Weren't they adorable?" Lissa lingered in the doorway.

Nate pasted on a smile, hiding his boredom as the 'happy' couple left. For a moment, a darkness hovered above Viv's auburn curls. He blinked, a frown forming as he studied her departing figure. Shaking his head in disbelief, he gestured to Lissa to usher in the next client. While he waited, he squeezed his eyes shut, pinched his brow, and prayed he'd imagined it.

No way was an AI sorrowful. They didn't have emotions.

But he had seen the darkness, and it wasn't near her husband.

Nate's ink had made sure of that.

2

7VVØ

Date: 2170.10.10
Nova's Lux Sector

THE INKJOB OPENING THE front door was a first edition, with repair marks scouring whatever skin its butler uniform didn't cover. Only one ownership tatt peeked out from under the collar—a falcon. Gibs knew better than to force his way into the mansion, badge or not, especially after the last time Butler had tossed him out on his ass. The landing platform was larger than normal but still without a railing. Thankfully, Gibs hadn't tumbled off the side and into the abyss.

He grimaced at the image of himself sprawled in the compacted litter beneath Nova. Recognizable amid the bits of him smeared and saturating the ground would be his cybernetic eyes and carbon-printed femur. He'd look worse than the inkjob they found this morning.

"Detective Gibson Shaw." Butler stepped aside with such gravitas that Gibs expected it to sweep an arm out in welcome.

The foyer hadn't changed since his last visit. White marble and bronze met imported wood, reminiscent of a hotel in the 2020s. Not the look Gibs would have gone with.

"Well, well, it's been a while!" Lawrence Walker strode into the ostentatious foyer, offering his hand in greeting. His crisp suit in steel gray whispered as he moved.

Gibs stared at the hand but didn't accept it. Doing so would mean all was forgiven, and that wasn't the case. He scowled, placing the blame for Dad's mental state on this Walker, and rightly so. Lawrence had aged well. Fine wine and old money had minimized the toll of living. Dad had never looked this good, especially with a blaster hole through his temple.

Best friends since kindergarten, Dad and Lawrence had supported each other through the rollercoaster of life. Lawrence had been there when Gibs's paternal grandmother had died, and Dad had fallen into a morass of sorrow. Hoping to keep him busy, Lawrence had used his influence to assign Dad to the most controversial case in the precinct—the kidnapping of a diplomat's daughter.

Finding her tortured body—very much like the inkjob's this morning—was more than Dad could take. He'd found his absolution in whisky and a fully charged blaster.

Gibs leveled a glare at the man, resenting the role he'd played, no matter his good intentions. The cut of Lawrence's gray hair was sharp and stylish. Gibs scrubbed his unshaven jaw.

Pulling his hand back, Lawrence shoved up his tailored sleeves and gestured to his home. "What brings you here?"

"Thomas Walker's mutilated inkjob." Gibs studied Lawrence's facial cues. There was no reaction like looking at a tranquil lake with no ripples visible from above or beneath the surface. "We found the X10 entertainment model this morning."

Lawrence dismissed his words with a brief pout and a furrowed brow. "How's this your problem?"

"I'm doing Montgomery a favor." Gibs smothered a snort at the lie.

Doing his captain a favor? By not quitting? By not freeing Montgomery from the tight grip Tamara had on his balls? The poor bastard would learn soon enough. Or maybe, the ass liked Tamara's kinks. Gibs hadn't and saw it as a depravity of something intimate. Doggy style was as wild as he went.

"This way, Detective Gibson Shaw." Butler's baritone had a metallic twang, indicative of its age. The vintage inkjob opened a door leading off the foyer.

One glimpse painted the image of an extravagant, well-stocked library. Books lined the walls. They were antiques, made invaluable since the traditional publishing and printing industries collapsed a century ago.

As the door sealed Gibs in the dusty silence, he traced the spines of a row of stacked erotica—if he judged them by the bare-chested bodybuilders clasping distressed damsels.

"Gibs, this is a wonderful surprise." Thomas bounded into the library with his usual boisterousness, dressed in pale camel slacks and a periwinkle-blue buttoned shirt. Gleaming of wealth and prestige, his champagne-gold hair flopped across his tanned forehead with perfect nonchalance.

In his crisp uniform, unshaven jaw, and unwashed hair, Gibs felt like an unkempt intruder... Inferior, but this wasn't on Thomas, who'd never treated the Shaws as anything other than family. Gibs scowled, needing this meeting to end soon. It was too much of a trip down memory lane for him, one he hadn't asked for and didn't appreciate.

"This is business."

Thomas's demeanor didn't mimic Lawrence's poker face. He'd never been one to hide his emotions. "You found her?"

"If by her, you mean, your missing inkjob, then yes."

Thomas scanned the room as if searching for her, the hope on his face sincere. He'd worn the same expression every Christmas.

Realizing she wasn't with Gibs, his shoulders stiffened as if Gibs kept her hostage in the back of his chaser. "Where is she?" He clipped his words. Anger and desperation peeled through his pseudo-serenity.

"At Renovare awaiting incineration. Expect a call from their sales department." Gibs didn't pull his punches. He needed to see honest reactions with nothing masked by civility.

Thomas winced. He squeezed his eyes shut and pinched the bridge of his nose, his breathing irregular. "She's dead?"

Gibs pursed his lips at Thomas's word choice. Dead? As in not living? Yes, all inkjobs were. He twisted his forearm and activated his holo-wrist. Holographics reflected off his skin, showing the law enforcement's details of Thomas standing before him. He pressed the record button.

"This recording is for quality purposes and can be used against you in a court of law." He felt like an idiot speaking into his arm, but the department had rejected his request for an old-school cell phone.

"You've got to be kidding me," Thomas grumbled under his breath as he paced the length of the Persian carpet.

"Mr. Thomas K. Walker, do you agree to this recording?" Gibs waited and watched. To say no might mean Thomas had something to hide. He hoped his old friend agreed. This interview need not be a difficult one.

"Yes, I waive my rights. Just tell me, what happened to Olivia?"

Gibs arched a brow. He'd heard of nutjobs marrying their inkjobs or forming a romantic attachment, but he never expected a Walker to fall into either category.

"For the record, let it be known that Olivia is the X10 entertainment model found in Deadzone this morning."

Thomas stopped pacing to grip Gibs's biceps. "Do they have to incinerate her, Gibs? How bad is it?"

Pain he recognized—that of a broken heart—crawled across Thomas's face. What was this? Was he grieving? No. Not Thomas: the charmer, playboy, and renowned philanthropist.

"Your ownership tatt was barely discernible." Gibs didn't offer further details. He doubted his old friend could handle it in the condition he was in.

Thomas's shoulders slumped, and he stumbled back, collapsing into the bulky faux-leather couch, a sob escaping him as he dropped his head into his hands.

"When last was she off her charge?"

"At the mayor's ball last night." Thomas's fingers muffled his words, but he lowered his hands before Gibs could ask him to. "I took her as my date."

Gibs's brow hitched another notch. "What? No scatterbrained debutantes available?" He forced a teasing tone into his voice, hoping to calm his overly emotional ex-friend and prime suspect. There had always been a long string of idiots lapping up Thomas's superficial sincerity and short-spanned interest.

Come to think of it, Tamara had been one of them. She must have taken one look at the queue of eager women, and instead, targeted Gibs, his best friend. He was a fool not to have seen through her conniving tactics.

"You know how small our circles are, Gibs. I've dated all the debutantes in Nova. Olivia was a refreshing change." He flashed his old smile before letting it dissolve with a tremor. "When we returned last night, we made love, then I instructed her to recharge."

Made love? Gibs grimaced. No one made love to a sex toy, but it meant the DNA would point to Thomas. There went that lead. He'd hoped the vandal had used the inkjob before mutilating it. Still possible. There could be more than one deposit. He'd call Davis later.

"I don't know what Renovare has been doing, Gibs, but she's so lifelike. Her voice soft, enticing, and natural. I feel..." His cheeks trembled. "...*Felt* a connection as if she understood me and reciprocated my affections."

Thomas leaped up, shaking his wrist to call up an email on his holographics. "There, I asked for Renovare to install a charging station in my bed so we could sleep together." He shoved his forearm in Gibs's face, too close for him to read the glowing letters.

Gibs smothered a chuckle, fighting for professionalism. Had Thomas fallen in love with his sex toy? Perhaps he should invest in one, especially if she gave good head.

He dismissed the fleeting temptation as foolhardy. Sticking any part of his body inside a machine horrified him, no matter how enticingly feminine they looked on the outside. What if it clamped its jaw and severed his dick? He shuddered, revulsion and fear sliding down his spine like a rivulet of ice.

"This morning when I awoke for my usual...treat, she wasn't beside me."

"Treat?" Gibs gestured to his wrist, reminding Thomas he was being recorded.

"Blowjob—she's rather good at it. But she wasn't here or in her other station. Butler has no recollection of visitors or intruders, nor does the security surveillance show any unusual movements. There should be something of her leaving the station or house. Or someone breaking in to take her."

"Since she managed to leave, the footage had to be tampered with. I'll need a copy," Gibs said.

"Of course, whatever you need." Thomas punched commands into his holo-wrist. He chewed on his lip, hesitant to speak. Gibs had never seen his self-confidence this affected.

"Can you tell me what happened to her...when you find out?"

Gibs nodded, but for the benefit of the recording, he said, "No. The investigation security protocol is tight. You'll know when I solve and close the case." He dropped his hand on Thomas's shoulder and gave it an awkward squeeze.

Thomas leaned closer to Gibs's wrist. "Yes, of course." He pulled back and mouthed 'thank you,' then hurried to fill the silence. "Solve it first. I'll wait to hear your findings." He flashed Gibs a relieved smile.

"Interview concluded." Gibs tapped the red square, ending the recording. "I suggest you go for a psyche analysis."

Thomas stiffened at the implication that he'd lost his mind.

"Hear me out. It's only a matter of time before the media blows this out of proportion. Go for the assessment to prove your sanity. Prove you weren't drugged or hypnotized."

Thomas grimaced. "You're right to suggest it, Gibs. The Rights-4-Synths activists have been vocal and violent lately." He chewed on his lip again before saying, "Sorry about your dad."

"Thanks for attending his memorial." Gibs forced those words past clenched teeth.

The change of subject to something personal startled him, and he hadn't prepared his responses. Despite the manner of his father's death, many had attended and offered their respects. Thomas had stood beside Gibs in silence, sharing his strength. Without it, Gibs didn't think he'd have made it through the day.

"He was a good man, Gibs." Thomas grabbed a book off the shelf and pressed it to Gibs's chest. "This was Olivia's favorite. Take it. Read it."

"Inkjobs read?" Gibs couldn't keep the incredulity out of his voice.

"She said that she'd read it electronically, but it wasn't the same as the printed version."

With the ancient book clasped in his meaty fist, Gibs left the library. His mind spun, dazed, alarmed. He released a shuddering breath, fighting for something to ground him. Could Thomas have lost his fracken mind?

"Butler, show me the X10's charging station."

In a narrow closet, the nodules and power cords of an inkjob were mounted to the back wall. A small alcove in the sidewall held a few books, proving she read for *pleasure*. The concept was so surreal—like his toaster painted landscapes because it *enjoyed* the hobby. Two primary cables as thick as his arm snagged his attention—one for power and the other a data extension. He assumed Renovare scanned their products for diagnostics, but what if they downloaded video footage, as well?

"The security surveillance." Butler offered the data crystal on a silver tray.

With the memory device in hand, Gibs strode out of the Walker residence with more questions than answers. Something heavy pressed down on his soul, dampening his emotions. With agonizing spasms in his stomach a possible prelude to an ulcer, his whole world tilted on its axis.

3

7#|233

Date: 2170.11.10
Nova's Blue Sector AKA 'The Holies'
The Skin Canvas

NATE SLAMMED THE DOOR behind him, too high-strung to care that he startled his waiting clients. One glance soured his mood further. More inkjobs needing encoded tatts. He dropped his tablet onto the counter and shrugged his jacket off, cursing the rain that had drenched him between taxi and front door.

"Whoops, bad morning?" The mischief curling Lissa's lips twitched Nate's.

Drawing in a deep breath, he allowed his foul mood to fizzle out. "Bad everything."

She wiped away the misery of the previous night just by being herself. He splayed his fingers on his chest, fighting the urge to hug her, but he held back, not willing to cross that boundary—one that blurred each day Kylie spiraled out of control.

"Well, you have two inkjobs then a long session—Mr. Dilbert's dragon." Lissa dipped her head to read off the console before looking at Nate. Sunlight kissed her brown curls and picked out bronze flecks.

His heart leaped, skittering excitement along his skin and brightening his day. He stared at her upturned face, admiring the splatter of freckles across her nose. Facing the reception, he searched for a distraction to ground him. Despite the hell Kylie was dragging him through, he loved her. A dalliance with Lissa would ruin his work life and their robust friendship, never mind his marriage *when* Kylie found out. He wasn't foolish enough to believe he could hide it from her.

He studied the inkjobs and smiled. None of them had dark clouds hovering around their heads. Their owners' emotions were borderline depressed, with thunderous puffs of emotions swirling and fading as normal. If he tattooed any of them, he'd slip a little chemical happiness into their ink—a sort of cheer-up gift. Yesterday's anomaly with Mrs. Olivia Collins had to be a fluke. He chalked it up to an overactive imagination rather than face the possibility of sentient AI Instead of sharing the incident with Kylie, he might discuss it with Lissa. She wouldn't blow it out of proportion or read implausible conspiracy theories behind the discovery. Regardless of who he told, he needed to share his possible descent into madness with somebody.

Grabbing his jacket and tablet, he disappeared into his backroom to start the day. Lissa ushered in his first inkjob along with the usual steaming cup of caffeinated sludge—her idea of coffee. The morning flew by with Max Dilbert's arrival the highlight. To thwart a midlife crisis, the man had decided on a tattoo of a coiled dragon curling around his shoulder. Nate hadn't complained—the chance to allow his creativity free rein was a godsend.

Max was a reclusive man, preferring the company of his thoughts to mindless chatter. The soft buzz of the tattoo gun kept Nate energized, but it didn't calm his mind, granting it the freedom to imagine scenarios where inkjobs rebelled, slaughtered humans, and forced them underground. He snorted, the sound deafening in the quiet parlor.

Only owners knew of the safe code, chosen by them as a last resort, with the knowledge that it would destroy the product, severing the connection between the inkjob's spine and brain. There was an additional kill code Renovare issued to synth units in law enforcement, empowering them to place human lives above synthetics in case the safe code failed.

After the four-hour session, Lissa skipped into the back room, carrying a toasted faux-cheese sandwich. She bounced on her toes, her fingers twitching.

"Out with it." He chuckled before he bit into the sandwich.

"The law's in a panic. They found a broken inkjob in Deadzone."

He scowled. There went his evening. This news would bolster Kylie's ranting. "So, why are you so fidgety?"

She sighed, her smile missing, but still, no cloud formed around her. "The latest ownership tatt was one you did."

He paused, halting the sandwich halfway to his mouth. "Frack." Though, why that might bring the law down upon him, he wasn't sure, but her tone implied she feared as much.

"Rick said they couldn't identify it at first."

Had it been the media, Nate might have dismissed it as rumor, but despite Rick being Lissa's ex-boyfriend, he was also a 'Cent'—which meant anyone working at Nova's Law Enforcement Center.

"Did he mention a possible visit from the law?" Not that Nate had anything to hide, but such visits were never pleasant. He shoved the last bite of the sandwich into his mouth and leaned back in his chair, wiped his fingers on his jeans, then tugged his tablet closer.

"Nope, but he was super excited. The vandalism was the worst they'd seen. The captain put an experienced detective on the case. I can't shake the feeling they're treating it like a homicide." She stretched over his shoulder, her lavender scent tantalizing as she swiped his sketch to the right, loading another.

She paused on an elaborate design he was toying with—entwining flowers, blossoms overexaggerated with fluttering tiny fairies, their adorable faces in exquisite detail. He imagined it wrapping around a woman's torso, from hip to underarm, curling petals under a breast and along a shoulder blade.

He shifted in his chair, the heat of Lissa warming his back, her hair tickling his ear. It took all his focus to remain relaxed, to not drag her onto his lap for a kiss. He switched his attention to her soft, pale peach lips. *What the frack is wrong with me?* When he didn't think he could bear another excruciating minute, she traced a fingertip across a fairy's delicate wings.

"What do you think?" His voice came out hoarse, forcing him to clear his throat.

"It's stunning." She met his gaze, trapping him to the moment like a pinned butterfly. "Who's it for?"

This close, the burnt-gold flecks in her eyes glowed. He shook his head. "No one."

"Could you do me?"

He sucked in a sharp breath but didn't look away. Scanning her face, he searched for hidden meaning in her words. Her expression remained innocent, her request sincere.

"It's a six-hour session." He followed the gentle curve of her neck to the unblemished skin of her modest cleavage. Her rainbow-colored hippy dress hid her curves. He expelled a relieved sigh. Had she shown more of her figure, he might have succumbed. And doing so would cost him his marriage and his friendship with Lissa.

"When you have time?" She arched a brown eyebrow. Her chocolate eyes warmed as a sensual smile dawned across her face.

He nodded, desperate for space to breathe.

She squealed, danced around the room, and blessed him with sneak peeks of her dainty ankles as she swirled her skirts. He grinned, basking in her contagious youthful joy while shifting his tablet over his lap to hide the evidence of his misplaced interest.

"So why so angry? What did Kylie do?" Lissa flopped onto her chair, pinning him again with a look.

"She's struggling to finalize the mayor's vote. Between work and Rights-4-Synths meetings, yesterday was another frustrating day for her."

Despite her busy schedule, she made sure she was always home before him. He used to love that, knowing she waited for him. Now he dreaded seeing her and having to endure her mood swings.

Married for four years, he'd often boasted that their honeymoon period was eternal. But that had crashed down around him. She'd replaced her attentiveness and affection with screeching and the smashing of objects, preferably glass. He was at a loss on how to handle it. Sex was less frequent, and when she initiated it, the act had taken on a desperate, violent tone. That's why Lissa's softness appealed to him so much.

Grabbing the hand clasping the tablet to his groin, she squeezed. "Just give her time and space, she's fighting so hard for what she believes in."

Trapped heat, like a helium balloon, swelled inside his chest and exploded, spilling its fire into his belly and lower. Lissa's defense and admiration of Kylie broke through the shadows of insomnia and doubt that fogged his mind.

"Thank you. I needed to hear that." He grinned and gestured to her hip and waist. "It's going to hurt, the tatt."

"You'll be as gentle as you can be, and that's all I need to know." She flicked her hand in a dismissive gesture, but instead of leaving him, she hesitated. "Yesterday, with Mr. Collins, you had a strange look on your face."

Nate jerked back, spread his thighs to ease the throbbing, and placed his tablet on the table. He wanted to tell her why, but now, given the chance, his stomach churned as sandwich and bile coated his tongue. He grimaced.

Drawing in a deep breath, he met her curiosity with a slow smile. "I saw...*something* over her head."

"Something..." Lissa scrunched her nose and studied the ceiling, deep in thought. "Are you sure? I mean, wasn't Mr. Collins standing near her?" She giggled, but it was a nervous sound. "Inkjobs aren't real—everyone knows that."

Nate stayed silent. He agreed with her, having had no prior encounters with emotional synthetics. She swallowed her laughter and patted his hand again. He flipped his and caught hers, lacing their fingers before she could pull away. He cupped their clasped hands with his other and peered into her chocolate eyes.

"I double-checked, Liss. You believe me, right?" For an unknown reason, or one he didn't want to unravel, he needed her unwavering faith.

"If you saw it, Nate..." She shrugged, flashing him a shy smile. "Perhaps something went wrong with her programming. Have you seen other strange clouds?"

"No." He released her hand and leaned back, using the heel of his palms to rub his stinging eyes. "A glitch—that was all I saw."

He laughed, relief bolstering the silliness of his suspicions. Telling her straight after he saw the cloud might have prevented the tension stiffening his shoulders and the visions of an impending revolution from haunting him.

The doorbell chimed, and she darted into the reception area with her usual smile and exuberance. He released a long sigh, proud of himself for resisting the temptation. A deep voice reached his ears, and he rose to investigate. There weren't any more appointments for the afternoon, and he'd considered heading to a local bar instead of home.

Ricky Sanchez loomed over Lissa, his stance predatorial, his smile warm against the darker hue of his skin. Nate frowned, not liking the Cent's assumption that Lissa was his. If that was the case, they wouldn't be on-again and off-again. Despite Rick's crisp law enforcement uniform accentuating parts of his youthful body, Nate didn't feel threatened. He was as well-toned and handsomer with his sun-streaked hair brushing his shoulders and indigo eyes. Lissa should look no further than Nate.

He stilled. *What the frack?*

Smothering a groan, he ran a hand over his face and forced a smile. "Thinking of taking our Lissa to dinner?" He wasn't on the market, and she wasn't interested, regardless. "Close early, Liss. I'll head to The Broken Faucet for a beer."

She hesitated, her gaze switching between him and Rick's eager face.

Nate allowed her reluctance to soothe his ego, but if Kylie meant anything to him, he needed time away from Lissa's tempting brown eyes.

It took all his control to let her leave. Whatever he was going through, he couldn't drag her into it. Texting Kylie that he was working late, he donned his jacket, grabbed his tablet, and headed for the bar, craving something stronger than beer.

4

|=0|_||2

Date: 2170.12.10

Nova's Red Sector AKA 'The Colony'

GIBS GRIPPED THE LIP of his cup with his fingertips, raising it to sip the black coffee. The bitter flavor coated his tongue, and he hummed in approval. He might not live in a safe neighborhood due to the debilitating divorce, but he sure as frack could afford real coffee imported from Ganymede.

His appointment at Renovare was at eleven before they opened their doors to clients at noon. He doubted he'd meet with Lord Fields, the original creator of inkjobs. The man would be too busy to see an aging detective over a few vandalized products. And no one wanted the media to catch word of the mutilated X10, not with the fanatics protesting that inkjobs had rights. *Idiots.*

With his feet dangling off the platform, he watched the sunrise, casting its revealing light across the city's horizon, unable to penetrate the lower levels. High up in Nova's Lux Sector, where Thomas lived, the smog didn't linger, preferring to drench Gibs's home in a hazy film. There was talk of the city installing air filters, but he'd be dead before that happened.

Savoring the last dregs of his morning ritual, he listened to the couple arguing in their cramped home next door. Somewhere someone practiced their scales on a violin, and two levels down, an elderly couple high on rage fucked like teenagers.

With a quick adjustment of the UV lamp, a little nutrient-rich water, and the stroking of the leaves, he tended to his potted grapevine climbing the wire trellis he'd built. The seedling was all he'd brought with him when he'd left home. The greenery was in stark contrast to the metal gray of the walls. He dug his fingers into the soil and sighed, cherishing the grittiness and the fragrance rising to tease him. Peace consumed his chest, and he smiled. When winter came, he'd have to prune it and the miniature rose bush beside it.

Like Jackson had taught him. Gibs often wondered what life might have been like had his brother lived. Memories decades-old resurfaced, and he thrust them aside, as ruthless as he could be. It had been an accident, but for him, he had to blame someone. It made no sense otherwise. But therein lay guilt, what-if scenarios, and the recycling of his failure.

Vowing to nap in the chaser later, he clambered to his feet. Time to head over to the spire piercing the skyline like hands palmed in prayer. Renovare's factory levels descended into the Deadzone, and they relocated the entrance each year as the pollution thickened and climbed.

Before tugging on his coat, he slid his Glock into its holster and strapped his blaster to his thigh. With a vigorous rub of his face to wipe away the last vestiges of insomnia, he stepped onto his platform and called his chaser from its storage beneath his home.

"Good morning, Detective Gibson Shaw." The pseudo-joy of the feminine voice grated on his nerves, and he gritted his teeth, unable to change the default without ridicule. "The department has postponed your appointment at Renovare."

"What?" With a grunt, he shifted in his seat, stretching out his legs.

The chaser tilted, its engines whirring as it climbed out of the haze and headed toward Lux. He tightened his grip on the armrests; the loss of control prickled his spine and settled onto his shoulders. Rolling them eased the tension.

"Officer Martin Davis expects your presence on the Promenade."

"What? That's impos—" Gibs clamped his mouth shut. He sounded like an idiot questioning his chaser, but Martin never ventured above the Deadzone, so this request made no sense. "Reveal chain of command."

"Accessing archives. One moment, please." The windows tinted, shielding him from the unfiltered sunlight. Across its glass surface flickered the data the chaser sifted through. "Sec-alerts at 245 this morning reported the discovery of a synthetic. At 315, the system assigned the case to you and rescheduled the Renovare appointment. The investigatory teams were finalized at 322. Notification of such issued at 429."

He hadn't received any message, but that didn't alarm him. His home was a Faraday cage, and tapping into the building's network cost extra. He slumped in his seat in disbelief. "Another synthetic discovered?"

"Please clarify the question."

He rolled his eyes toward the transparent roof of the chaser. "Estimated time of arrival?"

"ETA is in twenty-two minutes and forty-two seconds."

He groaned, dismissing a nap as an option in his agitated state. "Call Davis."

"One moment, please." The latest show-business news played as he waited for the call to connect, ramping his frustration. Who gave a shit what those arrogant actors got up to? He'd rather listen to the weather report. On the right flickered the latest designs in weaponry—personalized advertisements he'd usually browse.

"Davis." Stress rasped the older man's voice, adding a wheezing quality to it.

"Tell me what you know. Any feedback for...victim one?" Gibs hesitated. If they'd found an unidentified woman's body mutilated, she'd be named a Jane Doe. A 'murder' case on an inkjob left their terminology lacking.

"Gibs? I don't got time for you now." Chaos—screams, and barks of anger—smothered Davis's voice. "This's an epic shit-storm. Just get here, and for frack's sake, make it quick." He hung up. With what Gibs knew of Davis, he had to be resenting traveling this far from the Deadzone.

"Activate emergency procedures," he commanded the chaser.

"Acknowledged. New ETA is thirteen minutes and nineteen seconds." The chaser dropped, speeding along the unrestricted pathway reserved for emergency and maintenance personnel.

He squeezed his eyes shut. The flickering lights whizzing past added to his building headache. It throbbed in tune with his heartbeat. His nostrils flared while he sucked in sharp breaths. *Frack, I hate my life.*

"Incoming call from Captain Stanley Montgomery."

Case in point. "Great." Gibs drenched the word in sarcasm, but the chaser wasn't fluent and patched the bastard through without waiting.

"Shaw," Montgomery boomed. His voice reverberating through the small confines of the chaser lanced pain through Gibs's skull. He winced. "Your rookie, Huxley, will meet you at the crime scene."

"A rookie?" Gibs curled his lips in disgust. Montgomery knew damn well he wasn't the best babysitter. "Who's fracken idea was this?"

"It came from the top, Shaw. I don't ask questions."

Damn bastard. Too lazy to manage his department. Silence thickened the air, and with a grumble, Gibs shifted in his seat. Montgomery waited for him to overreact, to throw a tantrum, and for frack's sake, he wouldn't entertain him even though he wanted to roar his displeasure. Every damn rookie assigned to him had ended up shot in the line of duty, had quit the force, or had spent hours in psyche assessments. He didn't have the time to babysit another non-committed youngster with a case of the delicates. Most weren't cut out for this kind of job. That or the academy was sending them out soft and unprepared. Swallowing past the lump in his throat, he stiffened his shoulders and leaned forward as if proximity to the console determined the clarity of his voice.

"My thanks to the top." He clenched his jaw then forced himself to relax. "I need a fresh pair of eyes on this case." *More like a spy.* He wouldn't put it past Senator Walker to have complained to the mayor after Gibs's recent visit. "Anything else, Captain?"

Montgomery cleared his throat. "No, that will be all." The connection ended.

Gibs let loose a string of curses mostly filled with 'frack' and 'ass-hat.' The urge to punch something gripped him, and he shook with the effort to restrain it. Acting out against the chaser would go on his record. Montgomery would find out and know he'd hit home with this rookie ploy.

A fracken rookie? Bitter bile flooded his mouth, washing away the remnants of coffee still coating his tongue. The morning had gone to hell, and his day wasn't looking any shinier.

The chaser dipped, weaved, then rose again, re-joining the traffic but only for a short while. It climbed higher, twitching his brow into a frown. That's right. The crime scene was on the Promenade. He twisted his lips into a harsh smirk. The location may have been the vandal's first mistake. Security was tight in Lux and anywhere else the rich frequented. The Promenade—dedicated to shopping and extravagance—had tighter security than the mayor's mansion in the Holies.

People scrambled out of the way when the chaser landed. The crowds were thick, the clamor as loud as on Davis's call. What the frack? Why weren't the department's Sec2s on duty? Nothing held back onlookers like skinless, faceless inkjobs in titanium.

Gibs withdrew his blaster and fired into the decorated screed flooring, burning an arc around the crime scene. Screams and curses followed as people dove out of the way, but he ignored them.

Tapping his throat, he activated the projector implant—standard issue to all law enforcement. "Step over this line, and I'll shoot to kill. And for the love of life, shut the frack up."

He deactivated his projector and faced the crime scene. Murmurs rippled through the crowds. At least the din had died down. Shops out of an Italian village lined one side of the Promenade, their faded plaster done to perfection. It was quaint—clean and constructed with the finest materials.

"Shaw." Davis ran up to spike the floor with barrier pegs, tossing glares at him.

Gibs holstered his blaster when the banners sparked to life. He strode toward the stuttering holographic shop front. Parts of the translucent mesh remained in place. That wasn't what snagged his attention.

There, in a grotesque pose, was a crucified inkjob. Skewered through its torso were metal spikes forming the shape of a sun. On the polished white stone of the shop's floor lay a few circular drops of green lube. Shining in the morning light, the inkjob's drained innards wrapped around the spikes, as if embracing them. The left eye was missing, with a few connectors jutting out. The right eye stared at Gibs no matter where he stood. He searched the ownership tatts for a symbol of the sun somewhere on her naked frame. She was ancient, with one or two clear spots for new tatts remaining. It would take him ages to track down her owner.

"It didn't happen here," he said.

"I figured that out already," Davis grumbled, cursing Gibs under his breath but loud enough for him to hear.

"What's soured your mood?" Gibs didn't care to wait for a response. "Found anything about yesterday's...Jane Doe?"

"Eve Roe." Davis sniffed, twitching his nose. "No biological trace from the labs, nothing on the heat-signature scans either, which means the inkjob fell from a higher level."

Gibs jerked back. The body hadn't looked crushed; perhaps the padded floor of Deadzone had cushioned it. If Davis said someone pushed the inkjob, he must've verified his suspicions. "Anything to confirm which level or height?"

"I checked whether the spot was below Walker's residence. It wasn't. And I've already surveyed the level. It's abandoned, cordoned off by the city as hazardous. Scuffed dirt, a few trickles of lube, but nothing to indicate a struggle." Davis spat something brown, which landed an inch from Gibs's boot. "The footprint's a narrow seven—a small man or tall woman. My money's on neither. I think an inkjob did it, to be honest."

I-thinks led to incorrect conclusions. Gibs scowled, shuffling away from the brown glob and Davis's natural stench. "What else?"

"The DNA's Thomas Walker's."

As Gibs had expected. With a nod, he prowled around the inkjob. Its death resembled art, as had the Eve Roe from yesterday. It was beautifully done, the rods piercing the synthetic body like a fork through tofu cheesecake. No way would a human lie still for such mutilation. Did the inkjob feel pain? Looking at the pinned body had him wincing in empathy.

Something shimmered the holographic bands, catching his peripheral vision. His head shot up, and he gaped. A tall, long-limbed blonde—dressed in a gray pantsuit paired with a red blouse—fluttered her fingers in a wave. Pinned to her hip was a badge he recognized. *Frack. A woman?*

She flicked her hair to the side, and tendrils of spun gold caught a stray breeze. Shoving her hand at Davis, she blessed him with a bright smile that split her ruby lips and dazzled the poor man. Cupping her hand in his, he blinked at her.

Tonight, Gibs would curse Montgomery in the safety of his home. For now, he interrupted the pair, not wanting Davis to drool over the crime scene. "Huxley, get over here. Did you read the dossier en route, or do I need to walk you through the previous Eve Roe?"

"Roe? Like Richard Roe?" Her melodic voice scraped across Gibs's nerves, sending ice sliding down his spine.

He scowled, not appreciating his body's reaction to her rose scent and breathtaking smile.

"My idea." Davis flashed a lopsided and yellowed grin while he chewed around his tobacco.

"Only Eves, no Adams?" Huxley pursed her pretty lips, peering at the inkjob. No embarrassment stained her cheeks, nor did she show any signs of vomiting though the lack of green lube serving as the inkjob's blood might have saved her from that. Gibs took both as good signs.

"Your thoughts?" He schooled his features, smothering the urge to smirk. What could an untried female rookie add to this investigation? Woman's intuition? *Frack, no.* Montgomery had sent him a distraction to ensure he failed to solve this case.

"It wasn't done here, and they terminated the inkjob before piercing it with the first rod." Huxley twisted to tap the nape of her neck. "Like the first one, a dagger to the spine severed its spinal cord."

"What?" Davis gasped, his face mottling red. "I saw no such wound."

"The scans of the skeleton show the blade marks scouring the metal vertebrae. They sprayed it with new-skin, hiding the incision. But with this one, they were too impatient to wait for the skin to seal." She presented a fine ass in her pantsuit as she twisted around the inkjob.

Davis scurried to the back, standing on his toes to see better. "Frack. How did you—"

"The labs sent the results about ten minutes ago. Looks like we have the same modus operandi." She hesitated before patting Davis on the shoulder as if offering him comfort.

He tapped his inactive holo-wrist.

"Davis, you would've noticed it soon enough." Gibs scanned the surrounding shops. Hidden among the décor, cameras blinked like the many eyes of a fly. "What does the security reveal?"

"Static: nothing coming in, nothing going out." Davis gestured to the body. "It wouldn't surprise me if it has an electronic disruptor implant."

"Or the vandal carried one. If it's here, it's short-range, or the holo-bands wouldn't work." Gibs sighed. "Send the security footage to me. Anything else?"

"The cleanup crew will be here soon." Davis tapped his unresponsive holo-wrist again, scowling. "It's not like the Deadzone where a body could rot for days. I figured Montgomery would appreciate a decent show."

Gibs hadn't donned sterilized gloves, hadn't activated his enhanced vision since none of that mattered. This simple case wasn't so easy to solve. And with the second mutilated inkjob, the 'killer' was becoming a problem. What circled his mind was the suspicion that he was dealing with a serial delinquent, and the artistic poses conveyed a message he couldn't decipher. As he stared at the inkjob's corpse, he couldn't see what the point was. What did the perp hope to gain? Notoriety, money, revenge, or the furthering of a cause... Any of those would suit.

"I'll send you the owner's details as soon as I source it." Davis gestured to the rods. "A star, by the looks of it."

"Sunburst." Huxley crowded Gibs, forcing him to step away.

He didn't stop there but broke into a stride, heading for his chaser while expecting the rookie to follow. She did.

"Get in," he said, climbing into his chaser.

She rushed to the other side and slid in, all graceful limbs and sweet perfume.

"Welcome, Detective Gibson Shaw, Officer Naomi Huxley," the auto-driver intoned.

"Deep cleanse." Gibs drew in a shallow breath, not needing his new partner's feminine fragrance to cloud his mind. *Why the frack did it have to be roses?* "Inform Renovare of our ETA."

"Your appointment is set for 1800," the chaser said.

"Inform them of my impending arrival, and mention the second crime scene. One's a coincidence, but two in two days is odd."

"One moment, please."

Silence claimed the space between them. Gibs relaxed, a burst of gratitude burning through him. Huxley not being a nervous talker was a plus. Listening to inane chatter all day wasn't his idea of a pleasant working environment.

"Renovare expects your arrival." The chaser rose.

Gibs swiveled his seat to face his...partner. He folded his arms across his chest and activated his enhanced vision to monitor her temperature and pulse. Now for the important questions. "Who the frack are you, and who did you blow to land me as your partner?"

5

|=1V3

Date: 2170.12.10
The Holies
Renovare

GIBS'S JAW STILL STUNG, and his reflection in the metallic coffee table hinted at the bruise forming. Thrusting his gray-laced black hair off his temple, he blinked at his hazel eyes and his unshaven jaw. Laugh lines implied he'd once been happy in life. He twisted his lips in derision, drawing his gaze to the bruise.

He'd chosen the crudest words, pushing Huxley too far, but he needed to see what she was made of, to test her boundaries. Grudging admiration engulfed him in warm waves he dismissed with desperate bitterness. There was no finding his partner attractive—he wouldn't stand for it.

He sliced a glance at her. She held her back ramrod straight and had crossed her slender legs at the knees. Her pinched ruby lips announced her foul mood, and he'd caused it. One day, over a beer, he'd explain his reasoning. But he wouldn't apologize. Not when some sick frack toyed with his career, assigning a rookie to him. And if he had any money to spare after the divorce, he'd bet on his ex-wife playing wifey with his boss.

He glared at Huxley while fondling his aching jaw. She had a mean right hook.

"Lord Fields will see you now."

He jerked back, snapping his gaze away from his partner. The receptionist wore a bronze-colored suit sharp enough to draw blood. He jumped up, running a hand over his uniform, conscious of each wrinkle. Beside him, Huxley glowed with grace and vitality with her hands shoved into her pockets in nonchalance. Where she was golden, the Renovare receptionist was somber—midnight black hair, dark walnut skin, and coffee-colored eyes. Her beauty was striking, so he glared at her, too.

"Thank you." Huxley gestured to the woman to lead the way.

He made the same gesture to Huxley. It wasn't as if he had an attack of chivalry, having dragged his manners from antiquity. No, he needed to see her hands, anticipating another strike. Her fury festered, and if he was lucky, he'd make it home with just a tongue lashing.

"I am Ms. Anna Zeta, and I will escort you to Lord Field's office."

"He's meeting with us personally?"

Gibs hissed at Huxley for beating him to the punch. He wrapped his fingers around her wrist and tugged with as much gentleness as a pissed-off divorced male could muster. "Let me ask the questions, *rookie*."

Huxley stared at his grip, then raised her gaze to meet his. "Of course, Detective Shaw." Instead of stepping back and breaking his hold, she closed the distance between them, her breasts an inch from his chest. "Synth." She nudged her head at Ms. Zeta.

Not liking Huxley's rose scent tantalizing his nostrils, he released her wrist. Nor did he like the fall of her hair feathering across his shoulder. He shrugged off her tendrils as if they held magical powers, as if where they touched, they enchanted.

"This way, please."

Huxley faced the receptionist, then in a graceful move he hadn't anticipated, she slipped behind him. He grunted and trailed Ms. Zeta, a little dazzled by the golden light from the setting sun casting bright angles on the polished marble floor. Embedded in the pitch-black stone were flecks of gold, and it wouldn't surprise him if it was real gold. Millions of people slaved, starved, prostituted themselves to survive, and Lord Fields had gold embedded in his floor.

The ceiling was vast, filled with shadows and light. Gibs's first thought wasn't how majestic the architecture was. No, he wanted to know who dusted those corners. Architects often had grandiose opinions of themselves and erected buildings as monuments to their greatness. The same applied to spaceship architects—he had grown up on just one of those marvels where everything looked surreal and beautiful but wasn't functional.

Home. He hadn't seen his mother in years. Not that their relationship wasn't an amicable one. They tended to live separate lives, touching base every three years or so, or in Mom's case, making surprise visits when her hippie ship docked close enough to Earth. He was due for just such a visit. Grimacing, he sent up a quick prayer that she would descend after he solved this case.

Ms. Zeta led them into a glass pod that shot upward the moment the doors sealed. Level upon level whooshed past, filled with blurring glimpses of employees attending to their tasks. As the pod rose, the sky darkened, and hints of the night's stars peeked through the setting sun. They drew to a halt on a whisper, and the opening doors were as silent.

"I leave you here. Good day, Detective Gibson Shaw and Officer Naomi Huxley."

Gibs hesitated as he stepped onto more polished stone. Around him was glass, allowing the cityscape to dance its way into the office. The glass walls formed the ceiling in a pyramidal shape, yet the room remained cool. In the center sat a curved piece of metal he had to assume was a chair. The accompanied desk was a sheet of glass jutting out of the floor like a bent finger.

He spun in a circle, ignoring the splendid view and the finest materials used to construct this impressive display of wealth. Where was Lord Fields?

"Make yourself at home, Gibs, Naomi." A voice reverberated through the air, gentle but authoritative. Gibs refused to squat on the floor, not because he'd lost the knowledge or the memories of doing so, but because he doubted he could rise again once he was sprawled on his ass.

Two holes formed in the floor, and chairs rose, strategically placed in front of the glass desk. He hesitated even as Huxley draped her figure into one. It was like a trapdoor. One false word and Fields could pull a lever, casting him into the bowels of Renovare, never to be seen again. He was paranoid and proud of it.

"Two illegal terminations alarms me," the voice continued. "I have seen the footage and case files. What is your view on the perpetrator? Yesterday's could've been a once-off, and our products aren't strangers to abuse. But two?"

"This's more than senseless synthetic abuse. It's symbolic." Gibs crossed the vast office to stare out the glass windows, his hands clasped behind him. "The 'artist' is trying to convey something bothering them. There's a purpose to each 'kill,' planned with meticulous detail."

"They had to know the synth, had to choose one based on their ownership tatts."

Gibs met Huxley's gaze in the reflection then asked, "Does Renovare carry any video footage from these...victims?"

"No, we only archive unique memories from retired synths, never from operational ones. That's a violation of our customers' privacy and the Pancras Treaty."

Color bloomed across her cheeks, but it wasn't fury in her eyes. She glanced away, shifting on her glass chair as if she was uncomfortable. "Do you have archived footage from retired synths that used to belong to the victims' owners?"

Lord Fields chuckled. "Yes, that we do have. Ms. Zeta will grant you access."

Spinning, Gibs raised his face to the voice. "Who gave you my case files?"

"Ah, Gibs, I cannot reveal my sources. Regardless, I'm Lord Reginald Fields, owner of Renovare. If I wanted a snapshot of your ass, it would be on my desk by morning." The insufferable man laughed again. "Ms. Zeta will see you out."

The pod opened to Anna waiting inside for them.

Gibs grunted then nudged his head at Huxley. As she strode past him and into the pod, he raised his hand to her lower back like they were on a date. Aghast, he snatched it back, his nostrils flaring. No chivalric behavior. None. The air thickened with tension, but his rookie didn't glance at him, content to stand in serenity while gazing at the cityscape's lights flickering to life.

The pod stopped sooner than expected when archives were relegated to a disused basement and never to prime real estate above the fog. Ms. Zeta ushered them out. She glided down a narrow passage—all sharp angles and hidden blue lighting, pausing outside a solid metal door. Lights sputtered around its edges, and when she pressed her palm to a carved panel, the color switched from blue to white. The door clicked open.

Yellow light flooded the narrow passage, bathing Huxley in a warm glow.

"Detective Shaw."

He jerked and raised his stunned gaze to Ms. Zeta and a grinning Huxley. "What?"

"You did not answer me," Ms. Zeta said coolly. "This way, please."

Heat burst across his cheeks, but he nodded, meeting Huxley's arched brow with his. Zoning out didn't mean he was dreaming of her. He shook his head and flicked his fingers, urging her to hurry.

"This is one archive room among thousands. Here, I will channel the feeds you require. Since it is late, Lord Fields has suggested you return tomorrow. If you choose to remain at Renovare, I am to provide a meal of your choosing."

In these small confines with Huxley and her alluring scent? Gibs would need a night to mentally prepare himself. Besides, he had Promenade footage to review. Something in those sec-vids might line up with the archived memories.

"Tomorrow morning is fine."

"Very well." Ms. Zeta retreated and led them to the pod. Down they went, smooth and silky; the night sky was darker, yet he could count the freckles splattering Huxley's cheeks. When the pod whispered to a stop, the doors opened to another Ms. Zeta.

"Anna, please escort Detective Shaw and Officer Huxley to me first thing in the morning."

"Of course, Bree."

Nausea tore through his innards, and he struggled with the bile crawling up his throat. Twins? He shook his head, gripping Huxley by the elbow as he hurried her to his waiting chaser.

The moment the chaser sealed them in and intoned its usual greeting, Gibs commanded it to take Huxley home. With the Renovare building behind them, he spun his chair to face her. Golden hair curled over her shoulder, and she looked as pristine as this morning. He felt like a frump, with exhaustion slouching his shoulders.

"What the frack? Those were synths?"

"It shouldn't surprise us; after all, they're the product." She snuggled her backside deeper into her chair and leaned back. "The Zetas are impressive as an introduction to their deluxe range."

"I couldn't tell they weren't human," he grumbled. "State of the art and certainly not anything they currently sell."

"How would you know?" Huxley popped an eye open while her ruby lips curled in a sensual smirk.

"Research, rookie, especially considering Thomas Walker's infatuation. And before you assume the worst, I didn't fuck any of them."

She arched a knowing brow. "Just checking, *partner.*"

Silence filled the chaser, and he pinched his lips. His mother's nasal voice reprimanded him, and he found himself blurting out an apology. And without alcohol having passed his lips.

"Sorry for the blowjob remark. Just not used to...partners."

"Women." She kept her eyes closed as if the day had tested her, too.

"Huh?" He allowed his gaze to travel along the arch of her throat, the stubborn tilt to her jaw, and the ruby softness of her lips.

"You're not used to women." She opened her eyes and leveled a stare at him. Here it came, the tightening of her jaw the only warning. "I get it, you had to test me and will do so until we've solved this case. Once I'm reassigned, you'll write a scathing report, and our forced courtesy will fade into distant disdain."

The chaser touched down outside her apartment. He snuck a glance and grimaced. It was far better than he could afford, at least three levels above the smog.

She opened the door but hesitated. "Or you can let me show you my awesome blowjob skills, and we can enjoy this case with a little more friendliness."

Gasping, he froze as her suggestion stabbed him with a bolt of need, twitching his semi-erect cock. He shifted in his seat, but the play of the city lights caught the twinkle in her intense gaze.

A tidal wave of relief swept over him, and he grunted. "Touché, Huxley."

"Good night, Detective Shaw." The door closed on her husky chuckle, leaving him in strained agony.

Frack, he needed a whisky and a cold shower.

6

SIX

Date: 2170.12.10
The Colony
Gibs's apartment

GIBS SWIRLED THE BURNISHED liquid and swigged it back. The spicy, intense flavor coated his tongue as fire burned a path down his throat and warmed his belly. It was the last of his whisky, and he'd have to order in. Sprawled on his couch in the nude, he watched the sec-vids for the twelfth time, hoping that committing them to memory might spark a clue.

His thoughts circled to Huxley, and he castigated himself for his inability to remain focused. A cold shower hadn't helped, but a hand flogging had. He spied his semi-flaccid cock lying on his belly and grimaced. Fracken woman.

He grunted and sat up in one fluid motion. His air con being broken made his home humid, and the moisture on his skin from his second shower had evaporated. It was time to head for bed. Still, he hesitated. Casting a gaze to the heavens, he pleaded for a clue, a shadow, a hand, a glimpse of something out of place.

The Deadzone vids showed nothing but shifting shadows cast by the smog. Not even when the body fell. With the ground padded so well by debris and litter, it didn't tremor the sec-cam. The body whizzed past it, then the cam jerked as it zoomed onto the inkjob lying in a heap. When it panned the second time, Eve Roe was in a new position—like stop animation but with a sec-cam the perpetrator had known about.

The Promenade vids were all static, but he had to try. Perhaps if he watched a few hours before the crime occurred, he might see something unusual.

In the distance, tinkling pricked his ears. He bounded off the couch to yank on his sleep pants. He slid his door open and stepped onto the platform, his neglected stomach twisting as if on cue. When he flicked his 'porch' light on and off, the tinkling junket dipped, with swirls and eddies, as it cut a swath through the smog. As he waited, he dug his fingers into the soil of his potted vineyard, a pixie cultivar. It brought him a small measure of peace, as it always did.

"Hey, Shaw, you up late. You working a case?" Eddie grinned, sliding his junket alongside the platform with a skill most Lux pilots lacked. "Gotta be with you still awake. The usual?" He didn't wait for Gibs's nod but started on a pizza base.

With his black hair pinned under a hairnet and his eyes protected by goggles, no one could guess Eddie was mostly Asian. Race had fallen away decades ago when everyone realized they had a bit of every race in their DNA. The one constant in his life, Eddie was the closest thing to a friend Gibs had since Jackson. Sadness rose to coat his heart, but a meal in his future smothered the loneliness.

"Meat supreme depending on the meat tonight." Gibs grinned, drawing in a deep breath filled with aromas that ranged from Chinese to Mexican to pizza. The big fast-food companies had tried to infiltrate the junkets, but no one could afford their prices. So instead, people bought variants of McDonalds or KFC, whatever Eddie could make.

"Tofu and pigeon for the most part, but for you, I saved a little bacon."

Gibs's stomach gurgled, and he blessed Eddie with a wide smile. "Heard anything? From Deadzone to Lux?"

"Strange things." Eddie shook his head while smearing rehydrated tomato paste on the pizza base. "Talks of a synth uprising, as usual—a new kid climbing the Shadows ranks—I doubt that. Oh, and your wife's screwing you over."

Gibs's scowled, hating having his name bandied about. "Ex," he muttered.

Eddie threw up his hands as if to placate, flinging grated processed cheese everywhere. "You got fans, Shaw."

"I take it everyone knows when I crap and who I'm banging?" He gritted his teeth, raising his face to the blurred stars, sending up another plea.

"Yes and no." Eddie shrugged. "Just you and your hand, my friend."

He fought the urge to look at his palm, glaring at Eddie, instead. At least, he was honest, and that was a rare quality. Gibs had to remind himself he valued it and not punch the messenger in the face.

He rubbed his guilty palm across his chin, exhaustion burning behind his eyes. "Got any whisky on you?"

"Sure thing." Eddie bent over mid-pigeon spread and pulled out two bottles from under the counter. "Take your pick, but it will cost you."

"I always pay, Eddie, you know that." Gibs grabbed a bottle and swiped his wrist over the pay console. Eddie slid the pizza into the oven—the heat hitting Gibs in the face. He stilled, not jerking back since it would take a second for Eddie to close the door. The cooler smog swirling around his bare chest refreshed him, and he sighed in relief.

"You've seen nothing criminal?"

Eddie's blank look had Gibs chuckling.

"I'm interested in anything targeting synths, other than the usual acts of hatred."

"The Shadows and Kicks sectors have been a little more violent, but they send those synths for repair or incineration before your enforcers hear about it. There's no way the Master would bring you or R4S to his door."

The Master, Gibs grunted, was an unknown face in the criminal underworld yet feared by all. The rights-for-synths advocates brought undesirable attention to the Master's business dealings. Visiting him or his bosses to ask about the two Eve Roes wasn't something Gibs would consider doing. Landing appointments was tough enough, but any nuggets of information he'd receive from the bosses would likely contradict each other. Worse, if they didn't like the look of him, he wouldn't leave there alive.

Another gust of hot air slammed into him just as a twinge of a headache beat behind his right eye. With a flick of his wrist, Eddie had the pizza in a box before shoving it at him.

"I'll keep an ear out, Shaw."

Gibs nodded. He pointed down with a slice of pizza to the unit below him before biting into its cheesy goodness.

"I won't forget." With a stiff wave, Eddie dipped his junket, stopping two levels lower at Mrs. Pakes'. Satisfied her kids would receive a meal that night, Gibs entered his home. Balancing the whisky, the box, and the half-eaten slice, he hit the 'door close' button with his elbow. He dropped the bottle on the couch and sprawled alongside it, balancing the pizza box on his chest.

The sec-vid looped, and he watched through heavy-lidded eyes. Four slices and two swigs of whisky later, a hesitancy snagged his attention. While shoppers 'meandered' with purpose and interest, this person lingered, and their head whipped at everything but the storefronts. Not once did Gibs catch a glimpse of their face, which implied they knew the placement of the sec-cams.

Dressed in a trench coat over a hoodie, Gibs couldn't determine the figure's gender. The shoulders were narrow, the build slight. He'd say a woman, but who knew these days, what with the overconsumption of soya? He'd read an article at the dentist's office about the impact of too much of anything—including coffee—affecting the growth hormone. Besides, a woman made no sense. Killing a synth required strength.

Killing? Gibs frowned. Why had he called it that? Had Thomas's ill-placed love affected him? His old friend wasn't prone to bouts of fancy. Wiping his mouth on a paper towel, Gibs activated his holo-wrist.

"Davis, check Thomas Walker's blood for narcotics." He grimaced, not prepared to see a close-up of Davis's nose.

"Do you know what the fracken time is?" A few curses filled the signal between them. "We need a warrant for anything Lux level—you know that."

"Fine, I'll have Thomas volunteer a sample." He hung up amid more cursing and shrugged, not feeling guilty. As law enforcement, losing sleep was the norm. Tossing the empty box on the floor, he replayed the sec-vid.

Chuckling, he paused it, rubbing his hands together with glee. The *woman* had stroked her fingers across the holographic storefront, and there, twinkling in the bright Promenade lighting, was a diamond ring.

He took a snapshot of it, sent it to Huxley, then called her.

"Shaw." Long blonde hair cascaded over a shoulder, and her smile was welcoming as if she'd anticipated his call. Her lips were still ruby-red and plump, making him doubt she'd been asleep or was alone.

"Find out everything you can about that wedding ring, then meet me at Renovare."

"Sure thing, Detective." She hung up, leaving him staring at the fading holographics.

"Fracken woman," he muttered, heading for a cold shower before bed.

Tomorrow, he'd investigate the benefits of owning an X10 for himself. Wondering if it would be warm as he fucked it had him shuddering. Pizza-flavored bile rose to choke him. Okay, maybe not. Maybe a visit to Nova's sex district—the Kicks—for a little relaxation would be preferable.

He'd stop over on his way to Renovare and ease his torment before he spent hours holed up with curvaceous Huxley. Nodding at his brilliant plan, he showered and hit the sack, sprawling out on his bed nude. After one last communication to the landlord to fix his air con or else, he was asleep before the holographics faded on his arm.

7

53V3/\/

NATE CRACKED THE DOOR open with cold dread sliding down his spine. Sultry music played from the living room. The savory scent of roast lamb filled their apartment. He stepped inside, guiding the door closed with a jutting hip.

He searched for warnings that this was a ruse. It had been months since Kylie made a romantic dinner. He was lucky if any meal was waiting for him. Hanging his jacket on the hook, he slid his tablet onto the table and ventured deeper into his home.

"Sweetheart?" He raised his voice above Nina Simone's.

"Just changing into something...more comfortable."

Her husky voice emanating from their bedroom had him toeing his shoes and socks off. Perhaps he could channel his unwanted arousal for Lissa into his wife and cease his daily torment.

"How was your day?" He uncorked the wine and sniffed, his mouth watering at the fruity, woodsy flavor.

"Good. I'll tell you why in a minute."

He nodded, a smile teasing his lips. Pouring the wine, he placed the bottle on the table and adjusted his trousers around his hard-on. Color caught his attention, and he lifted his head to admire the splash of crimson fabric Kylie wore. It barely covered her and accentuated all he'd missed.

She sashayed toward him. Dazed, he lingered on her curves. Time slowed, and her breasts quivered with each breath. The swing of her unbound curls was mesmerizing, broken only by her hand on his chest. He gripped her hips, relishing the feel of her soft flesh under his palms. He drew in a deep breath—his nostrils flaring—as he drowned in her blue eyes.

She ran her hand up his neck to curl her fingers into his hair, the sting of her nails grazing his scalp. He hissed—his heart rate spiked, pumping blood through his veins. She parted her lips to kiss him on the chin, along his jaw, and nipped his earlobe.

He growled, gliding his hands up her back to tug her closer, needing to feel her breasts crushed against his chest. She chuckled, slipping out of his embrace with a wag of her finger.

"Dinner first." She tossed her hair, playing peekaboo with her lustful gaze before blowing him a kiss.

"You first; dinner can wait." He looped an arm around her and lifted her against him. With long strides, he carried her to their room, sprawling with her onto their bed.

"But..."

"Not another word, Mrs. Dough."

In the aftermath of their lovemaking, with her draped across his chest, he stroked her hip. They hadn't had sex this good in ages. The past few times had involved a wham, a bam, or a no thank-you, Nate. Whatever had happened at work today had put her in fine spirits.

"So, how was your day, Kylie-love?"

"It was amazing." She gasped, scrambling up to fold her legs under her. Despite the shadows under her eyes, she sparkled with the vibrancy he'd fallen in love with. "I'm used to sorting retired synths' memories—" She grimaced, her bright smile fading. "Today, I saw something incredible."

"What?" He sat up to gather her hands in his.

"A synth cried. Not on command but on her own."

He stilled, ice drenching the lassitude from his body. "Real tears?" He cleared his hoarse voice, hoping she didn't notice.

"I can recognize synthetic expressions and emotions, Nate, Renovare pays me to. This was *real*." She snatched her hands back and bounded out of the room.

Returning with her work bag, she placed it on the bed and dug through it—all manner of items landing on the rumpled sheets. Then gripping her tablet in hand, she climbed onto the bed to sit beside him.

She bounced with excitement. "I saved it to show you."

Leaning into her to better see the image, his breathing slowed. Time spun as he watched tears slip down the synth's tattooed cheeks. She touched her face in surprise before meeting her gaze in the mirror.

"This is un-fracken-believable." He forced a bright smile, giving Kylie a tight hug to hide his concern. For hovering around the synth was a dark cloud, one he knew all too well.

"The strange thing is, when I went to fetch Supervisor Harris to show him, the vid on the main server was gone." She frowned, nibbling on her bottom lip as she replayed the scene.

"What did Harris say?" Nate furrowed his brow, trying to look like he was as confused as she was. He was grateful the image was missing because, in the hands of a rights-for-synth advocate, it would cause more damage than good.

"What could he say?" She shrugged—her dejected shoulders didn't alarm him as much as the cloud forming above her head did. He needed to nip this discussion in the bud or else his evening was shot to hell. "I wouldn't put it past Renovare to track my feed, but it's too cumbersome for them to have found and removed this one memory."

"Kylie-love, maybe they monitor your reactions. What did you do when you first saw it?" He gathered her against him, relishing the fading feeling of close companionship.

"You're right. I gasped, jerked, and jumped up."

His scalp tingled, and tension straightened his spine, and he stiffened, leaning away to grip her elbows. "Did they see you make a copy?"

She nodded with her eyes widening.

Fear and fury burned through him, blurring his thoughts. Despite the fire urging him to rid himself of the excess energy pumping in his veins, he stilled, scanning the room. Could Renovare spy on their employees from within their homes?

"Delete it, now."

She shook her head, clutched the tablet to her chest, and bolted off the bed. He followed her naked ass, ignoring the fresh twinge in his loins. She slammed the bathroom door in his face, and he gripped the door frame. Drawing in calming breaths, he waited for the dark spots in his vision to clear before slipping into the bedroom.

She punched the button by the door, activating the sterilization filter. It whirred and sprayed them with a fine mist.

"I'm sending it to the cloud," she whispered, running her fingers across the tablet. "I've deleted it." Her bellow startled him. "Are you happy now?"

"You better have or else, wife." His voice reverberated off the walls, loud enough in case someone eavesdropped, and she slapped her palms over her ears with a giggle.

She slid the tablet onto the vanity and threw herself into his arms. He caught her, crushing him to her with his hands gripping her ass. The kiss she gifted him with was all he remembered. Hot and intense, it pierced his belly with shards of need.

"Hungry?" She peppered kisses across his cheek.

"Later."

She squealed when he tossed her over his shoulder and carried her to bed.

8

319#7

Date: 2170.13.10
The Holies
The Skin Canvas

THE MOMENT NATE SAW her, he knew he had a problem. Lissa bounced around the reception area with her brown curls swaying as much as her hips did. He grimaced, wishing he could cast away this attraction for his dearest friend and focus on the progress he'd made with Kylie.

This morning had been the stuff of dreams. How their marriage used to be. She'd awoken him with kisses and a freshly brewed espresso. While he savored the bitter flavor, she'd dressed for work, donning each clothing item like an exotic dancer would strip them off. She hadn't made it past her bra before he'd pinned her to the bed.

He rubbed his chest, the warmth of love and contentment filling it, but lust was a tricky bastard, never satisfied. Enter Lissa. Her short summer dress exposed her bare legs, and with a flick of his hands, could be over his shoulders.

He scowled, waving at her as he hurried through to the back-room. Perhaps twice with Kylie hadn't been enough? He nodded. Tonight, he'd repeat last night's antics and rid himself of this lust for Lissa.

For once, he hadn't looked at the clients waiting for him. Another sighting of an emotional synth would only confirm his worst fears. If he hadn't undergone tests as a child, he'd worry he was losing his mind. He remembered the psychiatrist, her vape in one hand and her beady eyes narrowed on him. Her office had reeked of cabbage and peppermint.

"Morning, Nate." Lissa carried his coffee over to his side table. Thankfully, he was removing his jacket and hid his burning cheeks and guilty thoughts. "You have a full house. Renovare sold quite a few of their X10 models. Their skin is squeaky clean." She clapped her hands, rocking on her toes.

"No couples today?" He couldn't resist teasing her.

She shook her head, curls and purple butterfly earrings flying.

Drawing in a deep breath, he offered a smile. He would enjoy each precious moment and think no further than the now. As she skipped from the room, he chuckled, pulling the console out in preparation for his busy day.

Lissa's subdued return drained the joy from him. Behind her stood two auditors in blinding white armored suits and stoic features. They were security synths converted by Renovare to ensure ownership compliance. He sat up straight as if Kylie had chastised him for his poor posture.

"Mr. Jonathan Dough, this is not a cordial meeting." They crossed their arms and clasped their hands in front of them, their posture as stiff as his. Although come to think of it, he'd never seen a slouching synth.

Not cordial? No frack. He forced a polite smile and gestured for them to enter. They did so in unison, their gaits matching more from their programming than years of working together. He nodded at Lissa, who scurried out, leaving him alone for this unexpected interrogation.

"Dough's pronounced like Rough. How can I help Renovare?" Spinning the console toward them, he granted them access to his recent tattoo history. "I'm up to code."

That hadn't been fun either—standing in line to re-register The Skin Canvas as a service provider. Renovare should have considered more efficient ways of renewing contracts since he'd been up to code for years.

"Kylie Jennifer Dough is your significant other, is this correct?" Their combined monotone voices snapped Nate's head up with a gasp.

His mind replayed last night's dash to delete the stolen footage. Were they here for that?

"She's my wife." His hoarse voice had him rushing to clear it. Aware they monitored his heart rate, he drew in a calming breath and flashed a smile.

"She has served Renovare for five years, and it is time for her celebration. We have scheduled it for tomorrow evening and require your participation."

"Celebration?" He mouthed the word, trying to sift through the fog of guilt clouding his mind.

Taking his confusion at face value, they said in unison, "At each work milestone, Renovare wishes to thank their employees."

He had gathered that, but why not send a communication? Why not give the invitation to her in person? Why send two auditors to scare the hell out of him? His silence must have conveyed something because one stepped forward, offering him a black envelope. He took it with numb fingers and stared at their disappearing backs. Had Kylie worked for Renovare for so long?

"Nate?" Lissa hurried in, wringing her hands. Her cheeks were pale, but no cloud formed above her head. He was so grateful he didn't need to deal with a panicking woman.

"They delivered an invitation." He fanned his flushed face with the envelope—embossed on the cover was Kylie's name. It looked authentic, but he didn't trust it, not after last night. They had to know she'd stolen from them. With so many employees to monitor, they had to be draconian, or else Renovare's secrets would land in the wrong hands.

Lissa squeaked, jumped around him, and clenched his shoulders in a death grip. Nate raised his gaze to the auditor hovering in the doorway. Fear chilled his spine, twisted his gut, and seized his tongue.

"Ensure Mrs. Kylie Jennifer Dough brings her tablet for cleansing."

Nate nodded, unable to speak, to breathe. So they knew, perhaps even monitored their home as he'd suspected.

"We have erased her cloud files, and Renovare will not tolerate further violations." The auditor stared Nate down with a solid black gaze, red light flickering in its mechanical depths. "Lord Fields is looking forward to meeting you tomorrow evening."

When it left, Nate tilted in his chair, keeping his focus on the auditors until they climbed into their sleek, gray chaser docked at his platform. As he released his pent-up breath, heat bombarded his face and slithered down his neck, but his heart rate didn't slow. It took him a moment longer to realize that Lissa still gripped his shoulders.

Rising on unstable knees, he spun and gathered her against him, knowing he teased the tiger but needing her warmth. He rubbed her back, soothing the shivers raking her.

"That was scary." She pulled out of his embrace—her tremulous smile and inner joy precious to him.

Cupping her face, he feathered the pad of his thumb across her cheek, hoping to bring color to her pale skin. "Let's start the day. Maybe keeping busy will help."

She nodded and stepped out of his arms, the loss of her warmth immediate and disheartening. He didn't watch her walk away. With a furrowed brow, he flicked the envelope over, a little crumpled from their hug. Holy frack, wait until he told Kylie. Lord above, she better not steal another image or so help her.

9

/\/1/\/3

Date: 2170.13.10
The Kicks
The Sex Box

Six misted boxes lined either side of Gibs, a few occupied with squashed backsides and splayed hands against the glass. On the top left of each box were holographic stats, describing who or what occupied the box. He adjusted his tight trousers, grimacing as he brushed his hard-on.

Striding toward the central box, he activated the holographics panel to place his order. A face shimmered in the frosted glass, a fake sensual smile splitting her delicate features.

"Good morning, Detective Gibson Shaw."

Inkjob. He scowled, stepping back to scan the other brothels in the area.

"How may I assist you?"

"Human, a female, preferred sexual position..." Heat stained his cheeks as he tugged on his uniform collar. "...From behind." He didn't want to see the woman's face, to feel a connection he didn't need. Just a sexual release in an impersonal world.

"One moment, please."

The faces and stats of the available women flickered onto the panel; most were too young, and he didn't want a blonde for obvious reasons. He raised his hand to select the brunette, who looked to be in her forties.

"A good choice, Detective Gibson Shaw. Box seven for you and your party." Her smile looked forced, but he dismissed it.

"Party?" He spun. Behind him stood two massive skinless Sec2 inkjobs, their exposed mechanics coiled in shadow. In front of them waited a tiny man, his black suit sharp. His practiced smile coiled nausea in the pit of Gibs's stomach. Fury was swift to follow, clouding his vision red as he saw his lust-filled morning shot to hell.

"The Master of Shadows will see you now." The petite man's voice mimicked his stature—delicate—and each word brimmed with crisp enunciation.

Gibs didn't want to see the Master; he wanted to ease the ache in his loins. He gritted his teeth and shoved his hands into his pockets, gesturing with his chin for him to lead the way. Little Man turned, but the bodyguards waited until Gibs followed him before they latched onto his ass.

Ushered into a sleek, gray chaser, the fragrance of plush leather greeted him. The softness of the fabric hinted at authenticity. Holy frack, the World Animal Organization banned the slaughtering of cows for meat or their skin decades ago. Either the Master kept a few cows in the back, or this pseudo-leather was the best money could buy.

"Greetings, Assistant Elijah Schneider and Detective Gibson Shaw. The Master awaits you in The Scarlet Letter."

Silence descended in the crowded chaser. In the background, soft jazz began to play. Gibs knew better than to dig for information. He'd receive no clear answers, and whatever Schneider said might raise more questions.

The chaser dipped and weaved through the traffic, clipping it at a speed that should have had law enforcement on their tail. Since the demarcations on the chaser indicated it as belonging to the Master, enforcement granted certain leeway. Pressure from the mayor and other businessmen trickled down to the officers as well as certain rumors of violent deaths to those disrespectful. Venturing into the Master's domain was a definitive way of ending one's career.

Of the five sectors beneath Lux, the Parliament, the Promenade, and the Amphitheater, the Shadows was the cleanest. Laundry criss-crossed between buildings meters apart and miles above the Dead-zone. Children darted around on homemade mini-chasers, saved from plummeting deaths by the nets the Master had installed. They knew not the cost to their parents' souls for the privilege of living in the Shadows.

The platform the chaser landed on rivaled the splendor of Ren-ovare's. Lined on either side were more skinless inkjobs, their hands clasped in front of their groins. Gibs climbed out of the chaser behind Schneider, trailing him. He had to shorten his stride, but it allowed him the opportunity to bask in the morning sunlight spilling onto the platform.

"This way, Detective." Schneider gestured to the dark interior drenched in crimson velvet and silk. If a murder happened here, Gibs would struggle to see the blood splatter without his enhanced vision. Against the backlit bar waited a woman in a sexy, black cocktail dress.

Long auburn curls cascaded over one shoulder as she toyed with the swizzle stick in her bloody martini. Tofu olives clung to the spear she clasped between red-taloned fingers.

Her ruby lips wrapped around the olives as they would wrap around his cock. Gibs shifted, adjusting his trousers with a grimace. Frack, he needed to see to his…discomfort before it impeded his ability to work.

"Good morning, Gibs. Thank you, Schneider. That will be all." She gestured to the seat beside her, uncrossing her long legs, exposing her inner thighs for a second before crossing them at the knees. Gibs scowled and climbed onto the stool, leaning his elbows on the mahogany counter. Leather seats and wood? The Master had contacts, but this was insane.

"You wanted to see me?" He dipped his head as if it would smother his hoarse voice. When a bartender slid a coffee in front of him, he gripped it with gratitude, taking a big sip of the steamy liquid.

Once they were alone again, she sucked on her thumb with her dark gaze narrowed on him. Red flickered in her eyes, revealing her enhancements. "You and Eddie have been discussing me. As the leader of The Shadows, I do have eyes and ears everywhere. A fact I shouldn't have to point out to you." Her words, delivered in a clipped accent, hinted at an expensive education.

So this was the Master? Gibs wasn't certain. None of the gossip had revealed their gender. That he was a woman intrigued him. There was a grace to her movements, and the arch of her back was enticing, thrusting out her breasts. At first glance, he wouldn't think of her as a ruthless killer and leader of the Shadows.

That she knew Eddie wasn't alarming. Their discussion regarding her hadn't been negative or insulting. It didn't warrant this interview. In his career, he could count on one hand the number of officers who'd entered the Shadows and lived to tell about it. Waking this morning hadn't felt as if death awaited him in the penthouse of the Master. He scanned the bar, ignoring the gold filigree, handles, and other details. Skinless titanium inkjobs barred his one escape route.

"I have reviewed your file and your case notes." Her voice was husky, deeper than expected.

He grunted. Not that he would dare question how or who leaked the confidential information. That was a losing battle with no definitive outcome he could foresee. He needed to focus on what information he could glean and, frack willing, survive this.

"Dismembering inkjobs isn't something I tolerate. The cost is exorbitant, and when this impacts my profits, suffice it to say, I don't allow the culprits to live."

"I didn't imply the abuse was at your hands. I merely asked if anyone might have seen something. Witnesses are scarce, even on the Promenade."

She gripped his knee, and he jerked back, banging his other knee on the underside of the counter. Sharp darts of agony lanced up his thigh, and he rubbed it, trying not to glare at the Master. That was one sure way to get himself killed.

She grazed his thigh with her talons before giving him another squeeze. When she removed her hand, he released a silent breath.

"I know. I wish to help. Schneider will give you my personal line should you have any questions or need access to areas otherwise forbidden to you." The Master rose and with a sensual shimmy, tugged her dress in place. Gibs tried not to let his gaze linger. It wouldn't do well to find the Master attractive.

His heart rate skittered at the realization she was letting him leave. Until the chaser lifted off the platform, he'd withhold his relief.

"Thank you for your time, Master." He slid off the stool and accepted her manicured hand.

She raised his fingers to her lips and feathered kisses over his knuckles.

His breath caught, and he suppressed a shiver shooting down his spine to nestle in his balls. This day had gone to hell. The aching agony in his groin intensified.

Trailing Schneider, Gibs closed his eyes for a moment, sucking in calming breaths. The sunlight drenching the platform stated the hour. His appointment at Renovare loomed, leaving him with no time to finish his objective at the Sex Box. He wanted to howl his frustration. Spending a day in the small confines of the data room with Huxley would test every bit of his restraint. Perhaps if he snuck off to the ablutions, a quick flogging might buy him a little peace?

He climbed into the waiting chaser. Instead of joining him, Schneider grabbed him and pressed his wrist to his. The zing of data received activated the holographics under his skin—Master of Shadows with a number. Gibs didn't want to ponder the sincerity of her attraction or if she'd been toying with him, knowing where he'd been when Schneider had collected him.

She was a beautiful woman, able to entice anyone. Why she would choose him was beyond his understanding. The door sealed without another word from Schneider, and after the chaser greeted him, Gibs instructed it to take him to Renovare. He may be late, but he hoped Huxley would await his arrival, or better yet, start without him.

10

73/\/

Date: 2170.13.10

Renovare

The Holies

Gibs leaped out of the chaser the moment the door opened wide enough for him to do so. Clipping his shoulder on the way out didn't bother him. The pain was fleeting. He wanted out the fracken thing and the clutches of the Master. While he watched it lift off, he expected a bullet to pierce his skull or the chaser to explode. Air whooshed out of his lungs as the seconds ticked by, and he faced Renovare's entrance, relief tingling along his scalp.

"Greetings, Detective Gibson Shaw. Officer Naomi Huxley has just arrived. Allow me to escort you to the data lab." One of the Zetas, he wasn't sure which one, gestured to the pod.

He grunted, happy to be mere minutes behind Huxley and not hours. Why was she late? Had someone or something delayed her? The thought of her standing in front of The Sex Box making her selection hardened his cock, and he scowled at the unsuspecting inkjob. Accepting his silence as acquiescence, she headed for the pod.

The levels whizzed past. He scanned them for snipers, reflections off long-range weapons, or a kamikaze chaser. All he knew about the Master was her unpredictability and intolerance for the smallest slight. He hadn't even known she wasn't a he. Wait until he told Huxley.

He grimaced—since when had he started thinking of Huxley as a proper partner? One or two days of knowing her—is that all it had taken? A nice pair of legs and a fine ass? How fickle was he that his loyalty could so easily be bought?

As complicated as this case was turning out to be, he did need fresh eyes. And having Huxley around ensured the investigation went according to code. If he discovered the person to blame was Lawrence Walker, or frack, the mayor, he needed his evidence to be above reproach.

"Lord Fields has insisted we provide lunch for you. I will request your preferences closer to the time." Zeta paused outside a door that opened at her touch.

He nodded and walked through, facing the inkjob as the door closed, sealing him inside.

The aroma of coffee greeted him, and he spun. Huxley smiled at him. Beside her on the console rested two tall cups of the real deal, imported from Ganymede. He would recognize that smell anywhere. While the Master's coffee was as expensive, it had been a sample and nothing like his usual morning dose.

"Morning, Gibs."

"Is that for me?" He gestured to the coffee, not wanting to assume. When her smile broadened and she nodded, he burst forward, needing its delicious strength and heat to soothe his jumbled nerves.

"Bad morning?" She rose, crowding him to cup his bicep. Warmth from her fingers burned through the cloth of his uniform. Concern furrowed her brow and pursed her lips. Her rose fragrance enshrouded him, so Gibs switched to breathing through his mouth. Only thing was, he couldn't sip coffee and breathe at the same time.

He filled her in on his interview, skipping over where Schneider had found him. If she had any idea how much she affected him, his days would become a living hell.

"Wow, I didn't know the Master was a woman. Are you sure she wasn't a puppet, a trick to lure you away from the true kingpin?"

"Kingpin?" He smirked, appreciating her word choice. Laughter bubbled in his chest, and he released it, the carefree joy unexpected and precious. Her slap on the arm brought him back to the moment. He sipped his coffee and chose the chair beside hers.

Cradling his coffee to his chest with one hand, he punched the buttons to activate the console. "Does it matter if she was a puppet? She had the authority, and it dripped from her voice, saturated her mannerisms. Not for a moment did I doubt she could flick her fingers and have me killed."

"Holy frack, Gibs, you could've died."

Gibs kept his focus on the screens, not wanting to see the horror on Huxley's face. He gestured to the vids to bring her back to their task. Any distraction would serve the purpose.

"Found anything yet?" He sipped and rolled the hot liquid over his tongue.

"The usual disrespect for property but nothing worth noting. I've sorted the vids by date across Lux owners. I haven't come across sexual memories. I suspect it's Renovare's attempt to protect the appetites of the elite. I'd never be able to vote for the mayor again if I found out he was as depraved as his ex-wife claimed."

Silence fell while they watched vid after vid of retired synths falling into routines and numbing Gibs's mind. If it wasn't for the constant flow of coffee Zeta supplied, he might have slammed his forehead onto the console mid-drool.

"Oh, about the picture you sent me." Huxley spun her chair to face him. Her lipstick had worn off, revealing natural plump lips. "The ring's not a standard design. And that's good because it means not trawling through hundreds of stores for the buyer."

"It's also bad because we can't determine which store made it." He bit into the cinnamon-tofu cakes Huxley had brought. He froze mid-chew when she dabbed his mouth with a paper towel.

"I have Davis running the image through the database. There's bound to be a record of its manufacture and sale." She navigated to the next vid queued, blissfully unaware of how her touch had impacted him. If he wasn't awarded a medal for outstanding service or—in this case, survival—there would be fracken hell to pay.

"Someone with your influence could fight for them, not stand by and condone their mistreatment." An electronic placard hid the woman's face—the flickering holographic slogans announcing her as an R4S advocate. She besieged the owner to do more than be a product consumer, to create laws and a foundation for justice for all.

"I'll add your plea to my gun's rights for freedom to defend itself."

Gibs grunted. He knew that voice: Lawrence Walker. What made his skin feel like thousands of stinging bees was that he agreed with the old man. A tool didn't need rights when it couldn't make informed decisions. It was like asking a toddler if they wanted to live in the outer reaches of space on a hippy colony. Gibs had orbited Europa for years, holding hands and singing Kumbaya around the solar heater.

It stood to reason he had married the first woman who had been normal, which wasn't as cracked up as he thought it would be. He and Tamara hadn't seen eye-to-eye on many things—their backgrounds too different to find common ground. Sex and affection had given way to abstinence and resentment.

He might as well have beribboned her in bright red and gifted her to his captain for Christmas. Frack, he hated failing at anything, including marriage. Failures invoked all the emotions he'd squashed since Jackson's death.

"Gibs." Huxley's voice pierced his morbid thoughts. "Want to take a break, breathe in some fresh-ish air?"

"No, we'd need a Zeta-escort, and I just want this done with. It's turning out to be a dead-end, Huxley."

"What's wrong with Naomi?" She pierced him with her green gaze. "I call you Gibs."

"You're my partner for the duration of this case which requires a certain protocol. I'm too old to give a frack what you call me, but should I be familiar with you, the verbal teasing and bullying you'll receive at the precinct will undermine your career."

Color stained her cheeks with a delicious pinkish hue. Frack, if she wasn't made aware of her beauty, of the mountain she needed to climb to be successful, then her naivete would cost her more than her career. Hell, it might impact her reputation.

"Thank you." She dipped her head but not before he caught a glimmer of tears.

He leaped up, desperate to be anywhere but near a crying woman. "Chinese okay?"

She nodded, and he darted out of the room in search of a Zeta. The inkjob waited in the floor's lobby, and he placed the order, choosing a variety of dishes. Who knew how long they would be, but a large supply of food would tide them over.

He approached the glass façade of the building, taking a moment to watch the bustling traffic. A few days ago, he was in his normal routine, solving domestic murders and hunting down eloped spouses. How his life had changed. He'd never expected to 'meet' Lord Fields, the Master, or step foot on Lux again.

Resentment ate at him. As he leaned his flushed temple on the cool glass, he wondered when his bitterness had turned into resignation; part of the blame for the failure of his marriage did lie on his shoulders, but he wasn't one to reminisce about regret. Yet, here he stood, and all because he found his partner attractive and might have a serial vandal on his hands. He chuckled, grateful for one thing. His mother hadn't descended on him in a cloud of alien herbs and a crushing hug.

"I will bring the meal once it arrives, Detective Gibson Shaw." Zeta's calm voice pulled him back from the façade, and he faced her. She held out two black envelopes with his and Huxley's names embossed upon them. "We have prepared rooms for your convenience as well as evening garments for the celebration. Lord Fields is looking forward to seeing you there."

Gibs accepted the envelopes, frozen in place at this unexpected turn of events. He opened his mouth to reject the invitations. He didn't do well at these fancy things and hated making small talk conveying nothing.

"Lord Fields has invited the previous owners of the retired synths in case you have questions. He has ensured that they will not leave until they have spoken to you."

Frack.

Gripping the envelopes, he headed for Huxley, praying she could think of a valid reason not to attend. At the same time, it *was* the perfect opportunity to question people without warrants.

Double frack.

Gibs lacked subtlety, uncaring whether he offended anyone. Perhaps attaching himself to Huxley's side might soften his blunt words and unforgiving scowl. Perhaps, under the influence of champagne and organic food, loose tongues might reveal more than their synths' memories did.

11

313V3/\/

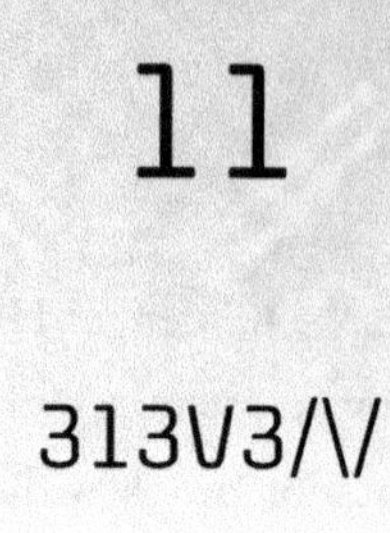

Date: 2170.13.10
Renovare
The Holies

"I CAN'T BELIEVE SUPERVISOR Harris said nothing," Nate grumbled, yanking on the knot of his tie. It squeezed his throat, cutting off his ability to breathe, and was it hot in here?

"I asked him the same question. He said it was procedure to receive the invitations via inkjob; adds a little pizzazz to the proceedings." Kylie's voice came from the bathroom where she was applying the finishing touches to what she'd termed her masterpiece.

"Pizzazz? Is that an official word?" Nate wasn't fond of Dean Harris, an old fart of a man who'd only held down the one job that had become his life.

"The system says it means glamor though why he couldn't just say so..." Heels clacked on the polished floor, and out stepped a vision in breathtaking blue. She glowed, and he trailed his gaze over her figure lovingly encased in a silken creation. Nate sighed, love and desire allowing a ghost of a smile to play across his lips. It wasn't often Kylie dressed for something special, and he vowed to change that.

"You look beautiful, my love." The lights of the neon signs outside flickered off her, and the kaleidoscope of rainbow colors made her appear ethereal.

"You should wear a tie more often." Kylie sidled closer to press her form against his in the pretext of fixing his tie. Her fragrance tantalized him, and even though he hated the tie, he held her tighter to him, gripping her hips. The night held the promise of sweet companionship and fulfilled desire.

"Ready?" Nate pressed a kiss to her temple, closing his hand over hers as it wrapped around his tie.

"Yes." Her smile swept him away, calling forth a myriad of memories from their time together.

He stepped away from her, grabbed her tablet, and gestured for her to lead the way. Renovare had sent a chaser over, more to insure they attended than out of thoughtfulness.

Kylie scowled at the tablet and grabbed a bronze clutch that matched her heels. He whispered a request that she only wear those later, then helped her climb into the chaser, admiring the glow on her cheeks.

"Greetings, Data Officer Kylie Jennifer Dough."

Soft music began to play in the background. Nate reached across for Kylie's hand, lacing his fingers through hers.

The trip to Renovare was quick but long enough for the play of nightlights on her face to fascinate him. "Never forget my love for you, wife," he said, tossing a smile at her.

"And mine for you, husband."

Nate's smile lingered. The cloud of depression and anger had been absent of late despite Renovare discovering Kylie's theft. When he had brought home the envelope and the confirmation that they knew, he'd expected a hurricane to descend. But the revelation of an emotional synthetic had pleased her far too much for the loss of her job or possible imprisonment to deter her.

The chaser touched down outside Renovare, and they disembarked amid other attendees. It stood to reason that she'd share the celebration with thousands of other employees who'd completed five years of service.

"Good evening, Data Officer Kylie Jennifer Dough and Mr. Jonathan Dough. Lord Fields will see you now."

"What?" Kylie stumbled, grabbing onto Nate's forearm.

He offered the inkjob the tablet and pressed his palm to the base of Kylie's spine, guiding her in the inkjob's steps through the crowds and up levels in a glass pod. His scalp tingled, and his lungs cinched. Paranoia darted his gaze from side to side, and he tightened his hold on Kylie. Each step was taken under the vigilant gazes of other inkjobs capable of doing untold harm. His creative mind toyed with the image of them marching to their doom, deep in the bowels of Renovare, never to see sunlight again. Lissa knew about tonight, which wasn't a comforting thought. Telling her may have placed her in danger, too. How could he be so stupid?

He kissed Kylie's temple and smiled at her, hoping to ease her tension. If Lord Fields killed them, there wasn't much he could do. He'd try though as any injury or death was preferable to Kylie suffering.

"Good evening. This way, please." A beautiful inkjob in a white gown greeted them the moment they stepped out of the pod. The security inkjobs backed off, but that didn't ease the throbbing between Nate's shoulder blades. One synthetic could kill them without breaking a sweat—the gender didn't matter.

The office was large, framed by floor-to-ceiling windows looking out on the mesmerizing skyline. Nothing else but a glass desk waited for them. Kylie slipped her arm around his waist, seeking comfort.

"No one has met Lord Fields, so don't expect this to be a face-to-face."

Her words provided some relief, and he released a held breath, pressing his palm to the cool glass. It didn't mean they wouldn't die, but it diminished the risk of the furious confrontation he'd expected.

"Your wife is correct." A voice filled the room. "What you saw, my dearest Kylie, was a glitch in a recent update, one we hid well from the populace." The man's voice moved around the room as if the speaker paced.

"The emotion was beautiful, intense. Will you be saving the data for future models?"

Lord Fields laughed, his joy sounding authentic. "I admire your love for my creations, but the world cannot handle lifelike synthetics. Their hatred is too real, their prejudice still in the infantile stage."

"I apologize for stealing a memory so precious. Had I known you needed it erased to protect the synths, of course, I wouldn't have hesitated." Kylie raised her face to the ceiling as if to make eye contact with the voice.

"I know, my child. I wish to aid your cause. Within your passion are the seeds of change and revolution."

A circular hole opened, and through it, rose a man in a tux. Small in stature but not petite, his Asian heritage shone in the ebony of his hair and the sharp angles of his jaw, but strangely not in his eyes or skin tone. He had a delicate face Nate would have loved to sketch, filled with dignity and character.

He studied Nate longer than was normal, exploding the tingles from his scalp down his neck. Fields's strange interest sparked a shiver Nate was barely able to hide.

Lord Fields strode forward to clasp Kylie's hand between his. "Would that suit? A headquarters from where you can coordinate your campaigns, a lawyer on standby to handle the legal side of things, and you placed on half-days to free up your time. And direct access to my PR department for any marketing material you need."

Nate opened his mouth to speak, seeing their monthly income diminish. The Skin Canvas couldn't keep them afloat. They needed Kylie's salary to survive.

The man shook his head at Nate, silencing him, and a smile spread his full lips. Ice slid along Nate's nerves. "I will, of course, double your salary if you're prepared to commit."

Kylie laughed, bouncing on her toes. She cast an eager glance at Nate and waited for his smile before nodding at Lord Fields. He pumped their clasped hands to seal the deal.

"Ms. Zeta will draw up the agreement and change of employment. Do enjoy the festivities."

He took a backward step onto the circle and descended. Meeting adjourned. Silence gripped the room as the hole sealed.

Nate wanted to take Kylie's hand and run, but she trembled with excitement, not seeing the offer as a trap. Working for Renovare meant Lord Fields controlled her campaigns, influenced her speeches. Didn't she see that?

Now wasn't the time to discuss it, though, for walls had ears. He'd need to pick the location, one Renovare couldn't monitor. Nate grimaced as he escorted Kylie into the waiting pod. He wasn't looking forward to breaking her heart.

12

7VV31V3

Date: 2170.13.10

Renovare

The Holies

GIBS SHIFTED, TUGGING ON the cuffs of his tux, hating that it fit him so well. How would Renovare know his exact measurements? That tweaked his ass, what with the Master and Lord Fields having access to his case files as if he'd posted it online. There was a mole. There were many, to be frank. He needed to talk to Davis and Huxley. They should keep their findings off the record until he'd found the culprit.

With one last glance in the mirror to check he'd combed his hair and beard, he admired the cut of the tux across his broad shoulders. He couldn't accept it as a gift, so the money Lord Fields wasted on it was a moot point. The tux was a loan, and he'd ensure Huxley understood that regarding whatever outfit the Zetas had provided for her, too.

He slid the data lab's door open. His breath caught, and he stilled, trailing his gaze up an extended leg peeking out through the gown's slit. A gold peep-toe heel added a sensual curve to her calf. In royal purple, the velvet enticed him to touch, to linger. With a sweetheart neckline and a partially bare back, there was too much skin on display.

Regardless, she glowed. A waterfall of hair draped over one shoulder exposed the graceful column of her neck. Long gold-and-diamond earrings dangled from her ears, brushing her collarbone.

Frack.

He pulled his jacket closed, preferring to stare at his blurred reflection in the polished shoes they'd provided. If he doubled his efforts in solving this case sooner, it might free him from her magnetic appeal.

"Gibs, you clean up well." She rose to her full height, a bright smile spreading her ruby lips. What was it with red lips today?

"Um, so do you." Then followed his words with a grunt. *Smooth, Gibs.* "I... You... That gown is beautiful." *From bad to flaming worse.* "Shall we?" He opened the door and stepped through, sucking in the cooler air of the passage like a lifeline.

He trailed behind her, mesmerized by the sway of her hips. Her enticing rose scent lingered, and he tried inhaling and holding his breath but couldn't. The words 'lovesick idiot' came to mind. Slapping himself in the face was tempting, and he might succumb to the idea if it didn't risk leaving a questionable mark. He didn't want her to know. His cheeks burned at the thought of it. Old detective swooning over his rookie partner? How the clichés abound.

Whether she knew it or not, she was an excellent distraction. Double frack.

Zeta waited by the pod, a polite smile contorting her synthetic features. "Your invitations extend to the VIP section where you are free to mingle with the other guests. Lord Fields requests that you behave above reproach since his reputation is on the line. I assured him that I will deal with any infractions."

As the pod descended, Gibs pondered how Zeta would deal with his blunt personality. Perhaps if he thought of this evening as a memorial, then he might treat the guests with a softer touch. He gripped Huxley's elbow to lean in, brushing his lips across her ear.

She stilled and glanced his way despite the shiver she did nothing to hide. He couldn't read anything into that. He hadn't meant to 'kiss' her ear.

"You take the lead on the questioning." He kept his voice low, not that it mattered since inkjobs had superb hearing. Huxley nodded and looped her arm through his as if they were on a date. He fought the urge to either jerk away or sidle closer to her. Frack his erratic hormones.

Boisterous laughter greeted their exit from the pod. Zeta cut a swath through the crowds, leading them to the dais at the back of the hall. Lights shimmered up high, casting illusory snowflakes in pale blue. A virtual snowfall drifted down onto the tables and around the mingling guests.

"Thank you, Anna. Gibson, Naomi, welcome to our celebration." In a crisp tux, an Asian man smiled, his voice stating him as Lord Fields. Not a black hair was out of place, and his skin glowed with good health. It didn't look as if he ever needed to shave, and for some strange reason, Gibs's beard itched in protest. Fields's dark eyes assessed them without expression, and Gibs bristled under the intense scrutiny.

"Thank you for the lovely gown, Lord Fields," Huxley gushed, sounding sweet and sensual at the same time.

"A pleasure but on loan since appearances matter." Lord Field leaned in close, his face softening with humor. "Not that I have any need to offer you gifts. You have nothing I want, not even your silence."

Gibs grunted, hating having the wind snuffed from his sails.

Huxley laughed again, but her grip on his arm tightened.

"Excuse me, my guests of honor have arrived." Lord Fields scurried off, and his fast-disappearing back slumped Gibs's shoulders with relief. The vise around his chest eased enough for him to breathe.

Spotting the bar, he met Huxley's slate-gray eyes. "Something to drink?"

"Oh, yes, please. Champagne or white wine." She scanned the guests milling about and nudged Gibs with her hip. "Off you go. I'll mingle. A woman alone attracts much attention."

Gibs nodded, too dumbfounded to speak. He headed for the bar, tapping on the glass surface as he waited his turn. "A white wine, preferably from the Chardonnay vineship. If not, a Riesling. I'll take a vodka."

"You know your wines," a woman whispered, trailing a manicured fingertip along his lapel.

"He should," Thomas Walker said before slapping Gibs on the back.

"I know my vineships," Gibs said, sparing his friend a welcoming smile. The woman must be his date—the smooth, cream skin and the glossy allure of her shimmering light brown hair told him she was a too-young socialite. "Skimming the barrel?" Gibs arched a brow.

Thomas laughed. "This is my cousin, Sienna. Cous, this is Gibson Shaw."

"Oh, I've heard so much about you." She trailed her heated gaze over his body like no debutante should. It didn't inspire lustful feelings in Gibs but quite the opposite. His bones ached from old age.

"You seem too cheerful after...y'know." Gibs flicked a nervous look at the young woman, unsure if she knew about Thomas's lost love.

"Ordered another, a perfect replica. Lord Fields was most accommodating. He assured me she would receive the memories Olivia had stored." Thomas grinned. "She's arriving tomorrow, and I can't wait." He bounced on his toes.

"Convenient and fortuitous." Gibs threw back his vodka without tasting it and nodded at the bartender for another. Sienna waved at someone in the crowd and waltzed off without a by-your-leave.

"How's the case going?" Thomas swirled the burnished liquid in his snifter—cognac, Gibs presumed.

"Slow. Nothing new to report." He leaned his elbows on the counter to scan the crowd. A few inkjobs peppered the guests. As well dressed as those in attendance, their tatts gave them away, with one or two standing out. The Wright brothers' first flyer marked a male inkjob on his neck. A female inkjob had a snake coiling around a semi-exposed breast.

Gibs shuddered, imagining how the vandal might use those against his victims. A splash of purple caught his eye, and he watched Huxley charm her way through the crowd. She headed for him, her gaze meeting his after every distracting encounter.

"Holy frack." Thomas's voice dripped with awe, and Gibs fought the urge to punch him. Hell no, not on his watch.

"My date." He flashed a warning. "She's off-limits."

Thomas threw his hands up as if in surrender, and Gibs scowled at his lie. Why did it matter if Thomas found Huxley attractive? The entire hall would find her irresistible. Despite his castigating thoughts, as soon as she reached him, he looped his arm around her waist and pressed a kiss to her temple. That his lips caught on fire was for his knowledge alone.

"Darling, your wine."

Huxley hid her surprise well, accepting the glass with a smile. "Good evening." She offered Thomas her hand, which he accepted to press a kiss to her knuckles. The fracken charmer.

"Thomas is an old friend, sweetheart." Gibs flared his eyes, asking her to play along. A bright smile split her cheeks, spreading her lips, and he lost his train of thought for a moment.

"Honey, I didn't know you had friends in high places." Her voice thickened, and Gibs couldn't say if it was with restrained laughter or pure lust.

Thomas tossed a chuckle at Gibs. "It's good to see you, Naomi. How's your mother doing? I heard she's still upset about that attempted chaser-jacking."

Gibs froze, shooting glances at them both. What the frack? How did they know each other?

"She is, Tom. It happened a few levels below Lux, so she's on this quest to have the zones cleared of 'scum.'"

"Since when have you been dating Gibs?" Thomas swirled his cognac, uncaring that Gibs was on the verge of killing them both.

"For a while now. I can't help it. There's just something compelling about him, y'know." Huxley sipped her wine as if she hadn't upturned his world.

Why play along when she knew Thomas? Gibs glared even as he twisted his lips into a stiff smile. They'd have a chat about this later. Come to think of it, what did he know about her? How had she been assigned to him? Who had pulled those strings?

"Any clues?" Gibs sought refuge behind his work, choosing not to find his ignorance embarrassing. "I'm thinking we research the tatts."

"Good idea." Huxley pressed a kiss to his cheek and rushed off to snag a passing Zeta.

"I'm impressed, Gibs. I tried to woo her for years."

"Woo?" Gibs arched a brow. He didn't want to reveal that there was no way in God's smog-infested world he could ever land such a woman.

"Naomi's the type of woman you shag *and* marry."

"Shag?" Gibs grabbed Thomas's glass to sniff. The warmth at his side drew his attention, and he slipped an arm around Huxley. Whether out of stubbornness or yearning, he chose not to think about it.

"Zeta will send a list of tattoo vendors tomorrow." Naomi sipped her wine, closing her eyes to savor the flavor. "This is lovely." She hummed her appreciation.

"Gibs worked vineships as a youngster." Thomas ordered another cognac.

Her eyelids fluttered open. "The ones orbiting Mars?"

Gibs shrugged, gulped his vodka, and relished the burn as he swallowed. He wasn't going to go into the horrid details of his childhood, nor how much he'd valued his father's rescue.

"Ready to interview the suspects?" She leaned in to whisper, her gaze snagging his.

He nodded, aware that this close, with her lips inches from his, he might have agreed to anything.

"Duty calls, Tom. Send my love to your father." She laced her fingers through Gibs's and tugged.

Waving his vodka glass as a farewell, Gibs allowed her to drag him through the crowd. Dread warred with excitement, and despite finding the sway of her hips fascinating, he cursed the distraction.

13

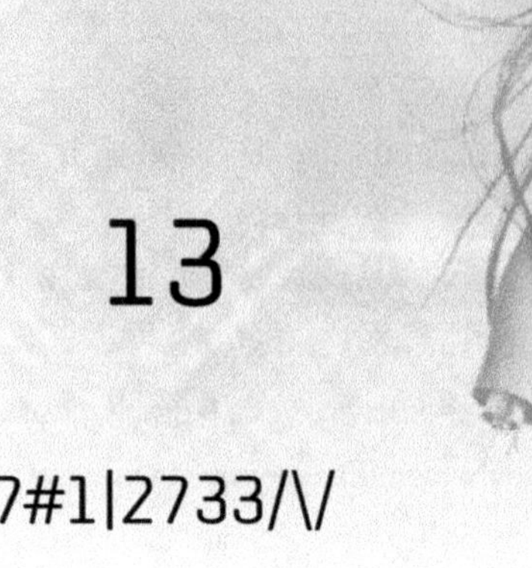

7#1|2733/\/

Date: 2170.13.10

Renovare

The Holies

GIBS TIGHTENED HIS GRIP on Huxley's elbow and tugged her into the room Renovare had provided. He twirled her past him, closing the door as soon as she cleared the threshold. She arched a brow but said nothing. As she tossed her clutch onto the bed, her pale hair cascaded around her and brushed her bare back.

"What a waste of an evening." He grunted. "Lies amid flattery. For once, I needed someone to be truthful." He gripped her shoulders as if to shake her then released her to pace, his long strides making swift work of the small room.

"You must read between their words, Gibs." She poured a glass of honeyed liquid into a tumbler and offered it to him.

He stared at it; as if adding alcohol to his volatile emotions was a good idea. Raising his gaze to hers, he let it meander along her dainty nose to her lips almost devoid of lipstick. His heart did a pirouette, and when he inhaled, her rose scent seeped between the cracks of his resolve.

With a shrug, she downed it and left the glass on the table.

Running his hand through his hair, he faced her. "Frack woman, spill it."

"Spill what?"

Gibs shook his head, struggling to focus. "Who *are* you?" He scrubbed his beard, needing the rough texture to ground the moment. "Who did you blow to land this case?" He was too far away for her to punch him again.

"You mean, to land you? Don't be modest, Gibs. It doesn't suit you." Huxley chuckled. "My uncle's the mayor."

Cold tingles swept through Gibs, traveling down his neck and along his spine to chill his semi-hard-on. He sat on the closest chair, wobbling it. A little too dazed to pick a question circling his mind, he opened his mouth to speak then snapped it shut.

"So no, my oral skills weren't put to the test. Uncle Charlie offered to find me a 'position' and, since he'd heard great things about you, he suggested you as my first partner." Huxley paused, running an admiring gaze over him.

Fire burst across his limbs, pooling in his loins, and spurred another bout of pacing. He forced himself to remain seated.

"I took my mother's maiden name, not wanting or needing Uncle Charlie's prominence for me to be successful."

Gibs flicked a glance at her. "Successful? You've made it worse, don't you see." He ran a hand over his face, disheveling his hair. "Enforcers can sniff out falsehoods like the bloodhounds of old. Which means, you're hiding something, and that could lead to distrust." He lunged out of the chair to grip her shoulders again and realized he might bruise her, so he rubbed her skin instead, marveling at the heated silkiness. "When they find out, and they will…" He groaned, losing himself in her gray eyes. "Well, I best be there when that happens."

"You can't protect me forever, Gibs." Her smile was soft…sensual, shooting sparks one way.

He grimaced, wishing he could adjust his too-tight trousers. Pacing eased the pressure a little. "Do you remember what I said about your reputation?"

A frown creased her brow, and with a fingertip, he eased it.

"No," she whispered.

Frack, had he spoken his thoughts aloud? He stepped away from her, breaking the enchanting allure of her scent. "Right. So, you gleaned nothing from the guests' inane chatter?"

Huxley's shoulders slumped. "They're fearful that it's the work of a Lux-hater, and so they squirreled their prized inkjobs away. It's why there were so few in attendance tonight." She fluffed her hair, scratching her scalp with a breathless moan. "Zeta should have the tatt results to us first thing. I haven't heard anything about the ring. You can follow up on that or sift through more memories. Your choice."

"I'll do the ring and a trip to Davis. You've got the hang of that damn vid contraption." Gibs tugged on his collar, ripping off the clip-on bow tie to toss alongside her clutch. He yanked off the jacket, hung it on a nearby hook, then undid the top two buttons of his shirt and rolled up his sleeves.

"That's it for tonight then? I could do with a shower and sleep."

"One more thing." He caught her wrist, halting her retreat. Her pulse beat against his fingertips, urging him to yank her into his arms. "Keep your findings to us and Davis. Someone's leaking our reports." He pulled her closer, gesturing for her to sit.

She did, exposing a fair amount of leg in the process.

He resumed pacing—the nervous energy too much to bear. "The Master and Lord Fields have both mentioned the case files, Huxley. For such a low-level crime, there are far too many high-powered people interested."

"Everyone knew how Thomas adored Olivia. Perhaps this is an act of a jealous ex-lover?" She shook her head, golden rivulets pouring over a velvet-encased breast. "No, that doesn't explain Eve Roe 2."

"Unless the vandal got a taste for it. Still, how could anyone overpower an inkjob, Hux?" Gibs pinched the bridge of his nose. "The motive's important, I agree." Releasing a long sigh, he met her worried gaze. "Don't keep the gown when it might be construed as a bribe. Keep nothing Lord Fields gives you."

She bit her lip, dimpling its natural lushness, and nodded.

His fingers twitched with the urge to caress her cheek. "Do you need an escort home? Want me to drop you off?"

"I'm staying the night to get a fresh start in the morning. Call when you find anything."

"Will do." He stepped back to let her walk past him but hovered, close enough for her warmth to reach him. "Let me know what Zeta said." Awkwardness made him vacillate between saying goodnight and kissing her. She flashed a smile, and the door closed behind her, drowning him in poignant silence. Would he regret not stopping her? *Yes.* Would he chase after her now? *No.*

He growled and spun on a heel to gather his uniform, making fast work of stripping off his tux. His clothing restored and feeling more like himself, he checked his Glock, holstered it, and left the room, the tux sprawled across the bed looking as if it had a good time.

Chasers queued, ready to transfer the guests home. Gibs hailed one and clambered in, ignoring the usual robotic greeting as he barked out his destination. Once more, he disembarked in the bustling Kicks. The air was filled with the stench of lust. Husky voices advertised their wares. Neon lights and holograms enticed the audio-impaired. The Kicks was a Venus flytrap luring all in need to their doom.

Spinning as he strolled, he checked that the Little Man and his 'guardians' didn't follow him. Content that he was, for now, alone, Gibs halted in front of The Sex Box's middle panel again.

"Welcome back, Detective Gibson Shaw. How may I assist you?"

Welcome back? He snorted. He wished this was a happy return, but he had yet to test their merchandise, and it had been a while since he'd visited the Kicks. Tamara, for all her female troubles, had thrived in the sexual department.

"Human. Female. Preferred sexual position, from behind." This time there was no hesitancy, no resulting blush.

"As you desire." A soft giggle followed, closer to the real thing than he'd expected.

The brunette from this morning wasn't among the choices. Gibs didn't want a blonde like Huxley and not a redhead either—too close to the Master. A brunette was the safest for his peace of mind.

"I want a brunette. Get me one." He leaned forward as if his preference revealed his inner turmoil.

"One moment, please."

"This going to take long?" a man slurred from behind him.

Gibs flicked a dismissive glance his way, faced forward, and waited.

"Your selection this morning was box seven. Candy has retired for the evening, but a friend of the Master is a friend of hers. She awaits you."

Friend of the Master? Gibs gritted his teeth. "Payment?"

"On the house. All your pleasure and desires are a gift from the Master."

Frack. As horny as he was, he didn't want to be indebted. Box seven lit up, the door slid open, and Gibs stepped to the side, allowing the man behind him to address the panel. The woman awaiting his 'pleasure' wore a white bustier, hugging a honey-tanned body made for loving. Long waves of brown-black hair fell around her, and dark eyes met his gaze.

She crooked her finger, and he approached her, admiring her breasts threatening to pop free. Garters topped her long legs—they had a Wild West style, frilly with delicate lace. White faux-leather pumps adorned her feet. The panel closed behind him, sealing him to his fate.

"Your name?" He slipped off his coat and tossed it over a nearby transparent chair, covering the cam behind the vodka decanter. The bed to the rear of the narrow room was on delicate claw feet, also see-through.

She pressed her body against his, bringing with her a sweet rose scent, nothing too cloying and no stench of old sex. With nimble fingers, she had his uniform open, grazing her nails across his bare skin. A shiver pebbled his nipples.

"Candy," she said, rubbing her parted mouth across his chest hairs.

He gripped her shoulders, reminded of doing this earlier to Huxley, and almost shook the woman. "Your *real* name."

"Sophia." Her dark eyes mesmerized him. Chocolate swirled in their depths.

Spinning her, he yanked her against him and grabbed her breasts, filling his palms. He pressed a kiss to the pulse beating at her neck. "Do you have time for me?"

"As long as you need." Her husky voice shot straight to his groin as he glided a flattened palm over the soft curves of her belly.

"An hour, no more." He dipped his fingers lower, drawing a gasp from her. As beautiful as she was, perhaps a little missionary wouldn't hurt.

14

|=Ø|_||2733/\/

Date: 2170.14.10
The Holies
The Skin Canvas

NATE GRUNTED A GREETING when he walked in, nodding at his waiting clients without making eye contact. A few of the inkjobs were new, with their unblemished skin and hovering clouds. Lissa flashed a bright smile, dipping Nate's frown into a scowl. It wasn't her fault he'd had an argument with Kylie that morning, and it sure as hell wasn't her fault he found her attractive.

He'd envisioned a romantic whirlwind of a night and a repeat in the bedroom department. Instead, in the chaser, he'd raised his doubts, his distrust of Lord Fields, and everything his proposal stood for. Nate had slept alone, Kylie's side of the bed cold when he'd awoken this morning. No coffee, no cuddles, and no sweet kiss goodbye.

"I'd offer a coffee, but by the looks of you, perhaps something stronger?" Lissa trailed him into the backroom, leaning her lush form against the door frame. A short sundress in periwinkle blue left most of her legs bare and catapulted his imagination.

He grunted again, pining for winter when she'd cover all that up and cease to torment him.

"How was last night? Did Kylie look beautiful?"

"Breathtaking." Before he could stop himself, he spewed the details of the Lord-Fields encounter and the subsequent argument.

"Oh, dear." Lissa shook her head, tossing her curls. "I see why you're miserable, but aren't you a tad paranoid?"

Nate glared at her, rising anger burning and cinching his chest. Her not taking his side left him speechless. He gaped at her, wavering between fury and disappointment.

Lissa was still nattering on. "…To have you concerned on my behalf would be amazing. She should've listened to you, perhaps even calmed your fears."

Just like that, his mood lifted. Nate's shoulders slumped, and he released a long-drawn-out sigh. "I'll take that coffee now, Liss." He flashed her a smile, wishing he could hug her. Therein lay too much temptation, so he busied his hands, readying his work area for the day ahead.

"On it, Boss. Renovare upped your vendor status, as well. You're fully booked until next Tuesday." Lissa rubbed her hands together with glee. "I feel a bonus coming." In a cloud of lavender, she left the room, granting a moment of semi-peace. Nate stared after her without guarding his expressions. Of all the emotions roiling within him, lust topped the list, but so, too, did frustration.

Renovare upping his status meant more business, but he didn't want it. It came with strings attached. He wasn't duped. This 'boon' was due to Kylie's new alliance with Lord Fields and not any hard work on his part.

"Any clouds?" Lissa placed his coffee on his side table, crossed her clasped hands in front of her, and rocked on her toes.

"A few. Looks like it's with the upgrades or new models only."

"Renovare wouldn't do this on purpose, would they, Nate?" She chewed on her plump bottom lip, and he zeroed in on that nervous action. "They could rebel. Start a revolution. People don't treat their 'things' well, you know."

"They'll recall them as soon as they find out, Liss. We have more chance of a rebellion from your toaster, sweetheart." Nate forced a smile, hiding that he'd considered the same possibility. If, or when, this happened, he only hoped he wasn't here at The Skin Canvas. He didn't have an inkjob at home where they could hide out until the initial massacre was over.

Grim thoughts, indeed. Renovare employees received a discount on inkjob purchases, but they'd decided against it. Lissa couldn't afford one, not on what Nate paid her.

"A strange call came in." Liss was back to chewing on her lip, dazzling Nate, who was left wondering whether she'd taste sweet or spicy. "They wanted to confirm that you'd tattooed a sunburst and a cat. I ran the sunburst through our database since we knew about the cat. The man sounded official, Nate."

"Not an admirer?" He winked at her, hoping to calm whatever fears she'd dreamed up. "Not Rick?"

"I wish. They made my skin crawl." Lissa shuddered. "They said both tatts belonged to the vandalized inkjobs."

He slouched, forgoing any more attempts to charm her out of her concern. "What else did they say?"

"That's it. Just how curious they were that you'd done both." Lissa paused, rubbing her chest, her brow furrowed. A soft mist formed above her head, and Nate bolted forward to drag her into his arms. No, not his Lissa.

She pressed her cheek to his chest and sighed.

Soft, feminine curves fitted against him; warmth, sweet lavender, and lust filled his chest, cinching his breathing. He cleared his throat, stroking her bare shoulder with the pad of his thumb.

"Don't worry about it, Liss. We're not involved, and you know how many inkjobs I tatt, so the possibility of both being mine is high."

"You're right, as usual." When she stepped away, enough to meet his gaze, she smiled. Her cloud had gone, but at this angle, she blessed him with a glimpse of her cleavage. She broke the contact and skipped from the room, leaving him alone for a moment.

He huffed, adjusted his jeans, and waited for his first client.

His heart rate had spiked when she'd mentioned the call, but sanity prevailed. He had done nothing, wasn't involved in the inkjob mutilations, and had nothing to fear. Still, it niggled his mind, just enough to cool his ardor the longer he dwelled on it.

Crossing that bridge when he had to was the wisest approach. He had enough on his plate without adding irrational fears. He needed to talk to Kylie, explain his concerns, ask her to be cautious, and perhaps, tonight, they'd have make-up sex.

Yet, despite burning through the lust with Kylie, his interest in Lissa wasn't diminishing. Fear of another sort, along with the sparks of excitement, skittered down his spine. Visions plagued him—of lifting her sundress to rest on her hips as he pinned her to the wall. Bending her over the table. Having her ride him in the receptionist chairs.

There was at least one silver lining to his new vendor status. There wouldn't be time to do Lissa's tatt.

It was all so unromantic, yet zinging through his blood was an eagerness that hardened him, harkening to his days as a horny teenager.

He was playing with fire, and he knew it, but knowing it and stopping it were two different things.

15

|=1|=733/\/

Date: 2170.14.10
Nova's Red sector AKA 'The Colony'
The Center

NOVA WAS LIKE A pie cut into five sectors. They called the blue sector where the rich middle class lived, the Holies. That wasn't saying much. The white sector was a squalid cesspool known as the Dump where the poorest of the poor lived, but even they had standards. None ventured into the Deadzone since it was where the Kicks tossed bodies and killed snitches. There would be no need for Gibs to visit the Dump anytime soon. Rarely did he venture into the green sector, the Kicks, but he'd been there twice in the last week. Memorable experiences both times. Thanks to Sophia, he was himself again and in control. He hadn't sampled the full bouquet the Kicks offered, and his tastes were tame in comparison to most men his age or younger. Or older, he grimaced, thinking of Lawrence.

That left the black and red sectors. Black or Shadows was for the Kicks' bosses, and their security was tighter than a virgin's ass. The red, or Colony, was Gibs's home, for now. The Colony was also the location of the Center, from where the precincts were managed. Delegation happened here, and in the bowels below were the morgues, labs, and cells for the less fortunate.

If he took a chaser high above the smog, he'd break through to the sunlight bathing the upper echelon of the Lux sector, whose denizens never bothered with the scum beneath them and had formed a caste system of their own. It mattered where you lived on Lux.

"Gibs, I trust this is important." Captain Montgomery strolled past, his suit crisp and expensive. He hadn't worn his uniform in years. Not like Gibs, who was a stickler for tradition even if he paired his with his father's tattered trench coat.

"Popping in to chat with Davis, sir."

"Very well. Carry on."

Gibs scowled at his boss's disappearing form, the elevator whisking him up and out of sight. What did he have that Gibs didn't? Authority? Class? He grunted and stepped into the antique elevator to descend into hell, so to speak. He was sure as frack his boss's cock worked just as well as his. So, it wasn't that Tamara liked. Maybe Montgomery's kink went deeper than Gibs's doggy style. He winced, trying to scrub the image from his mind.

Prestige? Perhaps Tamara sought re-entry into Lux?

The elevator shuddered, metal grating on metal as it traveled. Lights flickered overhead, and the stench of bleach and old onions filled the compartment. He twitched his nose but said nothing. When the doors opened not quite on level, he pulled himself up, only to be slapped in the face by a potent bleach odor. Dead bodies in floating gurneys lined the passages, their exposed feet stamped with bar-tags. One scan and their details would pop up on his holo-wrist. Glassed walls allowed a line of sight across the floor, piercing labs, morgues, and the central coffee station. He headed there first.

They didn't skimp on coffee here, and he helped himself to the imported stuff, inhaling and sipping with relish. A slow spin on his heels showed Dr. Margo Travis in the middle of an autopsy, her gray bun messy and unraveling further with each cut of her power saw.

Davis waved, several rooms back, latex covering his hands. Why he was here, Gibs didn't know. There was something strange about Martin Davis, something borderline macabre, but he did his job well, and that covered all manner of irregularities. Gibs snorted and poured another coffee. The problem with Davis was that he had too much character in a conforming world.

"What brings you here, Gibs? Where's the blonde? Got rid of her already?" Davis peered around Gibs in search of Huxley.

"She's trawling through memories at Renovare." Gibs pulled out a metal chair, praying the spindly legs held his weight. "I came in person for a reason, Davis. Had a run-in with the Master and Lord Fields, and they both mentioned reading the case files."

Davis jerked as if slapped, poured himself a coffee with six sugars, and pulled out a chair. His face contorted with alarm, not adding to his attractiveness in the least. The bright lights filling each ceiling panel reflected off his bald pate like a disco ball.

He shook his head, and Gibs half expected music to fill the room. "It wasn't me, if that's what you're thinking."

"I wasn't. Just thought it best to talk face to face. No communication along the usual channels. Keep your findings to the three of us."

Davis slapped his palm on the table as a broken-toothed smile cracked his face. "Keeping the girl?"

"For now. Got any more data for me? The owner of Eve Roe 2?"

Davis grimaced, threw back his coffee, and rose to pour another. "It ain't good, Gibs. I double-checked, just to be sure."

Gibs waited for the trembling man to fill his cup and resume his seat, but when a flask came out of his pocket, he arched a brow. Alcohol was fine, and he wasn't one to judge, but it wasn't advisable to indulge on the job.

"Charles DuPont."

Gibs blinked, unsure he'd heard correctly. "Frack." He cleared his throat, his vocal cords strangled. "Triple check it."

"I did. Eve Roe 2 belonged to the mayor, Gibs. I ain't going to Montgomery with this without making fracken sure." Davis offered his flask, and Gibs splashed a little of it into his coffee.

"I need all the details." Perhaps the vandal targeted Lux as Huxley had suggested? A Lux-hater widened his suspect pool to the impossible. There were too many people screwed over by the rich and famous. His pulse burned and throbbed at his temple. He rubbed it with an extended middle finger.

"Done." Davis stirred his coffee with a broken stylus. "Oh, and Margo hasn't received Thomas Walker's blood sample. Did you forget to ask?"

Gibs grunted and typed on his holo-wrist. He had to scroll forever to find Thomas's contact info, too lazy to use the search function.

"Tom, need a blood sample for a narcotics scan, and did you go for that psyche assessment?" As he waited, he sipped his tequila-laced coffee, twisting his lips in disgust.

"Fine, and yes, want the results?" Thomas's picture popped up, along with his response. The holographics striated both, but Gibs could read them just fine. That didn't mean he would stop pestering the department for a cell phone.

"Yes, please send the results to me. Good luck today with Olivia 2."

"Thanks."

Gibs settled his gaze on Davis. "Done. Send someone to collect the blood sample." He threw back his coffee, the tequila not enhancing the flavor as it incinerated his stomach lining.

Davis chuckled. "It pays to have friends in high places."

Gibs glared. "Does it?"

An uncomfortable silence claimed the small coffee room.

Davis shifted in his chair and took a long pull from his flask. "The blade marks are of a small dagger. The more I look at the evidence, the more I think the killer's a woman."

Gibs grunted at the findings, having come to the same conclusion. "If that's true, how can she overpower a synth?"

"We do every day. She must have the police neutralization codes."

Gibs rubbed his jaw, the headache pinging across his temple to settle behind his right ear. "Think it's an inside job?"

"Hell no."

"Just in case, trawl through all the wedding photos of the female officers. Maybe one of their rings matches the vandal's. And find out who manufactured the dagger."

Davis huffed, tapping his fingers on the table's metallic surface. "Frack, Gibs. It isn't as if I'm busy."

"Delegate, Davis. Get Montgomery to assign a rookie to you, too."

A hopeful expression didn't soften the harshness of Davis's face. "Can I have yours?"

Fury—hot, red, and fierce—tore through Gibs. His internal voice roared a no. "She's busy."

He slammed his cup onto the counter and stormed off, fighting the urge to rip Davis's head off. Gibs's attachment to Huxley made no sense and neither did his protectiveness. Working with Davis would aid her career, would improve her investigative knowledge, so he shouldn't begrudge her the opportunity. He froze, his finger hovering on the elevator call button.

Spinning on his heel, he stomped to Davis. "When she's done at Renovare, I'll send her to you."

Done. He released a shuddering breath. Striding toward the elevator again, he sensed that he might regret this decision. No more than he regretted having to ask Montgomery for the synth unit's details and their kill codes.

16

S1X733/\/

Date: 2170.14.10
Nova's Red sector AKA 'The Colony'
The Center

GIBS PACED OUTSIDE MONTGOMERY'S office. A familiar giggle told him all he needed to know. Montgomery was screwing his ex-wife, spreading her legs on his desk. Gibs grimaced, and bile rose and pooled in his mouth, bringing with it a decided tequila flavor.

"He's almost done." Montgomery's receptionist, a petite woman with gray streaks in her brown hair, flashed a polite smile. Her name-plate said "Mrs. Dennis." She was new and would last as long as the previous woman had.

"I'm sure he is." Gibs flashed an insincere smile. Dread engulfed him, thickened, at the thought of sex stinking up his captain's office. He rose, rubbing his damp palms on his thighs. "I can come back later when the room's been...fumigated." He scowled, having meant to say aerated. With a shrug, he headed for the elevator as the receptionist leaped to her feet and the captain's office door opened.

"Gibs, what a surprise." Tamara sashayed out, her legs working just fine. Had he known she'd spread it for any man, he might have had second thoughts about marrying her. Not a hair was out of place in her blonde bun, her lipstick perfect. Everything was pristine except for a telltale wrinkle over her left breast.

"Mara." He nodded. She hated him calling her that since it meant bitterness in some languages. It suited her better than Tamara ever would. "Captain, got a minute?" Gibs peered around her as if she were but an obstacle.

"It better be important." Montgomery pressed a kiss to Tamara's temple and swatted her backside. She giggled, her cheeks flushed.

Gibs closed the door on her face, chuckling at her gasp of outrage. "Owner of the second Eve Roe is Charles DuPont." He didn't hold back his punches, not with Mara's cloying perfume still lingering. Thankfully, it overpowered the stench of sex.

"Frack." Montgomery dropped into the chair behind his desk, his face paling. "Are you sure?"

"Davis is." Gibs paced the room, unable to sit. He studied the framed awards and certificates lining the office walls. Nothing in the Center had been revamped in decades, maintaining the look of a 21st-century police headquarters. "I'll have Huxley question him since he's her uncle."

"Frack, how did you...?"

Gibs arched a brow, silencing his sputtering boss. "I'll accompany her, of course, but as a show of support."

"Fine." Montgomery harrumphed. "Anything else?"

"Yes." Gibs faced the man—the gray in his temples, the dark blue eyes, the tall frame with a little fat in the mid-section. It had to be his bulging wallet Mara liked. "We think the perp's a woman, which means she knows how to deactivate a synth. I need a list of the members of the synth unit, all their details, and what the kill codes are."

"They change monthly."

"This month's will do." Gibs paused. Either the woman did the deed herself, or she bypassed the algorithms, getting her inkjob to terminate their own kind. That wasn't a simple task. Renovare had to have personnel who could do this. He'd been right. It was an inside job; he just didn't know whether the perp worked in law enforcement or inkjob manufacturing.

"I'll see what I can do."

"Thanks, Captain." Gibs hurried out of the office before Montgomery could stop him. His destination was Renovare, or Huxley, to be specific. He wanted the interview with the mayor scheduled as soon as possible. Climbing into his chaser, he ignored the usual greeting; instead, he bent his legs to rest both elbows on his knees, steepling his fingers. He'd forgotten something. It niggled at his subconscious.

Leaning back, he closed his eyes to run through the events of the past four days. He relived climbing out of his chaser in the Dead-zone, including the cloying stench, the smog clinging to his pores, the mildew coating his tongue.

Thomas's infatuation, his belief that Olivia was human in all the ways that mattered. Lawrence's dismissal of his part in Dad's death, and Butler's disdain which had to be in his programming. Gibs's pulse leaped as his thoughts circled Butler.

"The security surveillance." Gibs lunged for the glove compartment where he'd tossed the data crystal. It lay amid old biodegradable gloves in various stages of degradation, spare bullets for his Glock, a scratched pair of sunvisors, and Olivia's antique book.

He gripped the crystal, joy splitting his cheeks into a painful smile. Wait until he showed Hux. Gibs stilled…stunned by the excitement sharing this discovery with someone meant. Someone? He grunted. Naomi Huxley, to be precise. He wasn't this excited to share anything with Montgomery or Davis.

Frack.

He wiped the smile off his face and shoved the crystal into his pocket. The plan for today was to meet up with Huxley, visit the mayor at his residence, sift through the data crystal, and read that cursed erotic novel Olivia had 'loved' so much.

At some point, he hoped to have the synth unit's details.

Focus on the now, not on the why. Why was his stoicism gone? Why had he allowed a rookie into his guarded life? Why had he come to care what happened to her, her career, her opinion? He had to think of her as the daughter he never had. Easier said than done.

"Incoming call from Officer Naomi Huxley."

Speak of the temptress. Gibs drew in a deep breath to steady his nerves. "Patch her through."

"Gibs, morning. Listen, I'm done, and there's nothing here."

"Meet me at my place." He grimaced, not needing her and his bed close, but it was the securest place he knew. "We've much to discuss."

"See you in a bit."

She hung up, and he instructed his chaser to take him home. He made a mental list of what they needed to discuss, trying to avoid thinking about how he'd left his place this morning. The empty pizza box sat on his coffee table. Half-chewed crusts stained the paper towels. A half-empty whisky bottle nestled between two cushions, and a bottle of lube lay on the floor where it had fallen.

Thankfully, the home was closer to the Center than Renovare, and he was en route anyway. Huxley would need to hail a chaser, leaving him enough time to clean up. His tension ramped, and he had to force his shoulders to relax, the burn between them a sure indication that Huxley's opinion of his home mattered.

The moment his chaser aligned with his platform, he leaped out, nearly slamming into his too-slow-to-open door. He left it gaping, flicking his louvers up to let in more air. He grabbed clothing items strewn everywhere and tossed them into the shute. Discarded junket food and other paraphernalia landed in the trash or sink. He fluffed cushions and made his bed before tackling the dishes. It wasn't much and didn't take long. After a quick swipe of the counters, he headed for the bathroom.

The vacuum bots had moved into his room by the time Huxley stepped onto his platform. Detergent stung his fingers, but the aroma of brewing coffee masked much of his home's mustiness.

"Knock knock." Huxley hovered by the door. She wore her uniform today, hugging curves he shouldn't be noticing. Her hair swung in a high ponytail, and her lips were a lush peach.

"Come in. Want some coffee?"

"Please." She dropped onto the couch, sighing as it cupped her backside. "I didn't expect you to live in the Colony."

"Mara got our home in the divorce, and at the time, another sector wasn't far enough."

"That bad?" Huxley twisted to meet his gaze, understanding softening her features. It might have killed him if she'd pitied him.

"She's screwing Montgomery." Gibs held out her cup, offering her the bottle of artificial sugar with the other hand. He shouldn't have blurted that, but it was only a matter of time before she found out. Since he knew about Uncle Charlie, it made sense that he share his sordid connections.

"Ouch." She declined the sugar and brought the coffee to her nose, inhaling its addictive aroma. "I'd never do the captain."

"Too old?" Gibs sat in the single-seater and plunked his boots onto the table. Huxley followed his example and spread out. He admired her long legs, enjoying having her presence in his home.

She shook her head. "He's not you. Says much about your wife, though."

Gibs choked on his coffee, grabbing the cup with both hands to stop it from spilling. He flicked a wary glance at Huxley, expecting her to be teasing him again. She wasn't. Potent heat filled her gaze, mimicking the turmoil she invoked within him.

"Ex," he muttered. Folding his legs, he slid his coffee onto the table. "Davis found out who the owner of Eve Roe 2 is." Rubbing his face did nothing to prepare him for what he needed to ask her to do. "It's your uncle, Hux."

"I know. Zeta gave me the owners' list this morning along with the tatt parlor. I uploaded both to the cloud." She flashed a smile, but it was a sad one. "It's why I needed to see you. Want me to set up a meeting?"

"Please. I could go through the official channels, but that could take days. We'll need surveillance footage, too. Someone with access is targeting Lux." He pushed off the couch to pace. "Davis and I believe the perp is a woman. You saw the hand, the diamond ring."

"It's possible. They could also be transgender or someone who identifies as a woman."

"True, but bone structure doesn't lie, Hux. The shoulders are narrow, the shoe-size a seven." He sipped his coffee before placing the cup onto the table again. "Montgomery's sourcing the synth unit's details. I'll ask Lord Fields for the names of his staff with access to Renovare's kill codes."

"Looks like we're narrowing in on the perp, Gibs."

He didn't have it in him to break her hope. How many knew Renovare's or the enforcement's codes? How many shops manufactured daggers or marquise diamond rings?

"It's not all of Lux, so I guess that's progress." He dug into his pocket to extract the data crystal, holding it up between forefinger and thumb. "You have a choice. You can trawl through the sec-vids from the Walker residence, or you can read this book?" He pointed to where the bare-chested man adorned a paperback.

"A book?" She sat up. "Why?"

Gibs shrugged. "According to Thomas, it was Olivia's favorite."

"She read for pleasure?" Huxley gasped and scooted her backside forward, picking up the novel to thumb through it.

"Didn't Thomas tell you? He believed she was as human as the next woman."

Huxley stilled, her eyes wide. "I didn't think his infatuation went that deep, Gibs."

"He mourned her 'death.'" Gibs dropped into the chair, something clicking into place. "Didn't Zeta say they didn't store activated synths' memories?"

Hux's tongue rested at the corner of her lips as she skim-read a page. "Yes, something about not violating the privacy act and the Pancras Treaty."

"Then how could they replicate Olivia with what memories they had?"

"Holy frack, Gibs. They're violating..." Huxley gaped, her face paling.

"Exactly, but how do we prove this, and how does this help solve our case?" He rubbed his face, fighting the disbelief and helplessness.

"It doesn't. We can only tip off the auditors—let them investigate it."

"Lord Fields is aware of it, for frack sake." Gibs lunged forward to grip her shoulders. "You saw the Zetas, Hux. What else is he doing?"

"I don't know." She gripped his forearms, her mouth parting.

He sucked in a deep breath, then another, fighting the spots swirling his vision. "Could he be tampering with their emotions, making them more human? Deploying upgrades and releasing new models then sitting back and watching the shit unfold?"

"All speculation, Gibs. We'll need hard evidence." She rose, using his elbows as leverage. "There's no one we could go to. I'd say Uncle Charlie, but this places him in a political corner."

"Montgomery's out. He's a puppet." Gibs cupped her cheeks, wishing he could kiss her. He had to do the one thing he didn't want to do, and if he died, the taste of her lips was its own reward. "I'll speak to the Master."

"Frack." She slid her hands up his arms, squeezing him there. "I'm coming with you."

"Hell no." With his thumbs, he brushed the curls off her temple, ignoring their slight tremble. "She could kill you."

"I go with you, or I follow you, Gibs. Your choice."

Then she kissed him.

17

53V3/\/733/\/

Date: 2170.14.10
Huxley's arms

GIBS FROZE, STUNNED THAT Huxley's lips touched his. Yet he couldn't deny those were her arms looping around his neck. He groaned, pressing his hands to the base of her spine, sliding a hand to grip her jacket between her shoulder blades. He crushed her against him, marveling at her feminine softness, her rose scent, and the sweet, honeyed nectar of her mouth.

Tendrils of her hair brushed his face, and he struggled to breathe through his nose, not wanting to break contact with her for something as unimportant as oxygen. His recently satiated cock leaped to life, straining his pants. He pulled away, just a little.

"Hux, let me taste you." Their breaths mingled as he drowned in the storm gray of her eyes. He'd never seen anything more beautiful. The corner of her top lip curled upward as luscious pink flushed her cheeks. She rose on her tiptoes, gripped his biceps, and parted her lips.

Time slowed. The exact shade of pink staining her cheeks, the freckle just below her right eye, the intense passion threading her ragged breathing, and the sweetness of her mouth would remain with him forever. He grabbed her ponytail, tugging her head back. She moaned, her back arching, her neck exposed.

Exquisite, not that he could tell her so. To speak was to waste a precious moment. He brushed his lips across hers, testing the plumpness, now bruised red from his previous kiss. Excitement fluttered in his chest like heart palpitations.

"Gibs, please." Her breathless plea shot straight to his balls, overwhelming reason, and he angled his mouth across hers, testing the moist treasure within. She dueled him, challenged his authority, his control. A groan rippled along his throat. His nostrils flared as his vision focused on her, ignoring the world around them.

"Hux, I..." Feathering kisses along her jaw, he couldn't form words, couldn't tell her what she inspired in him.

"Frack, Gibs, I want you." She fumbled with his uniform, undoing snaps and ties with desperate eagerness.

He stilled, pulling away but gripping her shoulders to ensure she didn't lose her balance. He wanted her, too, but that didn't mean he had to take advantage of this. Something felt wrong. His instincts leaped in dismay. Her cheeks were flushed, her eyes glazed with her frantic movements as if something compelled her, intensified her emotions.

"Hux, did you consume something this morning?"

"What?" Unnatural heat poured off her body, and he chastised himself for not noticing.

"Think, Huxley." He shook her, sending her pony swaying.

"The chocolates..." She leaned her temple on his chest and sucked in deep breaths. "The ones you sent me."

Icy tingles rippled down his neck and spine. He scooped her into his arms and hurried to the door, slamming the chaser call button with his elbow. Frack, how could he be so naïve? Her behavior had been out of character, but her kiss had surprised him, robbed him of thought. He'd wanted it too damn much.

Time ticked as he waited for the chaser to rise. He settled his focus on her face, trailing each feature with vigilance. Her breathing was labored, and she met his gaze. Fear widened her eyes and darkened the gray of her irises. At least, she'd stopped trying to strip his uniform off him and was taking this seriously.

"Poisoned?" Her voice was too soft, fading, sending a fresh stream of fear through him.

"Hux, stay with me." He hugged her against him.

Her fingers slid along his shoulders like a caress of feathers, but her full weight hit him when she fainted. Panic set in then. He thrust her into the chaser, clambering in after her as he roared instructions. The chaser activated emergency protocol, taking them to the closest clinic.

Time slowed again, each second passing with him checking her breathing. Tears stung his eyes, and he blinked them away, needing to remain calm and strong. Frack, he cared—too much too soon. He hadn't noticed her feverish state because he'd wanted the kiss. This was all his fault. If he'd remained focused, fought her allure, stayed professional, whoever had targeted her wouldn't have had a chance to harm her.

A medical team awaited them as soon as the chaser touched down on the extended platform. They loaded her onto the floating gurney, and he ran after them until the door slammed in his face. Peering through the glass, he watched the medical staff press oxygen over her mouth while drawing blood. What else could they do?

He spun away from the scene, anger solidifying the blood pumping in his veins. "Davis," he growled into his holo-wrist.

It took an agonizing second before Davis answered. "What?"

"Huxley's been poisoned. Search her home for the chocolates someone sent her on my behalf. Test them. We need to know what we're dealing with."

"Frack, Gibs. How is she? Where are you?" Davis's nose bumped his wrist and sent his holographic striations spinning.

What patience Gibs had evaporated, tainting his vision red. "Davis, find the poison." His roar drew cries of alarm from the medical personnel and patients around him. He didn't care.

Davis jerked. "Right. On it."

Gibs collapsed into the closest chair, dropping his face into his hands. This made no sense. Why target Huxley? Why spur a romance when there was none? Well, none from her side. Was it a side effect of the toxins scouring her system? Shame hit him hard, burning his cheeks anew. He'd wanted her, relished the feel and taste of her, yet she suffered, drugged with who knew what. Had he been on his game, he'd have noticed sooner, reacted quicker.

If she died, it was on him.

Time ticked. He ignored incoming calls from anyone but Davis, who'd found a half-eaten box of imported chocolates on her bed. The real deal, according to his bald friend. *Friend?* Gibs grunted; the speed at which his life had changed left him reeling.

"Gibs?" A nurse addressed the waiting room, scanning the faces raised in eagerness.

He rose, running his palms along his thighs. "I'm Gibson Shaw."

"She's asking for you."

He froze, fear seizing his muscles. Was he about to hear Huxley's deathbed wishes?

"She'll be fine—just an overdose." The nurse huffed, running an accusatory gaze over him. One he recognized through her goggles and mask.

"Overdose?" He caught the nurse by the shoulder. "Of what?"

"Rage."

He stared after her disappearing black-overall-clad form, then burst into a jog, praying he didn't lose sight of her. *Rage?* That explained so much. He'd heard it affected the libido. By heard, he meant having to endure the screams and grunts from the elderly couple two levels down. The popular drug saturated every inch of the Kicks, of course.

Seeing Hux sprawled in the clinic's bed, her face pale and hair damp, tore through him, softening the walls guarding his emotions. What Mara had destroyed suffered a rebirth, light bursting through the cracks and splintering the ichor coating his heart.

"Gibs?" Hux held out a trembling hand, and he leaped forward to grip it and raise it to his lips for a kiss.

"How are you feeling?" He croaked the question as he shuffled closer to brush the hair off her temple.

Pink stained her cheeks, adding color to her porcelain skin. "I'm sorry..." She gestured to his gaping uniform. He'd forgotten about it.

"Sorry about what?"

"Kissing you..." She dipped her head to hide her tears, but he'd seen the telltale shimmer.

He forced a smile even as her regret streaked sadness across his soul. "You were under the influence." He hadn't been and had no excuse for his behavior.

"No, I'm sorry I needed drugs to gather the courage to kiss you." She smiled, her once-peach lips now too pale. "I'd prefer to do it when I'm aware of my actions and able to remember every detail. It's just a tantalizing dream now."

She nestled into the pillows, meeting his gaze with an intense emotion he couldn't decipher. It was warm, though, and his heart rate responded, recognizing whatever it was.

"Promise to kiss me when I'm well?"

He nodded, unable to deny her this, to deny her anything.

She sighed, sliding deeper into the blankets. "Thanks for saving me."

"It's what partners do." He kissed her temple, not bothering to resist the temptation. She had an excuse; he didn't. Now that he had the taste of her, there was no fighting this attraction. Not anymore. Not when her near-death had him realizing how much she meant to him.

"They say I have to stay for a few hours." She waved an accusatory finger. "Don't go solving the case without me."

He rolled his lips to smother a smile. "Yes, ma'am. I'll bring the book and collect anything else you need."

Her eyelids fluttered closed, but her breathing was regular. He trailed a fingertip along the curve of her cheek, brushing his thumb across her parted lips. A nurse entered, and he snatched his hand away, heat burning his cheeks and neck. He strode out of the clinic, heading home for the book then to her apartment for a few essentials.

"It's Rage," he said the moment Davis called him.

"Yes, a more potent version than what's on the street. Someone wanted her to die, Gibs." Davis ran a hand over his bald spot. "It's expensive stuff, too."

"I'll look into it." Gibs wasn't one to show gratitude, but he had to start somewhere. "Thanks, Martin. I'm taking her to my place this afternoon. You're welcome to visit."

"I'll be there at six."

Gibs pursed his lips as he climbed into his chaser. Now to convince Hux the safest place for her was with him, in his apartment and his bed.

18

319#733/\/

Date: 2170.14.10
The Holies
The Skin Canvas

GIBS STEPPED INTO THE small tattoo parlor, set up as he'd expected one to look: white walls, white faux-wooden floors, and white chairs with a backdrop of framed and mounted black tattoo designs. As soon as he'd parked his chaser, he'd activated his enhanced vision, needing to see the interviewees' heart rates.

A bubbly brunette greeted him, her bright smile implying there wasn't much going on upstairs, intelligence-wise. It was late afternoon. No one waited in the reception area although the last client was at the mercy of the buzzing tattoo gun.

"Hello, welcome to The Skin Canvas." Bubbly swept out her hand, gesturing to the empty chairs. "Nate will be with you in a moment."

Gibs paced, denying the offer of a beverage, preferring to spend his anxious energy before he collected Hux from the clinic. He'd fetched her things and forgone picking up the book. She would have plenty of time to read in the next few days. He hadn't been able to wait idly at home, nor at the clinic, so he'd trawled the files Hux had uploaded onto the cloud. That led him here.

The tongue-in-cheek name of the parlor was as welcoming as the receptionist. Gibs didn't put much faith in either. The sweetest of people were capable of murder.

The buzzing ended, and Gibs faced the backroom, waiting for the last client to appear. Laughter reverberated off the walls, the conversation ebbing and flowing between humans. Inkjobs didn't converse with such vibrant ease.

A man stepped out in a Renovare factory-worker overall, sleek in stainless-steel blue. He'd rolled up his sleeve, exposing a tattoo of a partial inkjob in a seductive pose. A ragged salt-and-pepper beard dominated his face, but his bright smile broke through.

"Thanks, Nate. Excellent work as always. I'll see you after my next milestone."

"Happy to oblige, Jamie." The man behind him was shorter and not as muscled, with a neat beard sculpting his jawline. An unraveling man-bun threatened to spill his gold-streaked brown hair. He'd shoved up the sleeves of his brown button-up shirt, exposing his tattooed forearms. Bubbly escorted Jamie to the door.

"Jonathan Dough?" Gibs didn't allow the man another second. He had somewhere he'd rather be.

"Yes, call me Nate. How can I help you?" He offered a polite smile.

"Detective Gibson Shaw." Gibs focused on the man's heart.

It skipped a beat, and his temperature spiked, but within seconds, both returned to normal. He had twitched, though, his smile wavered, and he stiffened his shoulders. None of that implied he was guilty of a crime. No, it was the usual response to having a detective question you.

Gibs pressed the record button on his holo-wrist. Tingles zinged along his nerve endings to the embedded chips. "As per protocol, I will be recording this session. Do you agree, Mr. Jonathan Dough?"

"Dough's pronounced like Rough, and yes, I agree to the recording."

Gibs nodded. "This recording is for quality purposes and can be used against you in a court of law. I'm here about two inkjobs you tatted: one with a cat and the other with a sunburst."

"Here are the files." Bubbly slid across the prepared file tablets.

Gibs scowled, not liking that they were forewarned of his arrival. He'd lost the element of surprise but not their bodily reactions his enhanced vision would reveal.

"Let the recording note the voice belongs to...?" He arched a brow at Bubbly.

"Melissa Lorenzo."

Gibs flashed a small smile that barely had time to bear his teeth. "How did you know I was coming, Ms. Lorenzo?"

"Someone from law enforcement called to confirm we did the tatts. Anything else we know about the crimes is from Officer Rick Sanchez, who's my...friend." Her sweet smile faltered, and concern furrowed her brow. "He won't get into trouble for this, will he?"

Gibs shook his head. It was best to lie regardless. Yet of all his concerns, a boyfriend revealing secrets of his case was the least of them. That wouldn't be happening anymore, not with their cloud storage. He hoped, but he couldn't put it past the Master or Lord Fields to have the account hacked.

"What can you tell me about the owners? Did they seem strange, behave in an abnormal way when they brought their inkjobs to you?"

Nate's right hand twitched, and a shadow passed over his blue eyes. Something lingered, alarming Gibs's instincts. His advanced eye recorded a small heart-rate spike, but Nate's nervousness soon subsided.

"Not really." Nate shrugged, shoving his hands into his denim pockets. "They and not their representatives must bring their inkjobs in. It's part of the ownership responsibility code of conduct they agree to when they purchase an inkjob."

Nate took the top file tablet from Melissa and activated it. "X10 model, brand new, belonging to Thomas K. Walker. His mannerisms were normal, nothing out of the ordinary." Nate raised his gaze, and his focus faded as he peered to the left, lost in thought, his temperature rising a degree. "A pretty thing, but all entertainment models are." He deactivated the tablet and handed it to Gibs. "That day, I caressed her cheek, marveling at how lifelike she was. Tiny hairs rose at my touch. She was an amazing work of art."

Gibs pursed his lips. "So *your* reaction was abnormal, not Mr. Walker's or the X10's?"

Nate chuckled. "You could say that." He activated the other tablet for Eve Roe 2. "Ah, yes, the mayor's. Had to book my studio out for that hour. Security, y'know." His brow furrowed. "This inkjob was old; finding a bare spot meant stripping her clothes off." Color stained his cheeks, and his temperature rose another degree. "I'd never had to do that before, and even though they're synthetic, my eyes and mind saw it as real. She was as beautiful as an X10, minus the refined, physical enhancements and in a matured-wine sort of way."

"You became aroused?" The physical signs were there, but Gibs needed to ask for the recording.

Nate stilled, flashing a look at his receptionist that told Gibs much. Eve Roe 2 had aroused him as much as Melissa did. The wedding ring on Nate's finger glimmered in the artificial light, adding another layer of intrigue. Gibs appraised the innocent allure of the receptionist. She had no idea how Nate felt. If she turned up dead, then Gibs would know the killer was tied to Nate somehow. Both inkjobs had sparked a reaction from the tatt artist. A jealous wife with too much time on her hands?

"In a way. Since then, I've stopped seeing them as human." His gaze flicked right when he said that, his fingers twitched, and his heart rate leaped.

Gibs grunted. A lie, but why? What did it matter whether Nate found them attractive or not?

"They're meant to be attractive, Nate." He accepted the deactivated tablet from him and tucked both inside his trench coat. "Thank you for your time." He headed for the door, but when he reached it and gripped the frame, he faced them. "One last question. Do you know any kill codes if an inkjob should go berserk?"

Nate shook his head without hesitation. "No, it's not needed when the owner accompanies them. They have their own safe words, right?"

Gibs nodded, forcing a small smile. "Thank you for your time."

He ended the recording and clambered into his waiting chaser. Nate had it right. He wouldn't need the codes, and there'd been no indication he was lying. Except for that once. Seeing the inkjobs as attractive was common enough that he need not be ashamed about it. So why hide it? Or was there more behind the thin lie?

He instructed his chaser to head to the clinic. Time for the true battle. He might have to reveal to Hux how he felt. Grimacing, he withdrew the tablets from his pocket, flicking a finger as he read the details provided. He couldn't see a connection, other than Nate's reactions to the inkjobs. Frack, the man might have reacted to all his clients that way. The Skin Canvas was a dead-end.

He tossed the tablets onto the luggage he'd packed for Hux. Being in law enforcement meant he had override commands to enter any home. Rifling through her drawers had excited and ashamed him when he'd buried his fingers in her delicate undergarments, thick pajamas, jeans, and shirts. He'd best not mention that he'd sniffed her perfume or rubbed her lingerie across one cheek.

"Lower air temperature three degrees."

"As requested, Detective Gibson Shaw."

"Call Davis." Gibs bounced his knee with barely restrained energy. He'd rather discuss the case than twiddle his thumbs. "Davis, I just came from The Skin Canvas. There's nothing there. I'll replay the interview when you arrive later."

"Frack, well, what did we expect? That the pieces would fall into place with ease?" Davis chewed his lip, shifting his eyes as if he had something to say but feared to. "Gibs, um, the chocolates?"

"What about them?" What else could there be? They were laced with Pure Rage; he didn't need to know more than that except who sent them.

"They had your fingerprints on them and no one else's. That implicates you in attempted murder."

His stomach wrenched as air rushed out of his lungs. "Frack."

19

/\/1/\/3733/\/

Date: 2170.14.10
The Holies
The Skin Canvas

"That went well." Nate smiled, relief drooping his shoulders. He shoved his hands into his pockets, rocking on the balls of his feet.

"Sorry, I blurted that out about Rick. I figured it was best to be truthful." Lissa folded her arms across her chest, shoving her breasts up and snagging his attention.

"You did well, Liss. Shaw *was* intimidating, and besides, it's best not to bring any distrust of your word. He'd disbelieve anything else we said."

"Right. I don't know about you, but I'm desperate for a drink." A mist formed above her head, and she trembled, her sweet nature unable to cope under the pressure.

He brushed a curl off her temple, tucking it behind her ear. "Sounds like a plan. My treat."

Lissa clapped her hands, her bright smile returning. He helped her close up, ignoring the internal voice screaming that this was unwise.

He needed that drink, and sharing it with Liss felt good. Perhaps too good? He wouldn't dwell on shouldn'ts and maybes.

The flagged-down chaser greeted Lissa as they always did but ignored him. He tried not to focus on the large amount of bare thigh she flashed. Chanting Kylie's name was a vain hope to redirect his interest. Lissa chatted about everything that came to mind. It was frivolous, easing what remnant of tension lingered.

The detective's brow had arched when Nate had revealed he'd found the inkjobs attractive. Had that been a surprise? He shook his head. It was commonplace, so why that reaction? He hadn't revealed his gift, unsure if it pertained to the investigation or if it would mark him as insane. Another psyche assessment denying his so-called insanity? No, thanks, he would skip it this time. If he hadn't shared this with Kylie, he sure as hell wouldn't share it with a detective.

Neither he nor Lissa knew anything about the mutilations. What led someone to do that baffled him. What was the pay-off? What did the person hope to achieve? He shrugged, choosing to peer out of the windows rather than look at Lissa. Wasting time thinking about the workings of a killer's mind was futile. He had other issues to worry about.

He snuck a glance at Lissa who'd slid forward on the seat to watch the passing scenery. Her sundress rode up. He indulged in a daydream, one where he slipped his fingers under her dress, along her smooth skin, and between the juncture of her thighs.

"Liss, how's your relationship with Rick going?"

She faced him with pink cheeks. "Um, the usual. He wants something; I don't." When she tugged her dress down, her fingers trembled. "He's stubborn, Nate. It makes me so...angry."

"Ah, Liss, you can't be angry. It's not in your nature."

"Then you tell me, how do I dissuade him?" She leaned forward, eager for guidance.

Nate trailed his gaze over her face, memorizing the dent in her nose, the swirling chocolate of her eyes. He lingered on her mouth, wishing he could test the plumpness with his lips.

"Date another man. Rick will get the idea."

"Or he'll kill him." She frowned, her lips pouting and just as tempting. "He's sworn to do so, Nate." She threw her hands into the air, the pink on her cheeks spreading lower. Her chest rose and fell with each shuddering breath. Above her head, a cloud formed.

"Date many then; he can't kill them all."

A slow smile spread across her face like a sunrise, resplendent with warmth and hope. "You're right. I can number them instead of name them and say I joined a dating service."

"Numbers don't lie." Nate grinned. She was too timid to do any of this. "How about I get you an inkjob for your bonus? That way you'll have a permanent bodyguard...or lover."

She stilled, her delicious mouth gaping, teasing him. Getting her an inkjob could save his marriage and thwart his daydreams. It was a brilliant plan. He couldn't be jealous of an inkjob, could he?

"You'd do that for me?"

"Sure, why don't we skip the drink and head for Renovare? Perhaps they have a handsome inkjob waiting for you to save him?"

"Frack! Now?" Her breasts jiggled as she bounced in her seat.

Nate closed his eyes and sucked in a sharp breath. This would dip into his savings, but it would be worth it if it saved his marriage. "An X10 for entertainment—maybe a few enhancements for security."

She squealed and threw herself into his arms. Seductive lavender and soft flesh engulfed him, and he returned the hug, relishing it for the once-off it had to be. She feathered kisses across his face, her breathless cries of gratitude hardening him more. Then she stilled, cupped his cheeks, and pressed a kiss onto his lips.

He buried his fingers in her dress, tightening the embrace. Holding himself immobile, he fought the temptation. If he kissed her back, it would be him taking advantage of her. He prayed she deepened the kiss, pleading with the universe to grant him this one moment.

"Sorry." She scrambled off him, rubbing her body along his in the small confines.

He swallowed a groan, running a hand over his face to ground him. Angling his body away from her, he crossed his legs to hide his hard-on.

"No offense taken." He forced a smile, then redirected the chaser to Renovare. Silence filled the space between them, and he kept his focus on the passing signs and buildings as the chaser headed for Renovare. He jerked when she ran a fingertip along his jaw.

"If you weren't married, Nate..."

He gasped, settling his gaze on her upturned face. A fire burned in her eyes, and she licked her bottom lip, relishing the taste of him. A soft hum traveled up her throat, and she dropped her hand to grip his thigh.

"Lissa, don't say such things. I'm barely holding myself together."

She froze, her mouth parting with a breathless moan. "You want me?"

"Yes, but I *love* Kylie." Confronted with his dreams coming true, he remained undecided. He could have her now, in this chaser, yet he hesitated and with good reason. A coy smile widened Lissa's lips. Her eyes narrowed as she trailed her fingers lower.

The bump of the chaser touching down matched his jerking when she cupped his cock through his denims. He escaped through the opening door, sucking in deep, calming breaths as he adjusted his jeans. Frack! Now what? Knowing she'd let him spread her thighs didn't help him fight this. He had permission, for frack sake.

"Come, Liss. Let's find you a lover." He dipped his head to meet her gaze, gesturing to her to exit the chaser. She did, a naughty expression accompanying the blatant reveal of her pink panties. He gripped her hand and yanked her out, ignoring the growl that tore from him. "Frack, woman, not now."

"Later then?"

"Yes... No!" He laced his fingers through hers and tugged her to the entrance. A woman approached them, a sales smile plastered on her face.

"My name's Rhona. How may I help you, Ms. Melissa Lorenzo, Mr. Jonathan Dough?"

He blinked at the inkjob, stunned she'd addressed him by name. No one or thing had ever done that except now and at Kylie's work function. Both times were at Renovare.

"I want an entertainment model that looks like him." Lissa brushed her hand from his shoulder down his chest, leaving behind an electric burn of desire.

"We don't manufacture the E7s anymore. They were an experimental model and only gifted to a chosen few."

"What?" Tingles burst across Nate's back and his shoulders and burned his nostrils, his vision blurred, and a pulse beat behind his eye.

"E7?" he squeaked. What was she implying? That he was an inkjob? Impossible.

Lissa frowned. "What are you saying?" She flicked her gaze between him and the inkjob.

"This way please." With a graceful sway of her hips, Rhona led them deeper into the display center.

Dumbfounded, he trailed her with fear and disbelief numbing his limbs. She gestured to an inkjob in a glass enclosure. He gasped, pressing his hand to his chest. There, staring back at him, was a face he knew well. His own.

20

7UU3/\/7Y

Date: 2170.14.10

The Holies

Renovare

"No." Nate bent over, gripping his knees as he fought for breath. "It's not possible. I have memories, I'm married, I feel love."

"E7s were experimental—Lord Fields's dabble with emotional range." Rhona tapped the glass, activating a holographic panel, unaware of how this news devastated him. "Renovare manufactured only twelve of them and grew them from birth. It proved Renovare's capabilities when the option of synthetic children was under debate."

"That means you grew up as a human, Nate. Each memory and life experience was yours alone. That makes you a human in my eyes." Lissa gripped his shoulder, her pity cloying.

He wanted to hug her and shrug off her sympathy, but if he couldn't calm his breathing and clear his vision, he'd faint. "Does Kylie know?"

"Only your parents know. Lord Fields wavered the cost of you if Renovare could monitor your growth." Rhona's sales smile remained in place.

"I'm an experiment?" Nate sat on the floor, his head spinning, uncaring that he was making a spectacle of himself. "I have a safe code?"

"It wasn't necessary. With an organic bone structure and muscle mass, you could grow, evolve as humans do. You wouldn't exceed the strength of a human man and therefore strain the law enforcement should they need to apprehend you."

"The strength of a human man," Nate echoed, his voice coming from far away. So not only was he a synthetic, he was a weakling, a runt. "There are twelve of me?"

"Initially, yes. Renovare manufactured six females and six males. Three females and two males are active." Rhona helped him to his feet as if he weighed nothing. "Your face mapping, manufacturing details, and schematics are in lockdown. I can, however, show you the trending faces for this year."

He nodded, not knowing what else to do. As Rhona droned on about the available options for the X10, Lissa looped her arm through his, and with her body warming his side, offered him comfort. His head ceased to spin, and his nostrils no longer burned. He could breathe at ease.

His thoughts whirled, and he grasped at the closest one, the most pressing. Should he tell Kylie? She had a right to know she'd married a synthetic...an inkjob. He grimaced. Even though she belonged to R4S, how would she react?

"You're still human, Nate," Lissa whispered, pressing a kiss to his shoulder.

He felt it through his shirt, felt the warmth of her lips, the tingle of excitement along his nerve endings. Did an ordinary inkjob feel that?

No, this had to be a lie; he wasn't an inkjob, a mindless machine.

"What happened to the other E7s? Were their deaths unnatural?" He pinched his lips, gathering his courage to ask the one bright hope in this misery. "Was there anything…odd about them?"

Lissa gasped, but she buried her face against his chest, not revealing his gift. He slid his arm around her, gripped her waist, and pulled her closer.

"There is nothing in the files about abnormalities. They died as humans do: suicide, chaser accidents, one in a burglary."

"No psyche assessments? You said Renovare monitored all aspects of their…our growth?" He refused to believe he was the only one with this gift. As the initial shock wore off, the thought that he had brothers and sisters who might share this excited him. He had an opportunity to understand his gift, its origins, and the freedom to not hide it anymore.

Rhona met his question with an unflinching gaze. "Yes, that is the protocol for new models. Unfortunately, there is nothing in the files regarding their mental acuity."

Disappointment devastated him, shuddering the air out of his lungs. "Do you have the names of my…the E7s?"

"Of course, would you like the list?" Rhona tapped on her holo-wrist and swiped her forearm over Nate's. The familiar zing confirmed the transfer of data, and along with it came a wave of excitement.

"Should you be so free with this information?" Lissa frowned.

Nate grunted; he didn't give a frack whether Rhona had violated protocol or the treaty of information.

"It is public domain." Rhona gestured to the console. "Please confirm your selection for your X10 model."

He scanned the stats Lissa had chosen, and the bright burn of jealousy seized his breathing. Tall, dark-skinned, black hair, and pale-blue eyes, the X10 was beautiful. The sculpted body was the kind Nate loved to sketch or tatt, and it would be one Lissa would spread her thighs for. He wanted to roar a no, deny her this when it had been his stupid idea.

"Frack," he muttered. "You can have him, but you're fucking me, Liss."

She chuckled, running her palm across his chest. "I thought you'd never ask." She trailed a fingertip along his bottom lip. "I considered doing him on the reception counter to get you to wake up."

Nate gasped, dropping his gaze to her upturned face. He just might watch, the idea of it sending fresh sparks of lust through him. The lure of forgetting his predicament was as tempting as Lissa. He wasn't human, could fuck her if he wanted to, but he was also raised by doting parents, their principles his code by which he lived. Being synthetic might break up his marriage as much as doing Lissa would.

Either way, he was screwed.

He swiped his wrist over the pay point, kissing her temple as he did so. "When can we collect?"

"The selecting of ownership codes and the naming ceremonies for the previous day's purchases are at 2 p.m." Rhona flashed a crafted smile. "Choose a good name."

Lissa skipped to the platform, tugging Nate behind her. His thoughts swirled, his emotions overloaded. The swing of her sundress, the flash of her thighs, and her bouncing curls were here, now, something for him to focus on, to distract him.

She ushered him into a hailed chaser, and the moment the door closed, she kissed him. This time, Nate kissed her back, claiming her mouth and the seductive thrill of forbidden fruit. None of that mattered, not with what he'd learned. For all he knew, Kylie was part of the deception. Like how he had to always sleep on the right side of the bed, eat organic food, and take the same expensive vitamins ever since his youth.

All stamped with Renovare's logo.

He grunted and slipped his hands under Lissa's dress, gripping her thighs. She moaned, her breathlessness spiking his temperature, the lust burning common sense from his mind.

There'd be an argument tonight when he confronted his wife, and he didn't give a frack if a hurricane formed above her head. Truth would win out, and his life would change. He just wasn't certain it would be for the better.

As Lissa yanked on his belt and undid the zip of his vintage jeans, lust blurred his vision and trembled his hands. He was as fracken human as the next man, and he'd prove it.

21

7VV3/\/7Y-0/\/3

Date: 2170.14.10

The Colony

"No, no way." Huxley shook her head, fastening her uniform with nimble fingers. "I'm not moving in with you, Gibs."

"Then live with Davis if it's me you dislike."

"Dislike? After the way I kissed you?" She snorted. "It's a no because I like my privacy."

He trailed after her stomping form, loving the sway of her ponytail and hips. Having her beneath him was only a matter of time, and he could wait, flex his patience for a bit. He climbed into his chaser after her, waiting for the door to close before he revealed the impending dilemma.

"Montgomery will have to charge me with attempted murder, Hux."

She gasped, the stubborn tilt of her jaw softening. "But..."

"My fingerprints are on the box of chocolates. There are no other leads."

"Frack." Squeezing her eyes shut, she pinched the bridge of her nose. "I move in for protection, and you're under house arrest?"

"Something like that." A house arrest with her would be wonderful.

"That makes no sense, not if you supposedly tried to kill me, Gibs."

He grunted, instructed the chaser to take him home, then faced her. "I'm calling the Master later to ask for help."

Her face contorted in disbelief, her mouth gaping for a moment before she snapped it shut. "Are you insane? She might demand payment of some kind, a favor, Gibs. It could be anything."

"What other choices do I have, Hux?" He ran his hand over his face, smothering some of his curses. "It's my fault. I should've remained professional, kept you out of the public eye."

"I call bullshit. Anyone with access to the files would know I'm your partner even if you squirreled me away in the bowels of the Center."

He gripped her shoulders and admired her upturned face. "It's because of the way I look at you, Hux. Don't you see that?"

"No, you're in the way of some nefarious plan, Gibs." She cupped his cheek, surprising him. The warmth of her hand reached through to him more than her words did. "This has nothing to do with us."

She lowered her hand, the loss of her touch acute, and pursed her lips, a plan formulating behind her gray eyes. "Is my uncle a suspect?"

"No, we need to interview him, gather what footage he has, but from where I stand, he can't possibly be involved in this." Gibs clambered out of the chaser, offering her a hand to help her out, then grabbed her luggage. "Davis will be here at six. We can run through what we know and what our options are then."

"But Montgomery could—"

"Yes, he could. And we don't have much time." Gibs dropped her bag on his bed, grateful he'd cleaned his apartment. "What do you feel like for dinner?"

"Do you mind if I shower first?" She gestured to her uniform, pristine even after her Rage ordeal. "I feel drained."

"Of course, my home is yours. Coffee?"

She nodded, and he darted out of the room, away from temptation. Closing the door behind him, he busied himself with the coffee, keeping an ear out for her and Davis. Even Eddie's bells would be a welcome reprieve from his chaotic thoughts. He wasn't close to figuring out who the inkjob killer was. If Montgomery charged him, threw him in a cell, Gibs would either have to rely on Davis and Hux to be his eyes and ears or give up the case.

He gritted his teeth. He didn't have an unsolved case in his records, and this one, sure as frack, wouldn't be the first.

"Good, coffee's ready," Davis said from the door.

Gibs jumped, smothering a yelp as he spilled hot coffee on his hand. He must have forgotten to close the front door.

"Sorry." Davis entered, lowering food containers onto the coffee table. "Picked up Chinese on the way. Where's Huxley?"

"Showering the Rage off her." Gibs ran cold water over the burn.

"I'm out. Be there in a minute." Hux's voice reached them through the bedroom door.

"Right, coffee and dinner. We can chat while we eat." Davis dropped onto the couch to unpack the containers. The rich fragrance of crispy pigeon filled the room, stirring up a gurgle in Gibs's stomach. He poured coffee into three mugs and carried them to the table. Milk wasn't needed—none of them added it to their coffee—but Davis drank his sweet, so he fetched the sugar bottle.

Hux opened the door dressed in black leggings and a baggy T-shirt, which slipped off one shoulder. She rubbed her hair with a towel, mumbling a greeting to Davis.

"How are you feeling?" Davis rose to his feet like a gentleman of old, waiting for Hux to choose a spot. When she curled up onto the single-seater, tucking her feet beneath her, Davis sat again.

"Better. Gibs says we have no leads, which I find hard to believe. Who delivered the chocolates to my door? My building has security—not the best but worth a look."

"I'll check it out in the morning." Davis offered her a container and chopsticks before diving into his meal. "The Rage is the purest, not something you can buy at the local market."

Gibs sighed, staring at his empty hands. He reached across to pick up his Chinese, deliberately moving slowly to make a point. Davis glared at him but didn't stop shoveling noodles into his mouth.

"There are no married women at the Center with that ring design, so that's a bust. The knife marks are from a spear-point blade, and thousands are manufactured every year." Davis shoved food around in his mouth to speak. "Thomas Walker's blood sample came back clean."

Gibs grunted, having expected as much. "I visited The Skin Canvas this afternoon." He tapped his holo-wrist, playing the interview. "Nate's heart rate spiked when he spoke about finding inkjobs attractive."

"Frack. Another dead-end." Davis threw his chopsticks into his empty container and dropped it onto the table. "I hate to say it, but we need another Eve Roe, one with clues."

"I feel as if I'm missing something crucial." Gibs placed his hand above his coffee cup when Davis waved his flask. "I'll watch Thomas's security footage tonight. How did the vandal steal Olivia? Inkjobs don't just walk out on their own." Lost in thought, he chewed on a strip of pigeon. "Montgomery promised to send a list of the officers on the synth-unit. With the situation as it stands, you'll have to follow up on that, Davis."

Gibs pushed Hux's coffee closer to her while she picked at her food. "Here's what I think we should do." He rose to fetch his whisky from the kitchen and poured a shot into his coffee. Hux declined with a shake of her head when he offered the bottle to her.

After pointing at Davis with his cup, Gibs paced his living room. "Davis, you stall the captain and the investigation into the attack on Huxley while you watch her security footage and follow the trail. Find who targeted her." He met his friend's gaze. "I'm trusting you with this."

"Hux." Gibs ran an admiring gaze over her bare shoulder and sighed, wishing the circumstances were different. "You head for Uncle Charlie and hide in his mansion. Spill the story to him, and ask for his help. Watch his footage, as well. Let me know how his inkjob left his home."

"And you?" She leaned forward, slid her half-eaten food onto the table, and scooped up her coffee.

"I'll head for the Master. Her political clout and her extensive access to all aspects of Nova should open fresh avenues. Let's hope she's feeling benevolent."

"What if there's another mutilation?" Davis put his flask down and mopped his forehead with a paper towel.

"Document everything, as usual, then upload it to our cloud storage. Hux and I will review your findings."

"Going into hiding makes you guilty, Gibs." Davis jumped up, his displeasure in his twitching fingers. "Why don't you explain the situation to Montgomery?" Davis threw out his arms in a pleading gesture.

"He might believe me, but to investigate and clear my name is time we can't waste." Gibs gestured to him to relax, to sit. Davis did, but a scowl furrowed his brow. "Montgomery can arrest me once we've solved this. A sense of doom is pressing on my chest—it's telling me that this vandal will raise the stakes and kill a human woman next."

"Do you believe that, Gibs?" Hux tightened her fingers around her cup, her knuckles white.

He nodded. "The first had claw marks, mild in comparison to the spikes piercing the second inkjob. The escalation has already started."

"Frack," Davis muttered. "I'll watch Thomas's footage tonight. You two get some rest." He rose, sliding his flask into his uniform's back pocket.

"Are you sure?" At Davis's nod, Gibs held out the data crystal. "Keep a lookout for something unusual. Thomas believed she had human traits."

"Right." Davis snorted, saluted Hux, and headed for the platform. "Keep me informed, and I'll do the same."

Gibs followed him, waiting until he hailed a chaser. Hux waved goodnight but remained silent and seated. He closed and locked the door, then cleared away the containers. She sipped her coffee, lost in thought. When she was ready, she'd reveal them to him, so he collected a pillow and blanket for the couch.

"Now what?"

"Off to bed for you; I'll sleep here." He gestured to the couch where Davis had rested his backside minutes ago.

She unfolded her legs and placed her cup on the table. "Don't you think we should organize everything tonight?"

"Might be wise, but do you want to after the day you've had?"

She rose and pressed her palm on his chest, meeting his gaze. "I do, or I won't be able to sleep. I'll call Uncle Charlie to start the process. You test the waters with the Master."

Gibs sighed, dreading making the call. When she disappeared into his bedroom, he activated his holo-wrist and sent a message to Schneider, detailing everything. No doubt, the Master was up to date with the number of informants she had.

After making his bed, he loosened his uniform, unholstered his Glock and blaster, and tugged off his boots. He would love a shower and to don his sleep pants, but the soft mumble of Naomi's voice said she was still on the call.

He softened the lighting and sprawled on the couch, sinking into its familiar depths. In the blur of pre-slumber, he could've sworn soft lips brushed his temple and the tucking of a velvet warmth of the blanket under his chin. Both were unlikely and incongruent with his lifestyle, so he lumped it under dreaming and let sleep claim him.

A HAND ON GIBS's shoulder jerked him awake, and he gripped it, yanking hard. A feminine gasp followed along with the realization he pinned Hux to his chest. Sprawled on top of him, he gathered her closer to him, nuzzling her cheek with his.

"Gibs," she whispered. "We have visitors."

"What?" He shook his head, clearing the cobwebs of sleep and erotic dreams. The opportunity to feather kisses along her jaw tempted him to linger.

"On your platform are two men. One wears Uncle Charlie's mayoral badge on his lapel. The other is a diminutive man in a gray suit. Alongside him is a Sec2 synthetic, all titanium and restrained menace."

Gibs twisted to see what awaited him, able to discern their shapes through the meshed louvers. Help had arrived. Relief slumped his shoulders, and he slid his hands lower to grip Hux's smooth thighs. He squeezed her before gliding up to fill his palms with her bare ass. Her breath hitched. As he kneaded her flesh, her breathless moan shot a dart of need to his groin.

"Gibs, now's not the time." Her rasping voice implied otherwise. He dipped his head to sip from her lips, pressing the tip of his tongue to her bottom lip, urging her to open for him. She did, tilting her head as she cupped his neck.

Moist, sweet, addictive descriptors flickered across his mind as he savored the taste of her, deepening the kiss as he once again forgot to breathe. He yearned for her more than he wanted this case solved.

"The Master wants Shaw." Schneider's clipped voice reached Gibs through the lust-filled haze. The Master's right-hand man on Gibs's doorstep proved she would help him. Still, he would have liked a few minutes more. He sighed, pressing his temple to Hux's as they fought for air.

"I'm not here for Shaw." The uniformed man said no more. Silence among the mayor's security was as valued as their ability to dispense pain.

"You're a good kisser." Hux kissed his chin. "I remembered that right."

He studied her upturned face in the pale light. "Why do I hear a but?" He chuckled, caressing his fingers along the dip of her spine, tugging her shirt up in the process.

"We need to deal with our guests."

"Then it's goodbye, Hux...for now." He snatched a quick kiss, needing to imprint the softness and moist heat of her lips into his aging mind.

"Until we solve this case, until you fuck me hard, it's never good-bye."

His breath hitched, and he tightened his grip on her waist. "Frack, woman." He shuddered. The burn of lust hardening his cock was her fault.

"Ms. Huxley." The burly bodyguard knocked on the door.

With reluctance and Gibs's unspoken permission, she climbed off him. "Just let me dress."

The man grunted, folding his arms across his massive chest. "You have five minutes, Ms. Huxley."

She huffed as she disappeared into Gibs's bedroom. He watched her long legs and swaying hair, wishing he could follow her. Instead, he rose, adjusted his hard-on, and opened the front door.

Schneider's stoic visage squelched Gibs's ardor. "Schneider, this is a surprise."

"Is it, Shaw?" The irritating man arched a brow but nodded at the Sec2.

Moonlight glinted off a synth's raised weapon.

Fire burned across Gibs's chest as he flew back from the blast, landing in a crumpled heap against his couch. He blinked in disbelief as Schneider entered his home. Gibs gaped with unsaid words. The warmth of the blood saturating his uniform did nothing to diminish the deafening roar as his mind struggled to understand what had happened.

Even Hux pressing her hand to his wound, drawing a moan from him, didn't shake him out of his stupor. Tears streamed down her cheeks, and he tried to raise his fingers to wipe them away. He couldn't. His muscles wouldn't obey. It had to be shock. A blast wound in the chest shouldn't affect his nervous system.

"You...shot me." His throat garbled the words.

Hux sobbed, stuttering into her holo-wrist to call Medical.

With an extended finger, Schneider deactivated her call. The mayor's security tore her off Gibs. Ice replaced her hot touch and spread outward as his life drained from him. She flailed, kicking, and screaming. Gibs struggled to help her, his shoulders twitching with the effort and spiking fresh pain through him. Disregarding his need to go to her, the Sec2 threw him over his shoulder. Gibs saw no more of her, but her cries and curses echoed in his ears.

Piercing agony and spots blurred his vision, both from the shift in elevation and the blood loss. Wafer-thin thoughts of Hux, the case, and his mother crisscrossed his mind as death circled him. He gaped like a fish out of water, his ribs refusing to let him breathe, leaving him unable to speak past the pain and helplessness crushing his chest.

For the second time that night, he let the blessed lure of darkness claim him.

22

7∪∪3/\/7Ƴ-7∪∪0

Date: 2170.14.10
The Holies
Nate's home

NATE STEPPED INTO HIS home, dropping his bag on the floor before taking off his jacket. He stank of sex, a delicious, wicked stench convicting him of adultery. What the frack did he care? He'd spill it all to Kylie in a minute, and her responses would decide which secrets he revealed.

"Kylie?" Gone was his earlier eagerness—the love for his spouse and his longing for her. The cloying emotion lining his heart now reeked of hatred. Could their relationship have survived the shaking of his foundation, the disintegration of what made him Nate? Perhaps, but he would no longer tiptoe around her mood swings and suffer through them.

"In here."

Here meant the small lounge they'd christened every inch with their honeymoon passion. He snorted. He'd been nothing but an X10 to her, a sex toy. Hovering in the doorway, he settled his gaze on her, focusing on everything he had loved about her.

A cloud engulfed her down to her forehead—a swirling malev-olent mass. Irritation crinkled his brow, but he didn't grimace at what the evening promised. It didn't matter anymore.

"Good, I need to talk to you." Not bothering to ask her how her day was, he chose the chair farthest from her. He scratched at the semen stain on his jeans—a marvel of innovation for an inkjob. What else had Renovare created and hidden in their build-ing—levels of hell disguised in prayer?

"Oh?" She arched a brow, swirling wine in her glass. Her skin was pale, translucent. He'd once admired its ethereal beauty. Now he saw it as an illness. The small confines of the data room meant minimum sunlight. She might be suffering from a Vitamin D de-ficiency, but that was neither here nor there.

"For her bonus, I bought Lissa an X10 inkjob today." He chuck-led, but it was cold, unfeeling, and did nothing to lighten the anger festering inside. For a few hours, their passionate escapades had, but when he'd headed for *home*, his memories of his life with Kylie had taunted him. "To my surprise, I discovered I'm not human."

She ceased swirling her wine. Her shoulders stiffened, and she straightened her spine. In slow motion, she unfolded her legs and leaned forward to grip the glass in front of her. Her skin took on an ashen tone.

She swallowed hard. "How did you find out?"

Electric tingles assaulted his cheeks, and he jerked, gritting his teeth to swallow the gasp. She'd known all these years and kept it from him.

"Frack how, Kylie. Why didn't you tell me?" He leaped forward to grip the armrests of her chair, forcing her to lean back to maintain eye contact. Fury burned along his veins, and the chair creaked under his *human* strength.

"Your parents wanted me to know before I married you. I wasn't to set my heart on children."

He stumbled back, pain squeezing his heart. Hoping to ease the ache, he thumped his chest. Could he have a heart attack? Rhona had implied as much. He was human but not and thus subject to their sicknesses and mortal existence. For so many years, they'd discussed children, the names they'd choose, where they'd live if Kylie fell pregnant. All lies! How well she'd played the doting wife eager for offspring.

"I want a divorce." He spewed the words like acid dripping from a burning tongue.

"No, I won't give you one. I love you. I sacrificed my time at R4S for you, your kind. Don't you see, Nate? You prove inkjobs aren't unfeeling robots."

"A poster boy for R4S—I should've known." He spun on his heel and headed for the door, wanting nothing from his so-called home. This illusion of what he wasn't. She grabbed his wrist, halting his escape.

"How can you not love me anymore, Nate? Doesn't my dedication, my disregard for your origins matter?"

He laughed, choosing not to share anything more, not his E7 siblings nor his affair with Lissa. Kylie's deception was grounds for a divorce if their marriage was legal in the first place. He wasn't human and, therefore, not bound by their laws.

"No judge will deny my request for an annulment, Kylie. You should be happy; after all, I will be the first divorced inkjob, setting a precedent." He gripped her shoulders as if to shake her. "Isn't that what R4S is all about?"

She shook her head, tossing her hair. He'd loved the color, loved how it shimmered in the light. Now, with tears streaming down her cheeks and her nose glowing bright red, he felt…nothing.

He sucked in a shuddering breath, releasing her before he bruised her. "I'm furious, Kylie, and with reason. I'm taking a break from us, from my situation. I'll see how I feel after some time and a little distance."

"I'll wait for you, Nate, I swear."

He studied her upturned face, not recognizing the woman he'd married and adored until a week ago. Worse, he didn't recognize himself. Perhaps he was letting his emotions run wild? He'd had too many lows and highs today, including finding release between Lissa's thighs. As expected, it had been an incredible experience, better than he'd imagined. Her innate joy had saturated their union.

He broke away, heading for their bedroom to pack clothes and toiletries for his E7 search. Earlier, he'd wanted nothing from his life with Kylie, but now that he was calm, he realized he was being foolish.

As he packed, conscious of a sobbing Kylie propped against the door frame, he called his parents.

"Why didn't you tell me?" The moment his mom answered, he attacked, not sure he wanted to hear their reasons or their excuses, but love compelled him to, at least, not have them worry while he was away.

"Donald, he knows," his mom called. Dad didn't talk to him often, not liking the holo-wrist and the world's dependency on technology.

Dad cleared his throat as his face filled the holo. "It was part of the deal we signed with Renovare, son." The tears in Dad's eyes must be an illusion. "Your mom couldn't have children, and when Lord Fields offered us a child…we snatched it up, no questions asked. We were so desperate for you that we signed everything, not caring whether it would cost us our souls."

"We broke our silence by telling Kylie. We didn't want her to blame herself because she couldn't fall pregnant." Mom sobbed, blowing her nose on a tissue.

"We love you, Nate. You not being human-born doesn't change that." Dad accepted the tissue Mom shoved at him but didn't use it.

"I'm too livid to think. I don't want to talk to any of you. Don't try to reach me, don't look for me. I need the time…" Nate broke off, a cacophony of emotions crushing his chest and seizing his throat. He shoved his things into his bag, anxious energy driving him not to care if he creased his clothing.

"Take as much time as you need." Dad mopped his eyes with clumsy movements. Nate doubted he'd cried in decades—not since Gran's death.

"Don't blame Kylie for our decisions." That was his mom, always thinking of others.

"Don't worry about my marriage, Mom. I'll call you when I'm ready to talk." He hung up then tossed in his last pair of jeans, zipping the bag shut. Snatching it off the bed, he faced Kylie who hovered in the doorway. Her tears spilled unhindered, and she'd folded her arms across her chest, curling in on herself. He'd never seen a cloud so dark, and he winced, admitting he was hurting her by leaving.

For once, he needed to think about himself. He didn't speak, just waited for her to shuffle out of the way. When she did, he strode past her and closed the front door on his so-called perfect life.

23

7∨∨3/\/7Y-7#|233

GIBS JERKED AWAKE, A cry of agony tearing from him when he jarred his shoulder. The stench of antiseptic assaulted his nose. He wore no shirt, no uniform. A crimson-stained patch and a strip of bandage shone in the artificial lighting. He lifted the sheet and grimaced—someone had undressed him.

A lamp beside him—the only warmth in the room—highlighted a pile of bloodied cloths and a used syringe dripping transparent fluid. The bed, a *wooden* four-poster, was massive, accommodating his height with ease. Thick velvet drapes shut out the sunlight, and Persian carpets covered the stone floors.

Where the frack was he?

Then he remembered kissing Hux and Schneider's titanium bulldog shooting him. Gibs swore, cursing everyone under the sun. It didn't change his situation, but it eased the tension pulling on his wound.

"You're awake." Master stepped into the room, all slinky curves and lethal seduction wrapped in a little black dress. Even in the soft lighting, her auburn hair glimmered.

"You shot me." Shifting on his ass, he tugged on the sheet and the mattress to sit up. He tried not to focus on his nudity. That level of vulnerability paled in comparison to the wound trapping him in this room. He'd run from here naked if freedom was the result.

"Your message implied urgency. I'm surprised you reached out to me." She sat on the edge of the bed and crossed her legs, drawing his attention to the pink stilettos tightening her calves. He wasn't as aroused as he'd been in their previous meeting. He had Sophia to thank for that.

"Yes, I was desperate, but I didn't expect you to try to kill me." He huffed, resisting the urge to glare at her since he was at her mercy.

"Try?" She chuckled, a husky sound that reverberated off the wainscotting. "My dear Gibson, if I wanted you dead, I would have instructed my Sec2 to aim lower." She flicked her hand.

He pinched the bridge of his nose, his nostrils burning as he fought for air, for calm. "But why have me shot in the first place?"

"You disappoint me, Gibs. Think, or would you prefer to bumble through solving this case, all while dodging your captain?" She picked at his bandage, running her palm over the edge as if to flatten a wrinkle. "Paisley Gibson Shaw, born to Margaret Shaw..."

"I don't need a history recap." He grunted. "It just proves you're well informed." He shrugged off her touch. "Mom goes by Cassiopeia. The name Margaret isn't as free of spirit as she'd have liked."

"Born on a hippy colony traveling the galaxy, you never knew your father."

"Is this necessary, Master?" Gibs sat up straighter, ignoring the sharp pull on his shoulder. He thrust a fist between his thighs, pushing down on the sheet to ensure he remained decent.

"I don't waste my time, Paisley." Master sniggered, holding two fingers to her lips. "What I want to ask you about is your brother."

Ice pooled at the base of his spine, and he stilled; the sharp shards of pain piercing his heart had nothing to do with his wound. Guilt was a slimy bastard, digging its claws into his psyche. He'd suggested they play above the plasma tanks knowing the area was hazardous. Mom was at one of her orgies again, or some 'campfire' party, leaving them in the canteen to entertain themselves.

Twisting a knife in Gibs's chest was the memory of the fear contorting his brother's pale face, his matching hazel eyes as he plummeted off the platform. He relived Jackson's death, the panicked dash trying to find help, to save him from drowning. By the time he'd managed to drag an adult there, Jackson's body had floated to the surface. He was facedown, and when they'd fished him out, his blue-tainted skin had screamed Gibs's guilt. Every detail haunted him. Jackson's swaying body in the bubbling, gelatinous liquid. How his hair had splayed out, his eyes unseeing. Claw marks scarred the sides of the vat: his last attempts to save himself.

"It was my fault." His voice was harsh, guttural—the pain shredding his vocal cords. "I convinced him to play in the gangways crisscrossing the plasma vats."

"Did your mom blame you?"

Gibs nodded. "In the beginning."

"You were twelve?" Master tapped his knee, and he shifted, closing his legs as if that could cover his vulnerability, both under the sheet and his raw emotions.

"I stowed away on the first ship leaving the Kerouac, landing on the Chardonnay vineship. That's where Dad found me four years later and brought me to Earth." Gibs chuckled, but it lacked mirth. "I was an asshole to him, blaming him for abandoning me, for not being there to save Jackson."

"Yet here you are, a decorated detective."

Gibs raised his face to the ceiling, sucking in a calming breath. "Satisfied?"

"For now." Master smirked, twisting her ruby lips.

"Does Huxley think I'm dead?" A steel band of ice and heat squeezed his chest. Yes, now *that* was an important question, one that had teased the edges of his mind since he awoke to this...situation.

"Yes, and she put on quite a show. I'd almost believe she's in lo..." Master's mouth gaped. "Why, Gibs, you sly old dog."

Gibs grunted, trying to maintain a stoic façade, not wanting to reveal his inner turmoil. The memory of Hux fighting to remain by his side was no illusion. He was in agony, knowing that she suffered, that she believed him dead.

"You're in love, too." A smile spread the Master's lips wide, not in victory nor mockery, yet it raised the hairs on the back of his neck.

Heat burst across his cheeks. He hadn't allowed himself the time to identify what Hux invoked in him but said so flatly, and by the Master no less, it forced him to face the truth.

"Yes, I love her." There, he'd said it. He might be handing the Master a way to control him, but he wouldn't lie, not when she'd already figured it out.

"Why the frack didn't my informants know about this?" Master bolted up and stormed to the door. "Schneider!" She paced, her auburn hair trailing her like a flaming star.

The little man hurried in, no expression marring his face. "Yes, Master."

"Open the block on this room, find Gibs a private channel, and let him speak to Naomi Huxley. Get Doc in here to check his wound, and for the love of frack, find him some damn clothes." She nodded at Gibs, almost as if to apologize, although he didn't know for what. "Come see me when you're dressed. Schneider will show you the way. We need to talk about inkjobs and Pure Rage."

With rapid taps of his fingers on his holo-wrist, Schneider opened a partition in the ceiling. Down slid a display screen, and before Gibs could focus on the image, Hux's face formed.

"Who is this?" Dark circles deepened her gray eyes, and her skin was ashen. Her disheveled hair cascaded around her like she'd just woken up. He couldn't speak, his voice having forsaken him now that he knew how he felt about her. Hux shifted, bringing her face closer to him as she peered into her holo-wrist. Disbelief widened her eyes. "Gibs?" she croaked before clearing her throat.

"Hello, Hux."

Tears slid down her cheeks, and she dashed them away with hurried movements. "No, it can't be."

"Shooting me was Master's idea of a rescue."

Hux's gaze flicked over his exposed chest, and frack, if his nipples didn't pebble. He restrained a shiver, barely.

"Are you well?" She traced a finger down the screen as if she could touch him.

"It's painful, but I'll live. Don't let anyone except Davis know I survived, and tell him face to face."

"Got it." She opened her mouth to speak, then dipped her chin. "I...I need you to take care of yourself."

Disappointment slumped him into his pillow. He couldn't shake the sensation that she wanted to say something else.

"You owe me a kiss."

He sucked in a sharp breath, crossing his legs to hide his growing hard-on. "You can have as many kisses as you want."

"Promise?" Her voice was huskier, or had he imagined it? When he nodded, she leaned back, wiping her nose with the collar of her T-shirt. "I'll carry on as if you died and continue the investigation as discussed." Her gaze lowered. "Can I reach you at this number?"

He arched a brow at Schneider who shrugged. "You can try." Gibs flashed a glare at the man, who didn't have a romantic bone in his body. Or any bone? Gibs swallowed a snigger, assuming his amusement was due to the pain meds.

"Take care of yourself, Hux. I expect a full report when next we chat, and you better not have shadows under those beautiful gray eyes of yours."

"Yes, sir." She saluted, then ruined it with a giggle.

The screen went black. Gibs sighed, sliding down under the sheets. Exhaustion drained what energy he had. "Thanks, Elijah."

The poor man flinched then nodded. "I'll source you a few items to wear while Doc checks on your wound."

"Take your time." Gibs burrowed into the pillow, crushing it in a tight embrace, wishing the softness was a specific woman's warm body. He could've sworn he heard Schneider say, "Save me from lovesick fools," but he didn't bother to verify it.

Lovesick? Yes, he was and proud of it. It proved he wasn't an emotionless bastard after all.

24

7VV3/\/7Y-|=0|_||2

GIBS HATED NOT WEARING his own clothes. Whoever's denims he wore, they were wider at the waist and shorter in length, exposing his ankles. He'd tugged on his work boots and yesterday's socks, his chuckle self-mocking. The unkind reflection didn't help matters, with the too-tight T-shirt and the gap between shirt and jeans, which bared his midriff. He needed a belt.

"This way, Detective." Schneider hovered at the door, running his gaze over Gibs, his lips twisting in amusement. The bastard had done this on purpose.

Gibs cupped his left shoulder and rolled it, wincing at the sharp tugs on his wound. The doc had visited, along with the stench of rum. He hadn't wanted the man to touch him, but his hands were steady, and Schneider glowered from the doorway.

Gibs's uniform was missing, and he felt naked without his Glock and blaster. Yet, there was a silver lining. He hadn't gone to bed wearing his father's trench coat. The blaster shot would've burned a hole right through it. He should be grateful he hadn't died, but hey, thanks for the new scar.

Wainscotting lined the corridor's walls, as well—a display of pride and wealth as if the thick, handwoven runner wasn't enough. He dragged his fingers along the wooden panels, testing their authenticity. The knots and dents remained. Frack, they were real. Gold adorned the door handles and the sconces, casting their warmth. The ceiling was molded in intricate patterns, and the air tasted old, which made sense since they didn't manufacture any of the décor anymore. These were antiques.

He trailed Schneider, passing closed doors. The silence deafened him, growing until he could kill to hear his elderly couple high on rage. Hearing no passing chasers, no screaming violin, no ding-ding of Eddie's junket was abnormal. It was as if the world had ceased to exist.

Schneider turned corners, uncaring that Gibs had to hold up his denims or expose his nude ass. He snorted; he'd pay to see the expression on Schneider's face if he did bare his ass. Then again, what had the man seen in the employ of the Master? Gibs's ass would be par for the course.

The little man paused outside a double door and rapped on it twice. The soft command to enter had him opening both doors and stepping back, gesturing to Gibs to pass him. Eager to have done with whatever this was, Gibs did.

He bit down on his inner cheek, smothering a gasp of amazement. Opulence, the likes of which he'd never seen before, adorned every inch of the expansive room. Not even on Lux did this exist. Wood paneling, sconces, and Persian carpets were as expected. Stuffed wooden chairs in embroidered fabric and a massive desk in a dark wood dominated the rear of the room. On one side, a fire roared in the hearth, burning *real* fracken wood!

The clink of ice snatched his attention. Against the opposite wall stood Master.

"I believe you prefer whisky?" She faced a drinks cabinet sloshing amber liquid into two crystal glasses. While cradling a glass to her bosom, she approached him, offering the other drink. He accepted. The heady aroma of woody spice wafted up from the glass, tempting him to take a big gulp to calm his nerves.

"Why did you help me? You could've dismissed my message, my plea."

"Now that's a good question." Master chose an armchair, twisting her body to rest an elbow on the wood, then cradled the glass in her hands.

Lowering himself into the chair opposite her, he waited. He wasn't about to drink something that might contain a drug.

"One that has an answer?" He swirled the burnished whisky and raised it to his nose to inhale, not removing his gaze from Master's face. Pressing the cool glass to his lips, he studied her expression, watching for eagerness, satisfaction.

She chuckled. "Come now, Gibs, you don't think I'd poison you after saving your ass."

Put like that, and with his distrust so blatant, he took a sip, then moaned. Smooth, woody, smoky flavors burst across his tongue when he swirled the whisky around his mouth. After swallowing, he sighed as the liquid fire burned its way down his throat and inflamed his belly.

"Good." Master threw back hers and rose to pour another. "You've decided to trust me. That's wise." She ambled to her chair but didn't sit, choosing to wrap her long fingers over the headrest. "I like you for some silly reason. Perhaps it's your misplaced honor; who knows?"

She trailed a finger along the carved wooden frame and shook her head as if deciding whether to say something. With a decision made, her jaw hardened, and she spun on her stilettos, striding to her desk.

"There's more to these dead inkjobs than we know. So, I'll need you to continue investigating from here. And since you're dead, you'll need a disguise, a new identity." She flashed a smile as if this delighted her.

"All right, but why? Can I leave...here?" He gestured to the room, meaning wherever the frack he was.

"There's been another mutilation. Davis is en route, and he'll be thorough. I'll get you there, too, but dressed in something a little more appropriate. Find who's doing this, Gibs."

"Why does this matter to you, Em?" Gibs threw back his whisky and rose, placing the glass on the side table.

"Em?" Her lips twisted with a mixture of surprise, displeasure, and humor.

"I can't keep calling you Master. Give me your name, or I choose one for you."

"No one has heard my true name spoken in decades. Em will do." She hit a button, and panels slid apart, revealing display screens lining the wall. Images from the crime scenes flickered to life, all from his case file. "This is your new headquarters. I'll place an assistant at your disposal, to run errands and such."

"Why does this matter to you?" He clipped each word, ignoring the fact that she'd gifted him this room in the interim. Like he'd hoped, he had her resources, her knowledge at his disposal—he should be ecstatic. Yet distrust was a natural instinct for him.

She sashayed toward him, pausing to run a fingernail along his exposed stomach. "I am heavily invested in Renovare, and whoever's doing this impacts my business. I don't like that."

"Nor do you like not knowing who's terrorizing your Nova."

A slow smile curled her lips. "That, too—a matter of pride, you could say."

A timid knock intruded on their conversation, and she commanded them to enter. Ice slithered down Gibs's spine, and he sat up straight, willing himself not to blink as Sophia strolled in. Her cheeks darkened when she spotted him, but she said nothing as she hurried across the carpet on slippered feet.

"Ah, Sophia, just in time. What news have you?"

He needed another whisky. So, he'd fucked a spy. It shouldn't have surprised him, and what they'd shared wasn't, in any way, special.

Sophia dipped her head in a bow. "A worker slipped flasks of undiluted Rage out of the warehouse." She flicked a nervous glance at Gibs. He was law enforcement, and he hadn't hidden that fact from her when he'd spread her thighs. "He's been...dealt with."

"Tighten security and dock the guards' pay." Em held out her empty glass to Gibs, shaking it for a refill. He obliged, not out of obedience but out of his need for a splash himself. "Who did he sell the flasks to?"

Sophia shook her head, her dark braid flying out to rest over one breast. She wore jeans and a T-shirt, in stark contrast to when he last saw her. "He didn't. The Cents took it."

Gibs froze, the uncorked decanter halfway to pouring. She'd implied his fellow law officers had confiscated the flasks. From there, someone had used them on Hux. The chances of that happening were high, and since there were traitors among his brethren, he didn't doubt Sophia's revelation.

"Frack." He splashed a good portion of whisky into both glasses, corked the decanter, and offered Em hers.

"Our Cents…" Sophia closed her eyes with a grimace. "They state the product went into the vault as per protocol, but no footage reveals who stole it from there."

"It's a start. I'm certain Gibs can take it from here?' Em arched a brow but didn't wait for his response. She downed her whisky and handed Sophia her glass. "If you need anything, ask Schneider. Oh, and Gibs…" Em paused at the door, a wicked smile curling her lips. "Since you're, shall we say, familiar with Sophia, I'd like you to meet your new assistant."

Laughter trailed her as she disappeared down the hall. He grunted, threw the whisky back, then faced the last woman he'd fucked as if his dirty deeds had come back to haunt him.

"Don't expect free sex." Her bold statement sucked the wind out of his sails, and he dropped into the chair closest to the fire.

"If you can, forget we ever…y'know." Heat not from the hearth singed his cheeks.

"Done. Now, tell me, what do you need?"

"Let me fill you in from the beginning." He gestured to the chair opposite him, and as soon as she sank into the plush cushions, he started.

"My wife left me for my boss, and due to her snake-like charm, I landed this case." Gibs drew in a long breath. He needed to get over Mara's betrayal. He *was* happy she'd done it, just not the fall-out afterward. "I'll start with Eve Roe 1 or Olivia."

Sophia was an attentive listener, asking questions only when something confused her. Gibs droned on, explaining how each clue revealed a chain of events he had yet to tie together. As the firelight shimmered off her ebony hair, he wondered what Hux would say when she found out about his salacious trip to the Kicks.

As a Cent himself, he knew one cardinal truth: no secrets remained hidden.

25

7VV3/\/7Y-|=1V3

Date: 2170.16.10
The Shadows
Gibs's new office

Gibs sighed, flicking through his new identity chips. They'd arrived within the hour, along with an outfit from the Kicks. He'd picked up a sleeve to sniff and was relieved to find it clean.

Leslie 'Lee' Wash. Em had a sense of humor, he'd give her that.

Sophia sat on the edge of his desk, swinging her foot. At the knock at the door, she shoved off the desk and flopped into an armchair. "Gibs, this is Viv."

A tattooist hovered by the door, holding a massive tool case in front of her.

He dropped the chips onto his desk and circled it to stand near the fire. If he was going to be shirtless, he wanted to be warm.

Tearing off his T-shirt, he dropped it onto the armchair and rolled his wounded shoulder. He wanted to be out of here and heading for the crime scene. Davis had already received notification that a new detective was on the case, a Lee Wash from Questa City up north—a transfer at the mayor's insistence—while his brethren searched for Gibs's killer.

"How long will this take?" He arched a brow at Viv.

"Not long when the tatts are something small. Master wants them all over your chest, torso, and back. I'll give you a collar and cuff definition." The blue-haired woman chewed on a piece of plastic, riffled through her opened case, and pulled out gloves and a wide scanning device. Permanent tatts decorated her toffee skin; detailed flowers and butterflies formed part of a bigger picture hidden beneath her clothes.

He gestured to her tatts. "Are yours real?"

"Yup, done by a tatt artist of renown." She waved with the scanner. "Any preferences?"

"Something tribal, massive angel wings, or chains. Nothing frilly, no unicorns, butterflies, and frack no to faces." He fought the urge to flex. He was man, hear him roar?

"How about a leopard over one pec?" She trailed her finger from his left nipple, over his collarbone to his shoulder.

He shook her hand off since it tickled. "Fine."

Viv swiveled the stick between her lips with a studded tongue as she scanned him from the waistband of his fitted denims to his neck. He watched her, preferring to study her unusual mannerisms than look at Sophia. Her presence taunted him, reminding him of his moment of vulnerability—finding release between her thighs. She was more stunning now with clothes on, perhaps because he knew what lay beneath the cotton and denim.

"Your wound will pose a problem. Two reasons: I'll have to alter the tattoo so that when it heals, it forms an eye or a void. And lastly, it's going to hurt like a bitch."

She didn't give him time, running the device over him, from shoulder to hip bone. A thousand needles bit into him at once, fire following its course. The tatts were semi-permanent, but that didn't mean they didn't hurt like hell. He shuddered, fighting to remain still. Grunting, he clenched his jaw and stiffened his muscles when he should be relaxing his posture to ease the pain. The frack-en instructor hadn't sat through a full-bodied tatt in one session.

The process was the same as a normal tatt, and over the next few months, his body would work through the ink and flush it from his system. He hoped.

Frack, if they *were* permanent, and Em had played a sick joke on him, he'd be super pissed. As it was, he'd carry them for a while. All as part of his disguise.

It was a waste of time. He was an hour behind Davis and hating the delay. His fingers twitched, wishing he could hurry Viv along and cease the electric fire now igniting his skin. The added heat from the hearth didn't help.

Sophia circled him with a canister in her hand. He trailed her movements with a concerned gaze. What did she intend to do? She pulled a wooden table closer, climbed onto it, and began to spray his hair, running her fingers through it at the same time.

The stench of burning flesh mixed with ammonia. Frack Em and her high-handedness. He understood she wasn't used to explaining her decisions, her plans, but if she wanted his buy-in, then she'd better include him.

His instincts cautioned him to remain respectful, but the woman had him shot. She owed him as much as he was indebted to her!

"Press your lips together." A second later, Sophia sprayed his stubble, then ran her black-stained gloved thumbs over his eyebrows. She rubbed a towel over his hair and beard, staining it black, as well. Tilting her head to the side, she assessed the results.

"And?" He wasn't fishing for compliments, and if he were, he doubted she'd be honest with him. She was a spy and a sex worker—neither was trustworthy.

Sophia pursed her lips, but her dimples revealed her amusement. "It might work. What with the tatts and these?" She held up a pair of reading glasses. "They're clear glass with a few minor improvements. Master wants your outings recorded, and these have direct access to the databases you'll need."

Viv targeted his back, cooking his skin with her scanner. Sophia grabbed a cotton swab and dabbed at his chest, drawing a hiss from him. She met his gaze before continuing. "These look...good." Flashing a flirtatious smile, she leaned to the side to address Viv.

"Thanks, Phia." Viv didn't pause her scanner, despite the sexual tension rolling over his shoulder. Right, as long as they didn't do it on his desk, he'd be happy.

"Almost done?" Sophia rushed to gather his new clothing and unzipped his jeans before he could stop her. If Hux had done that, he'd have a raging hard-on. Thankfully, he was no longer interested in either of the women torturing him.

"Frack, woman! I can dress myself." He had to use his voice to stop her. Grabbing her hand would impact the scanner's path.

"It's not as if I haven't seen it, Gibs." She huffed but stepped back, leaving his fly open.

"Please extend your arms out as in a crucifixion." Viv shifted as soon as he assumed the position. "Biceps are trickier, the muscular indents, the curves..."

"Just do the upper arms then." He frowned. Who would see more than that? He understood doing one's job with thoroughness, but this was temporary.

Viv shrugged. "All right and matching tribal bands around the wrists."

The pain had become intolerable, and he gritted his teeth, squashing the need to roar, to demand she stop. She was close to finishing; he could endure a little while longer. He squeezed his eyes shut, focusing on the case, the clues, on Hux, on who might be behind her attempted murder. Sophia circled him again, the touch of her cotton swab blurring into the fire inflaming his body.

"Holy frack, Viv. These wings are stunning. I love how they curl around his shoulder blades and dip into the dimples above his ass. What's this? Latin?" Sophia was a hairbreadth away from resting her chin on his shoulder as she spoke to blue-haired Viv.

"To thine own self be true. Master's suggestion. She said it suited him." Viv lowered her scanner and assessed her work with a critical eye. "Almost done." She packed her device into her tool case and removed a red canister. "This might sting."

Fracken hell, sting? A thousand insects chewed his flesh as she sprayed him, then ice drenched his skin, and numbness set in.

"Painkiller, antiseptic, and sealant in one." Viv packed away the canister and yanked off her gloves, tossing them inside her case. "No infection and no irritation from your clothing. Good luck, Detective Lee Wash."

"I'll escort him to his chaser, and come see you, honey." Sophia followed Viv to the door, trailing her fingers along her forearm.

"Sounds like a plan." Viv kissed her on the cheek, waved at Gibs, and closed the door behind her.

He arched a brow at her, a smirk twisting his lips. "So, what's your preference?"

Sophia shrugged, but darkness flittered across her eyes. "Viv and I have been 'together' for a while, but I do what the Master needs." She draped his garments over the back of an armchair, eagerness to end this task clear in her efficient movements. "People reveal many secrets when you withhold gratification."

He furrowed his brow, trying to recall if he'd said anything during their shared hour.

"You were a favor for the Master. I wasn't there to milk you for information." She sniggered at the word 'milk.'

"Did you enjoy...?" Heat stained his cheeks. Trying to hide his embarrassment, he sat to tug off his boots and socks, then rose to slide off his denims. Her focus didn't waver from his face when she held out his new pants.

No color stained her cheeks. "Yes, surprisingly, but I don't experience an emotional connection with men. With Viv, it's more intimate as if she understands me, knows what my soul needs."

He nodded. After all, what was sex but a connection between two individuals, and without that connection, it was just mindless, a fleeting pleasure, not impacting them as people.

Pulling the pants on was a sensual delight. They were butter-soft, clinging to his legs and calves. He zipped them closed and sighed, running his palms down his thighs. "Kickers wear this?" He sat down to pull on fresh socks and his work boots.

"This disguise is from Questa's Center. Beige pants, dark-blue tunics, magnetized in a diagonal strip. The walnut-colored double-coat is tailored to fit your shoulders, and it's heavier at the back because of the meshing. Questers don't like being shot in the back." She dangled entwined belts on a forefinger. "Crisscrossing belts hold your weapons: a standard dagger and two laser pistols, refill canisters, and one or two smoke bombs."

"I want my Glock." He felt naked and vulnerable without its heavy presence.

She laughed. "Nope, that's a Gibs trademark. You're Lee Wash. I'd suggest you practice drawing them their sharpshooters, cowboy."

Despite his best efforts, he chuckled.

"Mirror." She addressed the screen-paneled wall, and their reflections appeared.

He gaped, turning from side-to-side. Holy frack. Black hair lightened the green in his eyes, and the stubble dominated his face, sharpening his jawline. The coat broadened his shoulders and fit him to perfection. The crisscrossing tunic exposed the new tribal tatts covering his chest and curling up his neck. The V matched the draping of the belts and the lethal weapons weighing down his hips.

"And these." She held out his eyeglasses and venti-mask—black-wire ribbing and fine mesh designed to mold to his skin and nose. As a Quester, his lungs couldn't tolerate Nova's unfiltered air.

He slipped the glasses and mask on but left the latter dangling below his chin. Once he held it in place, it would seal, and he'd need to depressurize it to release it. Frack, he didn't recognize himself at all.

She held up a finger. "There's one more thing."

He yelped when she pressed an inject-gun to his neck. A sharp spike of pain lanced up his throat as if he'd developed an infection.

"What the frack, Sophia?" He paused. "My voice..." A deep resonance vibrated his words.

"The vibration is temporary until your vocal cords adjust. Sing something in the chaser." She darted to his desk and returned with the new identity chips. One by one, he pressed them to his holo-wrist to scan the information. He had to assume the data would infiltrate his neural network and hide what made him Gibson Shaw.

"Ready?" She held the door open for him.

"Where's the crime scene?" Gibs waited in the hallway for her to lead the way. Who had the vandal targeted? The enforcement commissioner? A celebrity? An admiral?

"Renovare." She didn't leave the level, leading him onto a platform close to his office. "Em is livid."

"How...?" He raised his hand to pinch the bridge of his nose but bumped his glasses instead. "Their security is military grade."

Sophia shrugged and gestured for him to climb into the waiting chaser. "That's for you to figure out, Detective Wash."

26

7UU3/\/7Y-S1X

Date: 2170.16.10
The Holies
Renovare

GIBS CLIMBED OUT OF the chaser, the venti-mask muffling a silly nursery rhyme he hummed.

"Fever, fever in the night; lock your lips nice and tight." The tune was stuck in his head now, and he hated its simple yet annoying cadence. Something about a pandemic in the year 2122 that had wiped out millions. "In the morning, you'll be done; call the grave man, one more gone."

He paused to scan the empty platform, surprised by the emergency lights flickering across its surface that indicated they would accept no customers today. Not that he could recall a time in Nova's history when Renovare had closed its doors to business.

Extra Sec2s lined the circumference, and above his warbling voice, Davis's ranting reached him.

Whistling the fracken nursery rhyme as he approached the entrance, Gibs scanned the circle of Sec2s guarding the crime scene and Davis pacing around them, throwing his arms in the air in mid-rant.

He grinned, his friend's behavior humorous to him although he doubted Davis would agree.

Gibs wanted to tease him, but Lee Wash and Martin Davis were strangers. "Officer Martin Davis?"

Davis stilled, then spun on a heel to glare at him. "Right, the import. About time you showed up. Tell these idiots who you are so I can work on the crime scene."

"I'm Detective Lee Wash." In his deeper voice, his temporary name sounded strange, like an out-of-body experience. He fought the urge to look for the source of the voice.

Six Sec2s relaxed their posture in a coordinated movement and marched off, joining those cordoning off the crowds.

"At last." Davis didn't face the scene; instead, he shoved his sweat-drenched face in Gibs's. "Listen here, Wash. You ain't this case's lead detective. Gibson Shaw is."

Heat burst across Gibs's chest like a rubber bullet hitting its mark. That Davis was this fond of him surprised and delighted him. He had thought the man tolerated him at best.

"Shaw's disappearance is a separate case." He assumed. After all, what could Hux have said? That the Master shot him and took his body? "Need help with that?"

"Frack no. We didn't ask for your assistance, interference, or whatever this is, in the first fracken place."

"Mayor DuPont believes otherwise."

"Frack." Davis removed his glasses and rubbed his eyes. "It's a re-election year, isn't it?"

"He did mention something about the Luxers getting antsy."

Davis sighed, the wind draining from his sails. "Once we solve this case, Shaw gets the credit, okay?" He leveled his beady eyes on Gibs, daring him to argue. He didn't. He was having a hard time hiding his laughter. "Right. Let's have a look at the poor thing."

Poor things—the plural being the operative word. Seated on their haunches and still in their work clothes, two Zetas faced each other, their arms raised above their heads. Knees, temples, and palms touched each other, forming praying hands in silhouette. Both had their eyes removed.

Green stained their white blouses, and three feet behind each backside lay their stuttering mechanical hearts in pools of congealing lube. The perp had taken the time to button each blouse post-removal of the hearts.

Gibs grimaced. He hated it when he was right. The mutilations *had* escalated though what had inspired the perp to do so, he couldn't say. He lifted black hair off the nape of the closest Zeta. The same modus operandi: a blade severing the spinal cord. Leaning against each other was supportive as well as symbolic.

"How did you know to look...?" Davis huffed, gesturing to his drones to start photographing the scene. "You had access to our case files?"

"Read them on the magrail over from Queste." Gibs shrugged. "I assume the ownership tatt is Renovare's company logo?"

"I'm assuming the same, but with their hearts extracted, the tatts will be shredded." Davis crouched, having pulled out a goliath pair of tweezers from inside his uniform. He pinched the top button and undid it, then with amazing skill, peeled the shirt open. On the edges of the shredded synthetic skin, the top of the dark-gray tatt peeked out.

"They place the tatts over the hearts?" Gibs raised his gaze, searching for security cams. "No footage?"

"Nothing, as usual." Davis rolled back onto his heels. His gaze shifted to behind Gibs, to the platform, and a smirk curled his lips. "This is going to be good."

Gibs spun, curiosity driving him. His breath hitched at the vision crossing the platform. Long-limbed, curvaceous Hux strode toward them, her uniform leaving nothing to the imagination. Swaying at every step was her blonde ponytail. But her lips weren't the ruby red he had expected to see. They were nude, pursed, forcing his gaze to her pale cheeks. Darkness shadowed her eyes as if insomnia plagued her. Yet, despite this, she was beautiful.

"Lee Wash, frack." Her tempestuous-gray glare was ice-cold and dismissive. "What do we have, Martin?"

Gibs's chest swelled with blossoming heat. His body trembled with the urge to lunge for her. She was breathtaking, her feisty nature unrivaled. "And you are, buttercup?"

"*Officer* Naomi Huxley, Gibs's partner." Her expression was fierce, with narrowed eyes, a furrowed brow, and pursed lips, but the moment she faced Davis, a bright smile dented her cheeks. "Sorry I'm late, Martin. I had an argument with the mayor about his decision. We don't need help from some unskilled, QC asshat."

"Yup, said the same to Montgomery, but we're stuck with him, Huxley." Davis shrugged. "We must deal with it as best we can."

"Fine." She pouted, then circled the crime scene. "Frack, I know these inkjobs. These are Lord Fields's personal Zetas, Anna and Bree."

Hux leaned closer to the inkjobs' faces, horror darkening her eyes. "What you got for me? Anything? Something? Hell, I'd take a single fracken fingerprint about now."

"Same old, no clues, no footage, and Gibs was right."

He was. Dragging his gaze from Hux's lips, Gibs shook his head to clear his lustful thoughts. He could reveal himself to her, but he needed her disdain to add believability to Lee Wash from Queste City. Telling her meant she would have to be on her guard, masking her words and expressions. He grimaced, drawing in a deep breath through the annoying venti-mask.

"Yup, it's escalated but it's still not human. I don't know if I'm ready for that level, Martin." She pressed her fingertips to her temple. "We've got to stop this before it reaches full-blown murder."

"Who can we talk to for data?" Helplessness struck Gibs, and he paced, filled with nervous energy. "Someone had to know how to reach Lord Fields's inner sanctum, how to disarm two inkjobs, and how to remove their hearts."

"Their anatomy is based on ours." Hux glared, her tone frosty.

"Listen here, cupcake, a tool is required to penetrate through the ribs unless the perp is an inkjob or a human with super sharp nails and impressive strength." Gibs smirked, having clipped his words, as well. If she played the bitch, he'd be the bastard. It suited him, helping him to vent his sexual tension somehow.

"*My name is Huxley.*" Venom deepened her voice.

"And the ability to disrupt the security cams." Davis's voice was far away, his focus on raising the hair with a gloved hand to photograph the entry wound. "This one had time to heal."

"We had an aggressive system virus that triggered a blackout. It is protocol to evacuate all personnel during a system malfunction."

Gibs whipped his head up and gaped at the Zeta standing to the side. Frack, that was fast. Lord Fields must have felt nothing for the Zetas to have cloned another so quickly.

"And you are?" Striding toward her, he activated his holo-wrist and chose the recording function. He didn't need to read the rights to her—she wasn't human.

"Cara Zeta, and I speak on behalf of Lord Fields." She clasped her hands in front of her as the terminated Zetas had done. "I am to assist you, Detective Lee Wash, in whatever you need."

"Why him?" Hux gasped and stomped across to Gibs, jabbing his chest with her forefinger. "I go where you go. I look at the same data you do. You share, or so help me, I'll have you off this case so fast, your venti-mask will fall off."

"Whatever you say, sweet cheeks." Gibs grinned; he couldn't help himself. Unfortunately, his eyeglasses didn't hide his humor, and she huffed, throwing her hands in the air.

"Fracken Quester, coming to Nova, thinking he's all we have."

Something was there under Hux's muttered words. Did she hold a grudge against Questers? "Is it Questers or me you hate?"

She spun on him, both hands thrusting him back. Her strength surprised him when he stumbled before catching himself.

"Don't you ever imply such a fracken thing. I am not a racist, nor is it wrong of me to be wary of your kind, Detective Wash."

Gibs arched both brows. Was she aware that she'd contradicted her anti-racist claim by calling him 'your kind'? "Last time I checked, *my kind* is human."

Davis flicked a worried gaze between them, inching away from the crime scene and toward the platform. Gibs sighed. He'd have to play this right. What would a QC detective do in this situation? Shrug it off? No, he'd teased her with derogatory names; he'd have to respond accordingly.

"What about me offends you, Officer Huxley of Nova? My poor eyesight? No? My dependency on a venti-mask to breathe? No? My irresistible charm and oft-times thoughtful nature?"

Curious as to what she'd say, he folded his arms across his chest and waited. He'd never have said she held grudges or had any streaks of hatred in her, but then, he'd known her for all of five days. Either he delved into her history or waited for her to reveal it. The latter would be better for their relationship, but as Lee Wash, her discrimination might spur him to investigate her past.

"Like. I. Said." She clipped her words with enough ice to drag a shiver through Davis. "I am not racist. I just don't like strangers. Especially ones here to 'help.'"

A good response, one which raised more questions than answers. She'd diverted the issue, steering his focus away from the pain lingering in her eyes, the reason behind her erratic pulse at her jaw and her shallow breaths. He stared at her for a minute, taking the opportunity to study her features until she glanced away.

Without removing his attention from Hux's profile, Gibs addressed the new Zeta. "Cara, I need a list of Renovare employees who can disable an inkjob. I want security footage from the day before this incident until now. I want stills of the crowd milling around." He gestured to the human faces peering through the gaps between the

Sec2s. A perp often hovered to watch their masterwork unfold. He'd trawl through Eve Roe 2's crowd footage for common faces.

Zeta nodded and scurried off, leaving Gibs alone with a scowling Hux and a once-again distracted Davis who poked at the lube pooling under one heart.

Gibs dipped his head to snag Davis's attention. "I would like access to your case files; the last date in the current one implies either the case has stagnated or you've taken your findings offline."

Davis rolled a shoulder, his lips twisting as a fine sheen of perspiration peppered his forehead to his receding hairline. "Um, sure. I'll upload the drone's scans and whatever the cleanup crew discovers."

Gibs offered Davis a curt nod. His professionalism was above par. "Officer Huxley, I'd like to review the memories mentioned in the file. Perhaps you missed something."

She squealed, her cheeks a bright pink as she clenched her fists at her sides too close to her blaster. "I didn't..."

"No offense intended. Fresh eyes and all that, honeybuns." Gibs smothered a chuckle, enjoying poking the bear. "If you could show me to the lab?"

"Fine, frack. Martin, I'll see you back at the Center." She stomped off, the sway of her hips their own enticement.

Gibs hurried after her, a bark of laughter slipping from him when she threatened to shoot anyone in her path. The crowds cleared like a knife through a roasted pigeon.

27

7VV3/\/7Y-S3V3/\/

Date: 2170.16.10
Solus City, west of Nova
A shopping sector

NATE REMOVED HIS SUNVISORS, squeezing his eyes shut against the unbearable glare as he rubbed the bridge of his nose. How anyone could live in Solus, he couldn't understand. Solar harvesting was the city's bread and butter, but it was hell on his cornea. Just before sunrise, he'd left Nova and Lissa's bed and caught a magrail. Two hours and a hired chaser later, he'd mopped up his sweat, fought a killer headache, and had permanently damaged his eyesight as he watched his 'brother' serve his customers.

Cuppa Joe, his coffee bistro, was as impressive as The Skin Canvas. It was well situated in a shopping district, and opposite the Pie and Pigeon stall, Nate could observe his twin without revealing himself. Pride swelled his chest, that they shared an entrepreneur code. He clipped his sunvisors on, keeping his head dipped.

Where Nate's shaggy hair fell to his shoulders, Joe clipped his short and brushed it to the side. Same build and height, same smile. Nothing hindered Nate's perusal when Solusians opted for eye enhancements. No one wore sunvisors.

The lunchtime crowd dwindled, having received their caffeine fix along with tofu-dominant pastries. Nate pushed off the counter, swiped the pay point, and crossed to Cuppa Joe. He'd debated in his hours of vigilance whether he should reveal himself, should destroy Joe Bailey's life. Thinking about how his parents and Kylie had kept it from him left his body trembling with restrained emotion. Yes, he'd tell Joe and all his 'siblings.'

"I wondered when you'd come over."

Nate jerked back. Joe gestured to the closest table and sank into a seat.

"How long were you aware I...?" Nate dropped in the chair, scraping the legs on the steel-patterned flooring. He wasn't cut out for this stealth bullshit.

"Sunvisors highlight strangers." Joe chuckled, leaning back to gesture to the barista. "But I've been waiting a while for one of you to visit me."

"You have? You knew about me? Us?" Nate frowned, sucking in a deep breath to calm his erratic heartbeat. He was muddling this.

"My parents told me as soon as I could understand." The waitress slid the cups onto the table, and Joe pushed a cappuccino across to Nate.

"You didn't think to tell me? To introduce yourself?" He stared at the intricate lacework dusting the foam, its fleeting existence intensifying its beauty.

"You looked happy, Nate." Joe shrugged. "Wyn's on her way if you want to meet her."

"Wyn." Nate tested the name on his tongue.

Joe's parents had the finances for two E7s, and Renovare must have thought to test whether they would behave as true siblings. No other family had more than one E7 except the Baileys. Joe and Wyn's names were on the top of the list Rhona had transferred, and they lived the farthest away. Time out of Nova had felt like a godsend.

"How did you find out?" After sipping his coffee, Joe rubbed his thumb along the edge and sucked the foam off.

"At Renovare when I tried to purchase an X10 for my assistant." Nate didn't want to think about that; he'd prefer to focus on what happened in the chaser afterward.

Joe grimaced. "I'm sorry. That must have been brutal."

Nate shrugged, not wanting to dwell on how his life had changed, spinning in a downward spiral until his emotions ricocheted between love and hate. He loved Kylie or *had* loved her, and with his parents leaving messages, begging him to remember how invested he was in her, in them, it had intensified his confusion. Despite his pleas for them to give him time, they couldn't. They cared too much. He rubbed his chest, the ache there growing harder to ignore.

"Finding out your parents and wife hid it from you...priceless." Nate forced a smile as if it didn't bother him anymore.

"I reckon you have family matters to deal with."

Nate smothered a snort by sipping his coffee. "I plan to check in on the others. Got any advice, any warnings?"

"Mitch Lewis is a mean son of a bitch. I'd steer clear of him. He knows he's an E7, but he doesn't give a rat's ass. Spends most of his time dodging law enforcement and screwing over hardworking citizens." Joe slammed his cup down. "He tried to swindle money out of me. I'm pretty sure he'll try the same with you."

"Thanks for the heads-up."

Joe gestured for another round of coffees. "Dina Le Roux is in the public eye up in Queste—some hotshot celebrity."

"I saw her name on the list, but I didn't think it was the same woman." Nate chuckled. "Never liked her acting, to be honest."

"Best not tell her that if you head north to try to see her." Joe rolled his shoulders as if readying for a fistfight. "Her Sec2s are formidable. I'd reach out to her first before leaving Nova. No use wasting your time if those bastards won't let you through."

"All right, and the last sibling?" Nate pulled a cup close as soon as the waitress slid their coffees onto the table.

"Ah, yes, the accountant. He's in Nova. Yes, I know the list says in Elega across the oceans—it's a lie. Here's the kicker. He doesn't look anything like us. Some sort of glitch during manufacturing is my guess."

"Morning, Joey." A woman intruded with a kiss to Joe's temple. A long walnut-brown braid draped over her shoulder, and the scent of lilacs teased Nate's nostrils.

"Hey, sis, meet Nate."

She spun, a bright smile splitting her cheeks. "*The* Nate, *our* Nate?" Graceful arms engulfed him, and he sighed, peace settling over his tortured heart.

"Hi, Wyn." He grinned, assessing the female version of himself. Tall, slender, with matching indigo eyes, her jawline angular but more delicate. In a white T-shirt and denim leggings showing off her curves, she was an attractive woman whom he would've looked at twice.

But now that he knew they were related, he saw only himself in her mannerisms and facial expressions.

Neither of them had clouds hovering above their heads, and Nate didn't know how to read that. He'd expected to gauge their emotions since he assumed all E7s could feel as much as any human. Perhaps they were happy? He'd monitor them, though. Any form of cloud would bring him hope that he was closer to a human than an inkjob.

"What brought you west?" Wyn dropped into a chair and snagged Joe's cup.

"Found out yesterday I'm not human." Nate blinked, a little dazed. Was it less than a day since his life had shifted on its axis? No, two days had passed. He'd wasted yesterday wallowing in self-pity.

"I'm so sorry." Wyn squeezed his hand resting on the table. "You have us now if you need anything." She shot a glance at Joe, who nodded.

"Thank you. I'm a little in shock, directionless…"

"…And as pissed off as a pigeon in a cockfight?" Joe laughed, thumping Nate on the shoulder. "I know that look, Nate. It's the same expression I get when I want to kill someone, something."

"My parents I can forgive. It's my wife I'm struggling to deal with. I don't know if I can ever trust her again or find what I once loved in her with this hanging over us." There, he'd summed up the problem. He flashed a smile, grateful for the clarity speaking to his new family had brought him.

"You'll figure it out." Wyn tapped his arm then cupped Joe's coffee for a sip.

"Sis, I told Nate about the others and just mentioned the accountant."

Wyn grimaced. "Thornton isn't too bad, except for the receding hairline."

"He's respected, though." Joe stole his coffee back, tossing a beady eye at his sister. "Works for the Master, or so I'm told. I haven't met the man, but he goes by the name Davis now."

"I know a Martin Davis, but I doubt it's the same man. Your Davis, I'll steer clear of. I don't want any reason to be under the Master's radar." As Nate saw it, out of the E7s, he'd gained two friends. The others were best left to their own devices.

"Wise. Staying for long in Solus?" There was an eagerness in Joe's tone. Nate couldn't decide if he wanted him to stay or to leave. "Mom left us for greener pastures years ago, but Dad would love to meet you."

"Stay for dinner, at least. You can catch a magrail and be home by midnight." Wyn bounced in her chair, her excitement rolling across the table. She reminded Nate of Lissa. He chuckled, nodding in thanks for the invitation.

"Why not?" he said and received another thump on the back from Joe.

28

7∨∨3/\/7Y-319#7

Date: 2170.16.10

The Holies

Renovare

"L ORD F IELDS WILL SEE you now," Zeta intoned, slicing through Gibs's obsession with Hux's ass.

Heat exploded across his cheeks, and he flicked his gaze to the new Zeta. "Cara?"

"I am Dawn Zeta. This way, Detective Lee Wash." She gestured to the pod.

Gibs stepped aside in a gallant gesture, indicating with an elaborate bow that Hux should lead. She huffed and strode toward him. Dawn held up a palm, stopping her approach.

"Lord Fields has requested Detective Lee Wash and not Officer Naomi Huxley. Please wait here."

Hux released a string of smothered curses and stomped her foot, her hands flying as she vented. Two Sec2s stepped closer, and she froze, tossing them a petulant pout as if they'd caught her throwing a tantrum.

"I want to know everything, Wash."

"Or what?" Gibs chuckled as the doors closed on another garbled rant. When he revealed the truth to Hux, he'd have a devil of a time surviving her reaction.

His holo-wrist pinged, and he barked out a laugh. She'd filed an investigative case on him at the Center. Receiving a notification proved the Master's omnipotence. Someone this thorough had to have anticipated any dissension in her ranks and business dealings.

He shivered, which raised the hairs on the back of his neck and stole his laughter. Owing the Master for the 'rescue' he had anticipated, but the more time he spent in the Shadows, the more she owned him. What would she ask as payment? Perhaps a frank discussion was in order this evening.

"Thank you, Dawn, that will be all." Lord Fields faced an extensive, panoramic view, his back to the pod and his hands clasped at the base of his spine. As soon as the soft whir of the descending pod faded, Lord Fields unfolded his stiff posture to rest his temple on the glass facade. "I don't like this, Gibs."

Gibs grunted. The Master must have spoken to Lord Fields, revealing his identity. It shouldn't surprise him that they were on such friendly terms. The two of them, along with the mayor, ran Nova. He strode deeper into the office, considering using the available chair to ease his exhausted and pain-riddled body.

"Neither do I. It's escalating, and now she's striking too close to the powers-that-be."

"She?" Lord Fields laughed, a cold sound lacking mirth. "Well, at least that's progress." He twisted, tossing Gibs an arched brow. "The problem is that Renovare only issues kill codes to the male workers."

"Frack." Gibs ran a frustrated hand over his face but met venti-mask and eyeglasses. "It has to be an inside job. Everything points to it." He depressurized the mask, unclipped it, and tossed the eyeglasses onto Fields's desk. Rubbing his face now that he was free to do so, he focused on the darkness around his soul, the mind fog, everything that hindered his ability to solve the case.

Lord Fields slipped around his desk and dropped into his chair, his shoulders slumped. "To strike at me and my closest synths implies I have weaknesses, Gibs. I cannot have the people of Nova believing I'm vulnerable."

"Release a statement saying it was a security exercise."

"That solves the publicity but not the fact that a *woman* waltzed past my Sec2s, lured my trusted Anna and Bree to her, then slaughtered them in this juvenile fashion. I *am* weak!" Fields thumped his desk with his fist, his hair flopping across his forehead. "How do you know it's a woman?" He flicked his fingers, and Gibs's case files appeared on enormous holographic panels—even the updated cloud files.

Sighing at their inability to keep even that data secure, Gibs approached the files, browsed the folders, then sifted through Eve Roe 2's crime scene security footage. He tapped the image of the woman, her back to him but her wedding ring visible.

"There."

"A wedding ring? That's it?" Fields bounded up, grabbed the image with a pinch of his fingers, and widened it, zooming in for more detail. "I've...seen that ring."

"What? Where?" The urge to shake Fields by his narrow shoulders gripped Gibs, and he folded his arms across his chest, forcing his body to relax, to breathe. One does not assault the richest and most powerful man in Nova and live to tell the tale.

"I don't know. I meet with hundreds of people a day, Gibs. Give me time; I'll remember." Fields gestured to his disguise. "If I didn't know who you were, I wouldn't have recognized you. Although, Master could have chosen a better name than Lee Wash."

"Agreed. Lee is too close to Paisley, and Wash is an anagram of Shaw."

"She has a wicked sense of humor, but sometimes, I don't think she plays with a full deck of cards."

Gibs met Fields's gaze but kept his face expressionless. When the silence stretched, and Fields's unblinking gaze didn't lessen in intensity, Gibs cleared his throat. "You can't expect me to speak ill of the woman who has me at her mercy."

"Well spoken, Gibs. She has chosen well." Fields scooped a data crystal off his desk and offered it to Gibs. "I've had Dawn transfer the case files, memories, security footage, and access codes to certain systems in Renovare. There's no need for you to wallow in a data lab when you can work in the secure comfort of your new office."

"Um, thanks." The bold, bright burn of a headache pressed behind his eyes. The political relationships between the mayor, Em, and Fields sent his thoughts into a tailspin.

Fields tapped on his holo-wrist, and the answering whir of the pod confirmed he'd summoned Dawn. "Send my warmest regards to Phia."

Right, Sophia. Had she fucked Fields as a favor for Em, too? How deep was Fields in Em's back pocket? Were those pockets interchangeable? A sharp ping of pain behind his left eye had him wincing. What he needed was a shot of something alcoholic.

Sliding the crystal into his back pocket, Gibs slipped on his eyeglasses, clipped on the mask, pressurized it, then followed Dawn into the pod. He'd need to talk to Hux and Davis again about securing their fracken case files.

Hux waited outside the pod, her cheeks flushed. As he disembarked, she paused mid-pace before scurrying toward him. "And?"

Gibs gripped her elbow, drawing a yelp from her, then escorted her with a little too much force to the waiting chaser. "Get in. Where's Davis?"

"On his way to the Center." She peered at him, raising a stubborn chin. "What happened, Wash? What did Fields say?"

Gibs glared at her and waited. His tense posture, continued silence, and the stroking of his blaster urged her to dive inside the chaser. She was all long limbs and ass as she clambered in, and he relished the exhibition. Before climbing in, he took a moment to wipe the smirk from his face. He was about to chastise her, and he needed her to take him seriously.

As soon as he'd instructed the chaser to take them to the Center, he spun his seat to confront her. "Fields has access to the cloud files, which means the Master does, too."

She gaped. "What? How?"

"I don't give a rat's fracken ass how! We have a mole, and it's either you or Davis. Who else has access to the cloud? Gibs? Would he share this information?"

Hux shook her head, her wide eyes. The violent tossing of her ponytail proclaimed her innocence. "No, it was Gibs's idea in the first place."

"Misdirection, perhaps?" Gibs watched Hux's lush lips whiten as she pinched them together, flushing her cheeks pink.

"He would never jeopardize the case. He's a man of integrity, a quality you know nothing about." Her defense of him was a balm to Gibs's soul. Frack, he loved this woman.

"How can you know that when you've been his partner for what, five days?" Gibs flicked a dismissive hand and held his breath, waiting on her response. Was it wicked of him to trick her into revealing how she felt? He activated his vision enhancement, then wished he hadn't, finding her erratic pulse, spiked temperature, and the rise and fall of her breasts mesmerizing.

"He earned my loyalty." She folded her arms across her chest, ruining his enjoyment.

Gibs snorted. "How?"

Hux huffed, unfolding one arm to toy with the stitching on her uniform and running a trembling finger along the seams. "He saved me when I ate poisoned chocolate, even insisted I remain in his home."

For a moment, that she thought him heroic tied his tongue. "He wanted to fuck you. Any man would've acted the same way."

Hux sucked in a sharp breath. She trembled, and tears shimmered on her eyelashes. The pain twisting her face speared him, but he persevered. She could be infatuated with an older man, with no worthwhile affection behind her youthful respect.

Meeting his gaze, she tilted her chin in defiance. "I'd let him fuck me as long as he's alive and well." She *knew* he was very much alive, having spoken to him yesterday.

Heat burst across his chest, and he wanted to lunge for her, to drag her onto his lap and kiss her. Spinning away from her, he stared at the passing scenery, searching for anything to thwart his urges. He'd have to remove his mask; he'd have to convince her it was him without her punching him in the mouth again. Feisty, breathtaking, adorable woman.

He studied her reflection, preferring that to looking at her. "You believe he's alive?"

"Yes." Her voice trembled, slicing guilt through Gibs. He'd find a way to make up for Lee's horrendous treatment of her. "Master would've killed him and left him for dead, rather than take his body."

"You were there?" Gibs twisted to watch the emotions play across her face. Fear, concern, and something else, intense and beautiful.

She nodded. "Someone sent Rage-laced chocolates, claiming they were from him. Gibs rushed me to the clinic and insisted on keeping me safe. Only his home wasn't safe for him." Hux pressed her fingertips under her right eye, catching her tears. "I didn't include any of this in my report, claiming I wasn't there. Davis and I believed it would keep the heat off him. You see, he asked Master for help on the case."

"And instead, the Master shot him." Gibs rolled his shoulder, the dull ache reminding him that he still sported the blaster wound.

"If I confronted the Master, assuming she'd allow me into her domain, what could she say? My Sec2 went rogue?" Hux sighed. "If Davis and I took it to Captain Montgomery, what could he do?

Would he jeopardize his career for his lover's ex-husband? Frack no. Investigating the Master would be political suicide."

"So you covered it up until you could solve the case, then Shaw could return as if nothing happened." Gibs arched a brow, implying she was naïve to think so. The pink of her cheeks traveled down the graceful column of her neck.

"Montgomery would have to charge him for attempted murder, but Davis and I are hoping to solve that, too. With Gibs somewhere in the Shadows, he's working both cases, and this time, with the Master's help. He's tenacious, trustworthy, a huge, old softie under all that grumpiness…"

"Enough, I'm not dating the man." Gibs removed his glasses to rub between his eyebrows. "You trust Davis?"

"Not anymore. Not if you say Fields has our cloud files." Hux narrowed her eyes as if she distrusted Gibs's word. "Unless you're sowing dissent. What evidence do you have that Fields has our files? After all, I don't know you, and you could be lying to me."

Gibs dug in his back pocket and waved the data crystal. "Everything Fields has on our case, the security footage for the last two days, and the memories you've watched already."

"Frack." She fell silent, chewing on her bottom lip. "You think Davis is our mole?"

Gibs shrugged then winced, his shoulder burning hotter the longer he went without his pain meds.

"You don't think Davis sent me those chocolates, do you?" Horror pooled in her stormy gray eyes.

He sighed, remembering she was a rookie and way out of her depth. She was his responsibility, both with the learning curve and for protection.

"Incoming call from Lord Reginald Fields," the chaser's feminine voice intoned. It had landed, but they had yet to disembark.

Gibs grunted, and Fields's voice filled the compartment. "Wash, it has to be an inside job. All my display models are missing their eyes. Only someone in my employ knows they're still active and recording. The virus not only deactivated my security but also access to the display cases."

Gibs gritted his teeth, their incompetence shoved to the fore. "Frack." With no shattered glass, they hadn't looked deeper, never thinking the perp had opened each case using the codes.

"I'm sending you a list of personnel with the security freedom to do all of this combined. Male or female, look into it." Fields ended the call, and the silence that followed was thick with tension.

"How many models were there?" Gibs scowled, replaying walking into the showroom and seeing the mutilated Zetas. "Six when you walk in?"

"Fifteen in total. Renovare keeps that many trending models at a time."

He met her stunned gaze with his. "Frack, Hux, how could we have missed this?"

"Gibs was right. This escalated quickly." She gave him a strange look, her keen gaze assessing before leaping out of the chaser.

Gibs grumbled. A man liked to be right, but in this case, he didn't appreciate it.

29

7VV3/\/7Y-/\/1/\/3

Date: 2170.16.10
The Colony
The Center

GIBS HEADED FOR THE captain's office *after* asking for directions. He'd taken a step toward the elevator before realizing he wasn't supposed to know the way. Hux flicked confused expressions at him, giving his body a slow appraisal, peering into his eyes, and leaning in to sniff him. Didn't she know what that kind of look or her proximity could do to a man?

She'd waltzed off, all limbs and ass, heading to the labs to find Davis, so the answer would be no. Gibs adjusted his butter-soft pants. They accentuated his hard-on as if it was a cardinal sin.

As Mrs. Dennis instructed, he chose a seat to wait. Mumbled words reached him through Montgomery's door but neither voice was feminine. No Tamara today although he'd have loved to run into her, tease her, flirt with her, then snub her.

"Oh, Felicity, is he running late again?"

There she was, popping her head in. The lighting didn't flatter her complexion, but Gibs flashed her what he hoped was a charming smile anyway despite the mask hiding most of it.

"Well, hello there." He may have deepened his voice just to add that extra level of testosterone to the temptation.

"Um, hello." Mara stepped into the room with a polite smile, not in the least affected by Wash's charm.

Either the full depth of his voice wasn't as impactful as he'd expected, or she didn't find his new tatts, dark hair, and form-hugging outfit attractive. Or his flirting was rusty. He planned to test out his voice on Hux. If she responded despite the way he'd treated her, then there was nothing wrong with his 'charm.'

"He won't be a moment, Tamara. Did you receive the flowers he sent?" Mrs. Dennis smiled, removing decades off her age and adding a timeless beauty. "He chose them—said you adored the color purple."

She did? Gibs frowned. He'd thought she loved red since every damn piece of lingerie she'd owned was crimson, burgundy, or maroon.

"He's so thoughtful, not what I expected after...you know."

Gibs shifted in his chair, expecting to hear her disparage every inch of her ex-husband.

"I loved Gibson, but I wasn't enough for him." She dipped her head so that her hair cascaded forward, hiding her face from Gibs. "I hope Stan finds him."

He gaped, his thoughts whirling, clashing with long-held anger and unforgiveness only to find they were baseless, drawn up by his broken heart.

"Do you think he's innocent?" Mrs. Dennis whispered, shooting judgmental glares at Gibs for listening in.

"Of course. Being a detective means everything to Gibs. He wouldn't violate the rules his father taught him."

Ice skittered along his nerves, and he felt weightless, without structure, as if his bones had melted. All this time, he'd wasted pent-up emotions on something he'd imagined. Mara didn't hate him, and she hadn't asked *Stan* to assign him to this mutilation case either. The case was turning out to be the highlight of his career.

The door opened, and Davis stormed out, mopping his brow. His gaze landed on Gibs, and he grimaced. What had Wash done to him since he'd left Renovare? Or did Davis know who Wash was and directed this anger at Gibs? If Davis was the mole, then his behavior validated his distaste.

"Ah, Wash, I'll see you now. Sweetheart, just another ten minutes, I promise." Montgomery curled his arm around Mara's waist and pressed a kiss to her temple. "You can go ahead. I'll meet you at the restaurant?"

"Oh no, you won't. I'll wait right here, Stan." She huffed, dropping in the chair beside Gibs.

"Captain Stanley Montgomery, I demand a moment of your time."

Gibs froze. Fear, horror, and the urge to cower slumped him in his chair. Mom? He twisted to peer at his mother, who flounced in amid swaths of color, vibrant movements, and strange fragrances, some of which he recognized. His stomach gurgled in complaint. She had herbal packets strapped to her love handles for headaches, her gout in winter, and an extra packet if her current beau couldn't get it up.

She leveled her hazel eyes on Mrs. Dennis, who had the courage not to shrink away from her stare. Perhaps this secretary would last longer than Gibs had thought.

Montgomery pasted on a polite smile. "How can I help you, ma'am?"

Gibs smirked, grateful for the mask hiding it. Montgomery had taken the polite approach, one which wouldn't garner him any favors. Gibs straightened in his chair, looking forward to the altercation, now that Mom wouldn't be picking on him.

"Don't ma'am me, boy. What have you done to find my son? I have the ear of the mayor, don't you know?" Her voice reached a high octave, piercing Gibs's eardrums. A memory flashed of Jackson and him cowering under his bunk bed after they'd done something to draw her wrath. Jackson would cover his ears and giggle, not realizing she could hear him.

Laughter rumbled up Gibs's chest, and he rushed to smother it. Yes, she did have the mayor's ear. The previous incumbent mayor had lost it in a duel, and somehow, the offending piece of cartilage had come into her possession.

"Your son?" Montgomery smiled in thanks at Mrs. Dennis, then ushered Mom into his office. As he closed the door, he winked at Mara, who tittered like a schoolgirl.

"I'll talk to you later, you hussy." Mom speared Mara with a glare and a wagging finger, cutting off Mara's tittering. Gibs barked out a laugh.

"I never liked that woman," Mara muttered. The feeling was mutual. Mom thought all women were whores. Stood to reason considering the way she fell pregnant with Gibs and Jackson. Trust one to know one.

"Why would she call you a hussy?" Gibs fluttered his eyelashes with 'sincere' curiosity.

"I married her son. He has your height and build but wore a permanent scowl. I loved him anyway." She sighed, staring off into the distance. "When I stopped looking forward to him coming home after work, I knew I had to move on."

"You find my son or so help me, Captain, there'll be hell to pay." Grumbles, mutters, and other calming tones followed the raised voice. "What? Do you think his father wasn't without influence?"

Grudging respect grew for Montgomery, able to remain so calm in the face of Gibs's mother. He sighed; there was only one way to solve this. He'd have to come clean to the woman and convince her to act the distressed mother. Mom would love that. She already believed she was the queen of the stage. It might be true on a desperate, bored-to-death-of-orgies hippie ship.

He bounded up and knocked on the door, opening it without waiting for permission. "Sorry to barge in, Captain, sir, but I do believe the mother of the renowned Detective Shaw might garner more information from his partner." He released the door and gestured toward the elevator. "I was on my way to the labs, and it would be an absolute delight to escort the lady."

Captain's face morphed from outraged frustration to blessed relief. "What a capital idea, Detective Wash." With surprising agility, he darted around his desk and out the door, blocking Mom's view of Mara. Right then, Gibs knew Captain Stanley Montgomery loved her, the poor bastard.

Like Gibs always did, he pinched Mom's elbow, right where she was ticklish the most. She jerked back, stilled, and raised her wide-eyed gaze at him, gaping like a fish. With a snap, she shut her mouth and allowed him to escort her out of the room and toward the elevator.

"What's going on?" Mom sidled closer to him to stage-whisper.

He winced and shook his head, asking for her silence, and ushered her into the creaking elevator, scanning the foyer for observers.

The moment the doors closed, she spun on him, yanking her elbow out of his grip. "There had better be a fracken good reason for this." She gestured to him, from his boots to his venti-mask.

"There's a mole." Gibs grimaced like that explained the pain he'd endured to disguise himself.

"This is Nova's Center." She huffed, folding her arms across her extensive bosom. "There's always a mole."

"Right. But this one has me in Montgomery's sights for a trumped-up attempted murder charge."

Mom gasped, and her cheeks flushed. "What? Your captain's an idiot. I'll give him a piece of my mind and anything else I can spare."

Gibs grinned, wishing he could be there for the show. "I need something infinitely better from you. I need you to play the concerned parent."

"I *am...was* the concerned parent." She frowned, confusion pursing her lips as she relived meeting Montgomery.

"Mom," he sighed. "Gibs is 'missing' to buy Detective Lee Wash from Queste City time to solve the case I was working on and unravel the mastermind behind the murder charges." He gripped her chin, forcing her to meet his gaze. "Please, keep the pressure on Montgomery to clear the Shaw name."

"Of course." Mom nodded, jerking her chin out of his hand. She studied his face above the mask, lingering on his eyes. "I didn't know you had a partner."

Gibs leaned against the side of the elevator's compartment and crossed his legs at the ankles. "Hux is a rookie, Mom, so be nice."

"I'm always nice." She huffed, sending up a miasma of medicinal odors.

"I mean it—no calling her a tart, a hussy, or a whore." When she opened her mouth to protest, Gibs leveled his matching hazel gaze on her. "You can stay at my apartment; just no orgies, please."

"I'm too old for those." Mom pouted.

"I call bullshit on that. There's a certain pouch on your person." He tapped his nose and stepped out of the elevator to hold the doors open for her. Past the cadavers under the flickering lighting to the coffee station, he led his mom, his focus on Davis and Hux huddled at the table. Both scowled when he entered.

"Officers Naomi Huxley and Martin Davis, this is Margaret Shaw, Detective Shaw's mother."

Mom threw a glare at him, plastered on a smile, and danced forward with an outstretched hand. "Call me Cassiopeia."

30

7#1|27Y

GIBS DROPPED INTO THE chair beside Hux and stole her coffee. She spun on him, then nibbled on her bottom lip as she waited for him to remove his mask. He would have to if he wanted to consume anything. He stilled too, lowering his focus to her teeth where they pressed on her petal-soft lip. Shaking his head, more to free himself from her dazzling beauty, he slid her coffee across the table.

"Prefer chai tea. Got any?" He deepened his voice to the same baritone level he had used on Mara. Hux's cheeks flushed pink, and she stammered, gesturing to two opposite counters for the tea. "Make me a cup, honeybuns. Let the men do the talking."

Just like that, his face hit the table skewing his glasses. Gibs groaned but despite the agony bursting outward from his nose and eyes, he 'clutched' his mask, checking to see it hadn't dislodged.

"Mrs. Shaw." Hux giggled, ruining her chastising tone.

Mom harrumphed. "I'm not disrespecting your mother, Detective Wash, but if you ever speak to a lady like that again…"

Righting his glasses, Gibs glared, well, he tried to, through his tear-filled eyes. The burn from his nostrils speared his skull, and for a moment, he thought his mom had busted his nose. He hadn't wanted to warn her about his behavior, needing her reactions to be real. Now, he was having second thoughts.

Gags and wheezes engulfed the room as Davis collapsed, tears rolling off his cheeks. He draped across the table, curled into himself, and slid off his chair to lie on the floor. Silent guffaws shook his shoulders. It looked like he might wet himself.

"Mrs. Margaret Shaw." Gibs clipped each word as he rose to his full height, taking a menacing step toward her. Hux leaped between them, pressing her palms against his chest as if to hold him back. He cupped her hand, trapping it there. Sparing her upturned face a glance, he pinned his mother with one of her legendary glares.

"As a rookie, one must endure all manner of abuse. It's par for the course with many lessons rolled into it. My mentor worked me like a slave, insulted and bullied me, and yet, here I stand, a detective with each accolade earned by the sweat of my brow." He pressed forward, forcing Hux to plaster herself to his body, as per his delicious plan. Looping an arm around her waist, he crushed her to him. He loved every soft curve molded against him. Her rose scent was an aphrodisiac on its own.

Peering into her gray eyes, Gibs allowed himself the opportunity to admire her features at a leisurely pace. "My derisive tone and my name-calling are not indicative of your skill sets. However, a stunner like you must realize that many will disparage your achievements. As Shaw's replacement, it is my duty to continue this tradition, to teach you how to survive both in the Center and out in Nova."

Hux gaped, patted his pec, then peeled herself out of his embrace. "I'll get you that tea." He could've sworn tears shimmered on her eyelashes.

"Fair enough. My apologies." Mom took the chair a red-faced Davis offered her, and they fell into a comfortable silence peppered by Hux brewing a fresh cup. An elbow to the ribs from his mom jerked Gibs out of the mesmerized gaze he fixed on Hux's ass.

"Um, Mrs. Shaw would like an update on her son's disappearance. What do we have for her?" Gibs nodded in thanks for the cup Hux placed before him. The tantalizing aromas of pepper, cinnamon, and cloves reached him through his mask and made his mouth water. A pity he'd have to leave it untouched.

"Gibs is fine, Mrs. Shaw." Davis contorted his lips into the semblance of a smile. "He asked for help from the Master and is annoying us with instructions. He'll hide out there until Montgomery drops the charges."

Gibs shook his head when Mom broke into a sob, real tears spilling down her pink cheeks. As he'd expected, she was rising to the challenge for center stage. Davis handed her his soiled handkerchief, the brown spots on it making Gibs shudder. Mom accepted it with the grace of royalty.

"I'm so sorry, Mrs. Shaw." Davis thumped her back like he would a glitchy drone.

"Do call me Cassie." She hiccupped, pressing the cloth to her eyes with excruciating care. Gibs would have tossed it to the floor and stomped on it. Something lethal had to be growing inside its fibers.

"Did you tell Davis about Fields's access to our cloud files?" He pinned his gaze to Hux's. "About the missing eyes?"

"Yes and yes. He knew about the latter—said the drones did a thorough 3D representation." She flicked her hair off her face, and the insipid lighting spun it in gold and silver.

Gibs broke the connection between them first, twisting to watch Mom charm the socks off Davis. Poor guy. A squeeze of Hux's forearm turned into a caress, and he snatched his hand away, heat staining his cheeks.

"I'll head out. With Fields's data crystal in my possession, I hope to have something in the morning." He nodded at Davis, then dropped his hand onto Mom's shoulder. He leaned down to press his mask-covered cheek to hers to hide his whisper. "For that performance, you can have *one* orgy."

She giggled and swatted him away, turning her smile to Davis again.

Gibs made it to the elevator, and despite the din of the cooling vents and the various machinery humming on standby, Hux's voice reached him. He paused with his finger on the call button then faced her, waiting for her to reach him. No, he did not admire the pull of her pants across her thighs and knees, nor did he linger on the light glimmering off the top button of her blouse.

"What is it, sweetcakes?" His earlier declaration had nullified the joy of teasing her. She didn't respond—there was no furious glare or stiffened posture.

A foot away from him, she hesitated, wringing her hands. "Where are you staying? I mean, what if we need to reach you? Um, to discuss evidence...clues?" Her cheeks flushed pink, and her focus darted everywhere but on him.

Gibs chuckled, tempted to scoop her into his arms for that kiss he owed her, but alas, his venti-mask cockblocked him. Then again, did he want Lee Wash kissing his woman? No, not when others might assume she was promiscuous. Kissing her as Lee toyed with her heart, as well. Expecting a volatile fight when she discovered his deception, he didn't need to add a broken heart to the mix. It sounded arrogant to assume he could entice Hux to fall in love with Lee, but he'd rather plan for it as a possibility than lose her.

"The Center put me up in a Kicks motel. Let me know when you need to chat, and I'll meet you somewhere."

She nodded with a furrowed brow as if his response displeased her.

"Create a new cloud file for you and me. Any progress we make, record it there. I'd rather have Davis believe we're struggling." Gibs closed the distance between them, cupping her elbow to lean in. "Fields thinks he's seen the ring before, and he's granted me access to Renovare's security system."

"From the start, the case intrigued Fields, but with his precious Zetas killed, he's all in." Her fingers twitched where they gripped his forearms. "Do you think he's sent us on a chicken run with fake memories?"

"The term is a goose chase, but no, the killings impact Renovare—their shares and their sales. And the killer striking close to him made this personal." Gibs pulled away when the elevator pinged. He stepped into the compartment and selected a floor, admiring Hux as the squeaky doors closed.

A static voice, with a thick accent he had never been able to place, announced the floor he arrived on. With hurried steps, he crossed the entrance foyer, hailed a chaser, and headed to his office. Someone tailing him wasn't a concern because once he hit the Kicks, he'd disembark, walk to the next platform, and hail another chaser. Passing into

Shadows territory would cancel any persistent tails, either by lethal force or misdirection. As a rookie, he'd once been a tenacious idiot, and once was all it had taken to teach him that lesson.

The moment he stepped onto his platform, he removed his glasses and pocketed them. Depressurizing the mask, he strolled down the passage to his office. By now, Schneider, Phia, and Em would know he'd returned.

Entering the vacant office, he unclipped the mask and tossed it onto the single-seater, taking a few moments to massage his abused skin. "Mirror." His reflection on the display screens showed no bruising around his eyes. He'd forgotten how fast Mom could move for someone of her size.

"Hungry?" Phia hovered by the door, a carton in her hand—strange yet delicious aromas wafting off it. "Roast *chicken* with tofu noodles?"

"Chicken?" As Gibs grabbed for the carton, Phia slipped it behind her with a giggle before offering it to him. He ignored his trembling fingers—no one would judge him. As delicacies went, chicken was top of the gourmet food pile in his book. Oh, and steak. He'd heard rumors of Luxers enjoying those sorts of meals, but never had such a succulent morsel passed his lips.

The decadent aroma had his mouth watering as he flipped the carton open. There, nestled on a bed of sauce-laden noodles, was a single piece of chicken—roasted a golden brown. Phia muttered to herself as she grabbed two bottles of water out of the fridge.

"How was your day, sweetheart?" She handed him a bottle before curling up on the couch, her movements creating squeaks on the leather.

"Bad, case-wise, bad, mother-wise, good, redemption-wise. I thought my ex-wife hated my guts. Turns out, I was the resentful one." He shook his head, then bit into the chicken, sinking his teeth in with excruciating slowness. Coating his tongue were juices his mouth hadn't experienced in years. He groaned and closed his eyes to fully appreciate the flavor. He settled a gaze on her while he chewed. "Why do you ask?"

Phia watched him, a smile on her lips. "Your progress must have pleased Master."

He shrugged, not ready to talk. A delicious heaviness settled in his stomach. He wanted to enjoy the satiated feel of a good piece of meat, one not made of textured tofu.

"I'm trawling through security footage tonight, Phia. You're welcome to keep me company, but in essence, I won't be needing anything."

"You know the way to your room?" The twist of her lips implied he didn't, and she was right.

"I'll sleep on the couch." He stared her down, challenging her to persist.

"You're a pain in my ass, Gibs." Phia leaped off the couch and approached the wood-paneled wall.

"Then we're doing it wrong." He chuckled before shoveling noodles into his mouth.

She clicked her tongue despite the smile teasing her lips. "Right, like I haven't heard that one." Throwing open a tall closet, she pulled out a blanket and pillow and placed it on the couch she'd vacated. "Behind door number two is an en suite. I packed a shelf with a few clothing items for you. Door three has beverages and snacks." She tapped her holo-wrist. "You have my details if you need me."

"Thanks, Phia. Have a lovely evening." He took a long draw from his bottle, trailing her with his gaze as she headed for the door.

"You didn't ask what's behind door one." Blowing him a cheeky kiss, she slammed the office door on the way out, her laughter drifting down the passage.

He slurped his noodles, eyeing door one as if it held something heinous. A carnivorous X10 entertainment inkjob? A stack of inkjob porn crystals because no one should pay for those unnatural yet visual delights?

He sighed at his empty carton, tempted to lick it clean. Instead, he rose and opened door two, hoping to wash his hands. For a moment, his reflection startled him. He jerked to the side then back, raised his greasy fists, then chuckled, laughing at his idiocy. Shaking his head, he washed his hands while studying the new him.

Perhaps door one had an arsenal?

Taking a fresh towel off the rack to dry his hands, he investigated the door. Flinging it open, the odor that hit him was as liberating as an orgasm. Chlorine-scented, crystal-blue water filled an aquatic therapy pool. The hum of its motor and the soft susurration of the gentle waves were music to his ears. He tossed the hand towel on the closet chair and paused.

On a stool rested a pair of swimming shorts and a rolled towel. He ignored it, stripped, and tossed his clothing where he stood. Within minutes, he was slicing through the water, the familiar burn in his muscles spreading joy from his chest outward. In the last week, he hadn't had a chance to follow his usual exercise routine, and in a land-locked city like Nova, swimming was a luxury. He paid a fortune to belong to a sports club with a pool.

Why did Em have this installed? Was it to prove how well she knew him? Was it to have something else he owed her for? He cut through the waves pushing him back. Here, like this, the water cleared the detritus from his mind. The clues in the case lined up. Despite Phia's assumption, he wasn't making progress.

He didn't have a suspect.

One thing had his instincts screaming. The perp worked at Renovare or knew the corporation's inner workings well. A technical vendor, perhaps, called in to handle cyberattacks or system-software upgrades? The security logs would reveal whether a scheduled visit had occurred.

There was something evocative about the extracted hearts, too, as if the perp had lost their restraint, taking out their grief, anger, or resentment on the Zetas. Such an action was one of confidence, knowing they had the time to structure the scene undisturbed.

The sheer audacity of it. In the Deadzone, that had been a trial, a sample. In a bustling shopping level, the perp had used technology to aid them. And with Renovare, without tech-savviness, they wouldn't have made it past the Sec2s.

What did that have to do with the wedding ring? Was that a misleading clue? He'd watch the Promenade's footage again, to check whether the woman played a role. His instincts had said so, yet he couldn't find the golden thread connecting the clues and pointing to the treasure at the end of the rainbow.

A shadow fell across the pool. He found his footing on the floor and rose out of the waist-deep water. Em waited, arms folded across her chest, and her tapping toe in a silver stiletto screamed her mood. Sighing, he waded to the side, pulled himself out, then grabbed the towel, dabbing at his face and chest, flashing Em his bare ass.

"Reggie is super pissed."

Gibs dropped his head, burying his face in the towel to hide his grimace. He wasn't in the mood to deal with anyone, having hoped for solitude. Tonight, he'd planned to solve the case or to find at least one person to fracken interview.

"He won't leave me alone; his agitation is spiking my blood pressure." Em didn't need his responses, carrying on the discussion with the knowledge that he listened or else. As she strode along the edge of the pool, Gibs wrapped the towel around him, tying it at his hip, choosing to be somewhat covered around a woman who oozed sexuality. He'd flashed his ass as if to say her presence didn't make him uncomfortable, when in fact, it stiffened his posture and raised the hairs on his neck.

"I plan to trawl his data crystal tonight. I need a suspect, Em. I have no one, and time's running out. Mutilating two inkjobs with additional symbolism in a tight-ass security complex is the perp throwing their elusiveness in our faces."

"Frack. Need any help?" She sidled closer, pressing her silk-draped body against his. His instincts bombarded him, and he shook his head.

"I need time alone with my thoughts."

"Is that why you sent Sophia away?" Em placed her palms on his chest, tapping his skin and trailing a forefinger along the edges of his bandage. She licked her lips, running an appreciative gaze over his tattooed form. "This look suits you, Gibs. One stop at a parlor and those tatts could become permanent."

"If Hux likes them, then maybe." He forced a smile, gripped Em's hip, and stepped around her, picking up the hand towel he'd tossed on the chair. "Thanks for the pool. At some stage, we'll need to talk about what this is costing me." He paused at the door to meet Em's gaze. "I'm under no illusions that you're helping me because you *like* me."

"What you'll owe me is the inkjob killer, Gibs." Fury poured from her, her fists on her hips, the narrowed eyes, the pursed lips. "And, if I decide you'll pay with your body, your life, your career, then it will be in full. I get what I want, always."

She sashayed past him, sliding her body along his in the too-narrow doorway. "Don't *ever* pull away from me again."

Ice drenched his heated muscles, evaporating the peace swimming had earned him. Frack, he was so screwed. He'd known this might be the case when he'd messaged Schneider, but he'd hoped the cost would be minimal like a naïve rookie fresh to Nova.

Now, not only had he rejected the Master of Shadows, but he'd placed Hux in her line of sight. Rubbing his temple where a headache was forming, he cursed himself with more colorful words than his mom had ever taught him.

He might have to break his heart to save Hux's life.

31

7#1|27Y-0/\/3

Date: 2170.16.10
The Holies
At home

THE EXCITEMENT OF ANY trip made the time it took to reach the destination feel short and the return journey exhausting, draining, and painstakingly uncomfortable. Not this time. Filled with the memories of his evening spent with his "new" family and the framed passing lights and shooting shuttles heading into space, time was as fleeting. The various videos Lissa had sent Nate of her fucking the X10 she'd named Bran left him with a raging hard-on eager for release.

And yet, he found himself in front of his door instead of minutes from Lissa's embrace. On automatic, he'd instructed the chaser to take him home from the rail station. His subconscious bringing him here was an unsubtle sign he needed to deal with his marriage. Just not tonight. He spun on his heel, ready to hail another chaser when the sound of Lissa's laughter reached him through the front door.

He jerked, finding it odd that Lissa would visit Kylie. After cracking the door open to listen, he entered, lowered his bag onto the counter, then headed for the lounge. Shattered glass, shredded fabric, and

221

strewn memorabilia littered the floor. On the wall, playing on their display screens was Lissa in the throes of lust, Nate's hands brushing the hair from her face as he leaned in to kiss her.

What the frack?

This was a recording as if Nate had a cam strapped to his forehead. Ice drenched his body, from his head to his toes. How had she recorded this...?

Frack, Kylie knew.

He cupped his left eye, shuddering. He'd been recording every second of each day of his life. Frack. And she had known of that, too.

"Kylie!" Nate stormed to their bedroom, ready to rip her apart. His vision tainted red, narrowing his focus. He panted, unable to breathe. Something squeezed his chest, radiating pain outward. How long had she monitored his day, his life? Was there a correlation between her thundercloud moods and him lusting after Lissa?

A tiny drop of blood slowed his steps, and he halted, dipping to flick the dot off the floor. He tested its consistency between his forefinger and thumb. Had she cut herself? He scanned the lounge behind him at the devastation. She must have. A few paces ahead, more crimson spots marred the floor.

"Kylie?" Concern cut through his fury, and he rushed into their bedroom.

On their bed, curled into a ball, lay his naked wife, bloody slashes across her body staining the sheets, and in the palm of her hand was an open packet of pills.

The silence deafened him. He cried out, leaping onto the bed to shake her. Words tumbled from his lips, pleas, curses mixed with gut-twisting sobs. Her skin was cold to the touch. He gathered her against his chest, wrapping her in his embrace, trying to force warm, inkjob life into her.

"Sweetheart, please, wake up." He rocked her, focusing on her face and the shallow but precious in and out of her breathing. He draped her onto the bed, tugged the sheet over her, slipped the packet into his pocket, and hefted her into his arms. On the platform, he kicked the light to summon a chaser, each second caught in a time loop, the wait endless. Contradictory emotions bombarded his mind, and what-ifs and accusations dazed him, forcing him to cling to one thought. He had to save her.

He trundled her into the chaser and instructed it to take him to the closest clinic. The chaser's protocol for such a call was to send a notification ahead, to place the emergency personnel on standby.

Patting her cheeks, he tried to wake her again, screaming at her that this was cheating, that she wasn't supposed to die, that in some sick, twisted way, he still loved her. When the chaser landed, he leaped out, holding the door open while the ER crew placed Kylie on a gurney, scanning her as they hurried her inside. He trailed them, his legs like bags of sand.

Not sure whether to follow her or to slump into a chair, he hesitated at the door. He had no one to call, no friends, and there was no fracking way he'd call his parents. He wasn't ready to deal with them. Yet, if Kylie died this night, would they forgive him? They loved her as their daughter.

He tapped on his holo-wrist, flicking to their number and making the connection. His mom's face appeared in an instant as if she'd waited, lying awake, needing him to reach out to her.

"Nate?" Her bloodshot eyes and red nose screamed her pain, and despite the fresh lances of guilt, fury, and betrayal spearing his chest, he softened his tone.

"Mom, this is bad. Kylie's in the clinic. I'm pinging you the location. I found her...drugged. I don't know with what." He ripped the packet out of his pocket and slammed it onto the counter. "This was in her palm." He kept his hand over it until the nurse nodded. Only then did he let her scoop up the packet and scurry away.

"Donald." Mom's clipped voice had Dad appearing in the image. "Kylie needs us. Nate, we're leaving now."

"Hold on, son. We're coming." Hearing Dad's voice filled Nate with relief. He slouched, energy draining from him, leaving him shivering. His parents would come, and they'd know what to do. Dad's calming, no-nonsense presence would fix everything.

"Excuse me, sir, I'll need you to complete the admission forms." The same nurse from earlier held out a tablet. He accepted with numb fingers, having ended the call a moment ago. Everything felt stiff: his joints, his movements, and his reactions.

He dropped into the closest chair and stared at the letters on the data tablet. They blurred, and he shook his head, trying to clear his vision. The splash of warm droplets on his forearms startled him, and he swiped at his cheeks, staring at his moist fingertips. Tears? Didn't that prove he was human? Did that matter when Kylie's life lay in the balance?

Time slowed, and the passing of patients and emergency staff tossed soft zephyrs of cool air his way, but they didn't calm his chaotic thoughts. What would he do if she died? He'd be free to be with Lissa, but he didn't want freedom at this cost. What had she taken? Where had she gotten the pills from?

He raised his head when someone took the tablet from his numb fingers. Mom. With a gasp, he rose to hug her, engulfing her in a tight embrace. She mumbled soothing words, in the same soft cadence she'd used when he was a child. Along with slow strokes up and down his back and Dad's intermittent thump on his shoulder, love, bright, bold, all-conquering settled in his chest. Nate sighed, a small smile twitching his lips.

"How are you doing, son?" Dad tugged Nate toward him and drew him into a quick hug.

"I've been better. I haven't heard anything yet." He scanned the waiting room, looking for the nurse from earlier.

"Donald, take him for a coffee. I'll wait here, complete these forms, and let Kylie's uncle know." Mom took the chair he'd vacated, and without a word, Dad steered him to the café, following the international sign for coffee.

He didn't speak, just pressed Nate into a chair at a corner table and ordered coffee from the clinic's inkjob. Silence stretched between them, thick with unsaid words, emotions, and awkwardness.

Once Nate cupped the hot cup of coffee in his hands, he told his father everything. The thunderclouds, Kylie's mood swings driving them apart, Lissa's allure, the discovery of the E7s, Joe and Wyn's welcome, all ending with how he'd found Kylie.

"She had a video of you with the other woman?" Dad gaped, his face tinged gray.

Nate glowered, not liking anyone calling Lissa the other woman. "Her name's Lissa, Dad, and she's sweetness and sunshine. If you're going to blame anyone, blame me."

Dad huffed. "She's a homewrecker regardless of her 'sweetness,' Nate. The elephant in the room is Kylie having access to your recordings. Fields assured us that Renovare had disabled that functionality for all E7s."

"When you agreed to the monitoring?" Nate shook his head, wondering if one day, his life would entertain the bored or serve as archival footage of life in the 2100s.

"You think it's a glitch?" Dad pursed his lips. "You could always sense our moods. We thought you were just a sensitive boy. Not once did we think you had a unique talent." He sipped his coffee. "And you use it to dose your clients? Isn't that illegal?"

Nate shrugged. "It's such a small amount in the ink, Dad. They leave The Skin Canvas happier, and besides, they sign a waiver. I put the chemical breakdown of the ink in the document."

"Would the drug work on inkjobs?" Dad winced. "Sorry, I didn't mean you."

"I am one, but I'm loved, I guess. As to the drug, I don't know. I'll talk to my suppliers, bring them into my confidence." Nate hadn't thought to dose inkjobs. Now, he'd hurry to include something in the ink to help them.

They sipped their coffee in silence until Mom pinged his holo-wrist. *The doctor is here.*

He bolted, abandoning his cold coffee. Dad followed. In a skin-hugging white uniform, the doctor chatted with Mom, tossing a calm smile when Nate hovered near.

"Mr. Dough, your wife will be fine. She took a dose of undiluted Rage." He frowned. "It's the second time this has happened this week, which means calling in the Cents. It's protocol, and I apologize for the inconvenience."

Nate nodded, his mind fogged, clouding his thoughts. Rage? How would Kylie know to find any? They lived in the Holies, the safest sector in Nova.

"May I see her?" He cleared his throat after he growled the request.

"In a bit. Her uncle is with her now and asked for a little privacy." The doctor grimaced. "I'll keep her for a few hours, just for observation. You may take her home then."

"We notified the Center, Mr. Dough. They've asked that you await their arrival." A nurse gestured to a closed door. "The clinic has reserved a room for the Center's use. Please wait in there."

"Of course." Nate forced an unnatural smile. "After I've seen my wife."

"I'll call you when she is free."

He nodded, spinning on his heels to enter the indicated room. A metal table surrounded by four chairs and mirrored walls cast it in dark, chilling tones. Yet, none of this phased Nate. Running into Kylie's uncle did.

He pulled out a chair for Mom and dropped into one opposite her. Dad hovered by the door, keeping it open with a hip as if shutting it would seal them inside. When he lunged into the room, and Kylie's uncle filled the door, the tension in the room chilled further. Dad chose the chair beside Mom and waited, drumming his fingers on the cold table's surface.

"I am Officer Martin Davis." Kylie's uncle mopped his sweat-drenched brow. "This recording is for quality purposes and can be used against you in a court of law." He leveled his gaze on Nate, his lips twisted into a sneer. "What the frack happened here, Mr. Jonathan Dough?"

32

7#1|27Y-7VVØ

Date: 2170.17.10
The Shadows
His new office

SPRAWLED ON THE COUCH, the remote gripped in one hand, the other shoved into his sleep pants, cupping his balls, Gibs flicked through the footage files. He sent some to the seen-not-worth-it folder, a few to the give-a-second-look folder, and left the remaining as key evidence he wanted to view repeatedly.

So far, the scan through Renovare's staff had settled on one man: James 'Jim' Nelson, which disproved the importance of the wedding ring. His wife, Shelley, also worked at Renovare in their Data Management sector. Could he be using his wife to case the scenes? Could Gibs be looking at a killer duo?

He shuddered. Not that he could recall the last duo of serial killers. Hell, his killers had always been one and done. With the new technology and enforcement tracking in place, a citizen couldn't shit without the government knowing about it.

He froze, his nostrils flaring. That was right, so how did no one see the delivery? Punching his holo-wrist, he called up the latest tracking information for the Holies, the Promenade, and the Deadzone. While he waited, he scanned through the security records of Nelson's comings and goings. He didn't deviate from his day-to-day schedule, from manufacturing to the canteen, back to the factory floor, and home. Shelley did the same, data labs to the canteen and back.

Searching through the chaser transit archives showed one trip to the Promenade two days before Eve Roe 2. No mention of the Deadzone, and of course, they were both on the premises during the mutilation of the Zetas. With their access to only two out of three crime scenes, was he chasing a dead lead again?

Gibs cursed, sitting up and tossing the remote onto the couch. He rubbed his face, forcing the exhaustion away despite the stinging in his eyes and his burning nostrils. What he needed was a stimulant, but since only caffeine was acceptable, he bounded up, heading for the deluxe coffee maker.

"Espresso." His voice was hoarse from disuse and still unfamiliar to him. He'd messaged Hux earlier, implying he'd developed a cold, his voice gone, and could only text her from now on. She'd sent the link to the mayor's security footage which had held nothing but an inkjob walking off the premises as if commanded to.

Could Shelley have access to inkjobs out in the field? Could she monitor them despite that doing so violated the Pancras Treaty? Gibs scanned the duties of a data management officer but found no reference to coding skills. The coffeemaker pinged, announcing his espresso was ready. He scooped up the tiny cup and frowned, hating the few sips it afforded him.

Grabbing a larger cup, he ordered a plain black coffee. As he waited for it, the dark flavor of the espresso still coating his tongue, his holo-wrist buzzed with the information he'd ordered. He flicked his fingers, tossing the spreadsheet onto the larger screens.

Who was near all three locations, seven days prior to each scene? After he typed in the search criteria, the dial spun, taking minutes and revealing thousands of names. He grabbed his coffee the second the maker pinged and sprawled out on the couch, scrolling through the results. This would take forever and cross his eyes by morning. He sighed, needing to add additional criteria.

Married or engaged. That took it down to half.

Technologically savvy.

A criminal record.

History of mental instability.

These left him with hundreds of names. Exhaustion thumped a headache at his temples, and he pinched his brow. He drew in a long breath, fighting the urge to sleep while searching through his fogged thoughts. Something formed and dissolved, just out of reach.

Access to inkjobs in any form—ownership, manufacturing, post-incineration.

Frack. Jim Nelson was a no-go. Neither his name nor Shelley's were anywhere on the list. After all this time, Gibs was back to square one.

Clearing the filter, he applied new search criteria—Hux's address in the Holies, a date, and a time span. One row of data appeared, and it was glorious. He grinned, sitting up to sip his coffee. Double-selecting the security footage played the image of a hooded woman delivering the box of chocolates. When she kept her face hidden, he scowled.

She'd hired the chaser from Renovare and headed for another Holies address after delivering the drugged chocolates. *Mm, interesting.* The address was blank, but her identity was...nothing. He spilled his coffee as he flailed in despair and frustration, cursing the screens, the stupid fracken case, and the fates that dared to assign it to him. Who the frack had the access to delete the tracking data?

Frack. He was back to the mole in the Center. And he knew of one.

He cleared the filter, punched in Martin Davis's name, and held his breath as the dial spun. The results showed his trips from home to work with no deviations other than known crime or food locations. It didn't spark alarms, but then again, this was a man who knew Deadzone well. It would be easy for him to slip out of the lower levels of the Center and travel to any of the crime scenes without the tracking recording it.

It stated his current location as at home, and his average departure time was set for six. Gibs would do an old-fashioned stakeout. He grimaced. He'd have to ask Em for some sort of nondescript chaser, one the tracking couldn't record.

What else could he look through? He accessed the folders on Renovare's data crystal and skimmed through the ones he'd already scanned. That left the memories folder of post-incinerated inkjobs. Only a few files were there, which was weird. There'd been hundreds when Hux and he had sifted through them originally.

Playing the first one showed an inkjob beneath a man. He scowled, pausing the footage in confusion. Was this some sick pervert's inkporn folder? *Frack.* He hated the concept of fucking an inkjob. The scene played out, and as the inkjob arched her back, her face contorted with pleasure, a natural gasp escaping her lips. Her cheeks flushed red, and she relaxed as if endorphins flooded her body.

What the frack? Had Renovare perfected the art of mimicking sexual responses in synthetics?

He watched the next footage, this inkjob shed tears and seemed surprised by them, wiping them off her cheeks to stare at her damp fingers.

What was he looking at? How did this help his case? Had Fields given him the wrong information? Gibs would ask the man tomorrow.

After switching off the footage, Gibs tugged the blanket over him, hoping to sleep a few hours before heading out on his stakeout. As he lay there, he sent Phia a request for a chaser or a cycle. Minutes later, still awake, he called up Hux's Center identity image and smiled, trailing a finger along the curve of her cheek. He was asleep in seconds, lured by the warmth in his heart.

33

7#1|27Y-7#|233

Date: 2170.18.10
The Holies
On stakeout

GIBS SLITHERED LOW IN the seat, trying to minimize his bulk even though Davis couldn't possibly spot him in the long line of chasers. Phia had come through for him. The taxi-chaser was as nondescript as he needed, except, it was ancient—its shudders, whines, and jerky dips set his nerves on edge. At any moment, he might plummet out of the sky to his death, his corpse lost to the wilds of the Deadzone.

Rolling his backside on the hard seat, he tried to ease the numbness there and his increasing urge to piss. Two hours and three coffees meant he had to go. He sighed. His age was catching up to him. Gone were the days when he could consume without a care.

Phia thought of everything. For the last hour, he'd snuck glances at the seat beside him where she had left a p-bot—designed for survival nuts who wanted to drink their purified urine. He snorted and un-zipped to angle his dick onto the cold curved lip. It softened the sound of his urine hitting the inside, but the designers hadn't bothered to warm the metal lip.

Once done, he capped the bottle and shook it, allowing the filters to do their work. There was no way he'd drink it, but he could pour it out of the chaser without blessing someone with a pissy day. Dropping the bottle onto the seat next to him, he rubbed his thigh where a pre-cramp burned. Frack, he would need to stretch soon.

Settling back to watch the entrance of the clinic, he recalled why he hated stakeouts. Silence, except for his breathing, left him with only his thoughts as if he needed to rethink this case for hours. He was at a dead-end, clinging to the hope that Davis would lead him to the killer.

What would his father say? *"Hit a slump, m'boy? You trawl through the evidence again. Visit the crime scenes over and over, and interview everyone. The tiniest detail could crack the case."*

Waste more time Gibs couldn't justify to Montgomery? Hoping for a big break, he was clinging to straws like a drowning fool.

He grimaced. Frack, he hadn't even told Hux where he'd be this morning. He activated his holo-wrist to do so when Davis stepped out of the clinic, his arm around a blonde. Beside him stood a familiar face...Nate Dough. Gibs scowled, not liking this. Since Nate hadn't tatted the Zetas, Gibs had dismissed the man as a suspect.

With his holo-wrist activated, he navigated to the recordings. His pre-Lee voice was first. "This recording is for quality purposes..." He remembered his surprise that Melissa had the files ready for him. Yet, this connection between Nate and Davis explained the call warning them Gibs was on his way. The woman between him and Davis was Nate's wife? Was she the connection?

Gibs called his partner. "Hux...ley." He coughed to hide his blunder. "Get me the files on Jonathan Dough's wife, spelled and pronounced like Rough."

"Well, good morning to you too, Wash. Where are you? I've got Montgomery on my ass because he can't find you." Her voice this morning did amazing things to his libido, spiking his heart rate. He snorted, trailing his gaze across her lips; it wasn't just her voice.

"I'm on a stakeout. I'll explain at lunch. Um, meet me somewhere?" Heat stained his cheeks as if he'd just asked her on a date. "You pick the place."

"The Pigeon-Fest at Holies Boulevard. I need to talk to you, too." This sounded serious, especially when she lowered her voice toward the end. "Eleven, and don't be late."

A tapping on the window startled him, and he ended the call without saying goodbye. Leaning against the chaser with his hand on the roof was Davis. Gibs checked his venti-mask was in place and opened the door. Davis stepped back to allow him to exit, his expressions switching between furrowed curiosity and narrowed suspicion.

"Morning." Gibs plastered a grin to his face even though Davis wouldn't be able to see it. "Had I known you'd be here, I'd have asked you to collect Huxley's results. The nurse said something about signing the information out." He huffed as if he hated being inconvenienced.

Davis relaxed his shoulders and ran his hand over his bald pate. "Sorry, this was kind of a last-minute thing." He gestured to the couple waiting for him—an irritated and fidgeting Nate and an exhausted Mrs. Nate. "My niece was...ill." Davis grimaced.

Gibs nodded as if appeased. Niece? So Davis had warned Nate as a filial courtesy? The way he spoke was reason enough to delve deeper. Most people mentioned the diagnosis as if knowing and pronouncing it correctly made it more serious than it was—an upper respiratory tract infection for the common cold. Davis's evasiveness was unnatural.

"I'm sorry she's ill," Gibs said when he realized Davis waited for him to respond. "I trust she's on the road to recovery?" Dad had taught him that commiseration often loosened tongues. Frack, the way this case was going, he needed every one of Dad's tricks.

Davis scowled, leveling a glare on Nate. "She better be."

"You suspect foul play?" Gibs focused on Nate. "I recognize that man—works at The Skin Canvas—has a thing for his receptionist." He smothered a shudder at ratting on the man, but the truth would out. It was a matter of time.

Davis whipped his head around, his brows arching to his non-existent hairline. "He what?"

"It was their interaction. Nothing happened yet, but where there's smoke, there's fire." Gibs shrugged, hoping to appear dismissive while every nerve in his body focused on Davis.

"I'll kill him." The little man trembled, his posture stiff, and his jaw clenched. A pulse ticked at his neck.

"Investigate first because if he hasn't done anything yet, we can't judge him for lustful thoughts. If we did, we'd have to tar ourselves with the same brush." Gibs forced a chuckle although he found nothing humorous. "I didn't know you had a niece."

"My adoptive parents had a daughter when I was four. My sister died in a tragic accident and left me Kylie to raise." Davis's chest puffed up like a proud parent. "I don't know why I let her marry that boy."

"Because she adores him?" Gibs smiled. Kylie had gripped the front of Nate's shirt and plastered her body to his. He embraced her with the gentlest of hugs.

Davis grunted. "Anyway, see you at the Center." He took two steps then paused. "Montgomery's looking for you."

Gibs nodded and waved, heading for the clinic. He'd pick up Huxley's results, a convenient excuse for his presence and quick thinking on his part, too. A boy of eight with a bleeding nose had first dibs at the nurse, and as Gibs waited, trying not to tap his foot, he called his mother.

"Mom, is my place still standing?" He chuckled, unable to stop teasing her. After Dad's death, their relationship had strengthened. Not that he saw her often. Absence made the heart grow fonder? Partially true, but with Mom, one visit was a large enough dose of her to last a while.

"Very funny, smartass." Her face shimmered into focus, and his place in the background looked off. Had she moved the couch? Was that orange on his walls? "I can't get used to you with this voice."

"You painted?" He gaped. When had she found the time?

"Of course. Who knows how long I'll be allowed to stay in your precious home." She flicked her hair back with a huff.

"I opened an account for you at Bohemian's."

She gasped, shoving her face closer to the screen. "Trying to buy my silence?" She wiggled her eyebrows then giggled. "Bribe accepted. I assume there's a limit."

He nodded and mentioned an amount. Her eyebrows shot up, and she pressed a kiss to the holo, tearing the pixels.

"Love you, bye."

He shook his head and switched off his holo-wrist, ignoring the pings from Montgomery and Em. He'd stop by the Center after this. As to Em, he didn't know what he was going to do. It might be a wiser course of action not to piss the woman off further, but if he didn't have a strategy, whatever he said could worsen the situation.

He redialed his mom. "I need to pick your brain. Let's do dinner."

"Okay, see you at six. I'll pick up something on the way home." She was in a mid-dress as if she readied herself for her shopping trip.

"We'll order from Eddie." This time, he ended the call.

Ten minutes later, the nurse helped him, and with a swipe of his wrist, he had the information. He paused outside the clinic to read Huxley's results, expecting nothing new. There was one addendum. He froze, read it twice, then whooped. His bold cry was lost to the breeze but loud enough to startle an elderly couple shuffling by.

Huxley's wasn't the only pure-Rage poisoning.

He spun on his heel and returned to the nurse for Kylie's file. This time, there was no delay. He paused on the platform to skim through this one: Kylie Dough, attempted suicide. That explained the 'ill' comment.

The image of a woman's body showed lacerations and the points of entry for Rage although, as suicide attempts go, this wasn't a planned one. How could she have known the Rage would kill her if she rubbed it on her skin? No, she had to have it on her hands when she held the knife or...shards of glass, according to the file.

His breath hitched.

Why would Kylie inject Rage into chocolates for a woman she didn't know? To implicate Gibs whom she'd never met? There was nothing in the news on the mutilations; nowhere was Shaw or Wash mentioned.

Frack.

He'd discuss this with Hux, but none of this made sense.

"Hux...ley, meet me at the Center; we'll head out to lunch afterward." Gibs pinched his lips at his near faux pas again.

"Ready and waiting." Her smile was wide enough to split her cheeks. "I was just about to call you. Seems we may have our first suspect."

He smirked. "Would her name be Kylie Dough?"

"No, it's a man, and Montgomery has him in the interrogation room." Her face filled the holo when she leaned in to whisper. "Gibs is all over the newsfeeds. The press have camped outside the Center, braying for him. You best hurry."

34

7#1|27Y-|=0|_||2

"WHERE THE FRACK HAVE you been?" Montgomery's face was mottled red. Spittle splattered those too near him. "Wash, in here now."

Gibs sighed. He shouldn't have poked his head into the captain's office. On one hand, as Wash, what did he care if he pissed off a Novan captain? But as Shaw, he couldn't afford to lose this job. He closed the door behind him and gripped the back of the chair. Montgomery paced the room, making wild gestures with his arms, mumbling and arguing with himself.

"I tolerated this subterfuge, Shaw, since the Master of Shadows, the mayor, and Lord Fields all supported this stupid, ill-conceived endeavor." He slammed his palms down, vibrating the ancient desk.

Gibs dropped his face to hide his shock. He was an idiot to believe he could fool his fellow officers. But he had to try though, what with the accusations that Davis mentioned... "Am I under suspicion for Huxley's poisoning?"

Montgomery jerked as if slapped. "What the frack? No, why would we consider you? Is this why you're in 'disguise?'"

Gibs lowered his face again. That son of a bitch, Davis, had lied to him. Fury burned through his veins, and he trembled, trying to restrain it. Pinching his brow, he sucked in a calming breath. "When we have time, Captain, I'll fill you in on my progress. For now, we need to deal with the mob of journalists outside."

Montgomery stilled and ran a frustrated hand over his face. "It's my job to handle them. You deal with the reason they're here." He gestured to the meeting room leading off his office.

Gibs frowned. This was unorthodox considering that this space hadn't received the technological upgrade needed to properly act as an interrogation room.

"Davis is in there now." Montgomery paused at his office door before leaving.

"What?" Gibs bolted for the room.

"Why are you here? Why did the Master send you?" Davis's irate voice froze Gibs's hand on the door. "She's involving herself where she shouldn't. Have I lost her trust?"

"We monitor all the Master's servants, as you well know." Schneider's impersonal tone sent ice down Gibs's spine. Davis worked for Em? When the frack was either of them going to tell Gibs about this?

Silence reigned, and Gibs tightened his grip on the doorknob. He held his breath, not sure whether they would reveal more information or whether he should enter.

"You have deviated from your path, Mr. Davis. I am to issue your final warning. Solve this case, or you will breathe your last." Schneider's presence was a conundrum; on that, Gibs agreed with Davis.

Davis giggled, bordering on hysterics. "Master has threatened my life before. What does it matter now?" His voice neared, and Gibs darted his gaze around Montgomery's office, searching for a hole to hide in. "Consider your message delivered."

Gibs bolted for the captain's desk, scrunching his tall form into the small confines underneath. Davis stomped past him, slamming the door shut. Schneider's highly buffed, black *leather* shoes appeared in front of the desk. Minutes passed with no further movement or sound. Gibs winced—his hamstring was cramping.

Schneider sighed. "I do not have all day, Detective."

Gibs jerked, banging his head on the underside of the desk. Groaning at the spike of pain lancing down his neck, he crawled out, tossing the stoic man a scowl. Scrambling to his feet, he continued the scowl while rubbing the egg forming on his crown.

Schneider's dark eyes warmed, but no smile formed. "You are cordially invited to attend a feedback session at eight in Lord Fields's office."

Gibs dropped his hand, slumped his shoulders, and threw his head back to blink at the ceiling. "Why...?" He arched a brow at the shorter man.

Schneider shot him a withering look, spun on a polished heel, and sauntered out of the office without fear of detainment. Gibs trailed him into the foyer, watching as the man entered the elevator and headed down. While Gibs waited for the next elevator, he stretched his hamstring. As soon as he stepped onto the ground floor, the noise from outside formed a muffled buzz with Montgomery fielding questions while camera drones peppered the sky.

Passing Schneider, Hux darted toward Gibs. He grimaced, but she wouldn't know the man. Her face was alive with joy and excitement, calling forth Gibs's smile.

"Wash, did you see him, the suspect?" She bounced on her toes, her flying curls and rose scent tantalizing him. "Montgomery kept him upstairs, not wanting any of us to catch a glimpse."

Gibs scanned the crowd. Revealing the truth, when it could be overheard, would involve too many fingers in his business—something he wasn't ready for. He forced a sad face. "He isn't our man. Some crackpot wanting jail time."

"What?" She followed her outcry with a groan, throwing her hands into the air. "Are we back to square one?"

Were they? He studied her flushed face. Dad believed nothing happened by happenstance. Gibs was meant to overhear Schneider and Davis. But how did this information fit into the many jagged pieces? Davis related to Kylie? Her husband a tattooist for Renovare? Lord Fields, the mayor, and Em having access to this investigation?

Gibs's stomach twisted, his hunger strong enough to eat the lining. "I have a lunch appointment with you, don't I?" He gripped her by the elbow and escorted her onto the platform, sneaking past the hovering press with their laser-focus on Montgomery.

Once inside the hailed chaser, he spun his seat to face her. "Something's come to light, and I don't know where it fits into the puzzle."

Hux wiggled her backside, cleared her throat, and flashed him an encouraging smile. "All right, shoot."

"I tailed Davis this morning." He paused to read her reaction. She watched him with an expectation and patience that was surprising for someone so young. "His niece is married to Jonathan Dough."

"The tattoo artist?" Her gaze trailed the markings peeking out from under his collar, and her lips parted with a sigh.

"Yes, and Davis must have forewarned them about my impending arrival." That still grated, but he couldn't change it. He frowned. "I followed him to the clinic. Kylie, his niece, was in for...can you guess what?" Hux shook her head. "Pure-Rage poisoning."

She gasped, color staining her cheeks. "So, whoever poisoned me did the same to her?"

Gibs wished this cursed venti-mask wasn't in his way. She was damn adorable, all-eager-eyed and breathless. "It was self-inflicted, or so they suspect."

"But how did Kylie get her hands on the stuff? Do you think she poisoned the chocolates?" Hux squeezed her eyes shut for a second. "And why me? Why implicate Shaw?"

He shrugged. "The enforcement tracking showed a woman delivering the chocolates." The chaser drew alongside the platform at The Pigeon-Fest, and he clambered out, turning to offer Hux a hand. They strolled into the restaurant and took the first table available.

"Ah, so you want me to delve into her life?" Hux slid into the chair Gibs pulled out for her, flashing him a smile. "Do you think this information might clear Gibs of the charges?"

He sighed. "Here's the kicker. Montgomery hasn't accused him of anything."

"But...Davis said..." Hux gaped, her cheeks paling. "Why would he lie?"

"I don't know. He hates Nate, wishes he hadn't married Kylie, and we know he's the mole, right?" Gibs leveled his gaze on her, waiting for her to confirm it.

She nodded, chewing her lip as she studied the menu. "I used Uncle Charlie's tech support to set up the encryption, so it had to be Davis who leaked the information."

"I thought as much." Gibs folded his menu, planning on ordering their pig-in-a-pigeon burger despite the cost. He needed bacon. "Here's what I want you to do. Investigate Kylie; go as far back as you can, pre-Nate. I suspect Davis used her to scout the scenes. If her wedding ring matches the security footage, then we'll know."

He placed his order after her, then sipped his purified water.

"What will you do?" Hux nibbled on a breadstick, tapping her fingers on the table.

Gibs grinned. "Arrest Kylie."

"But..." Hux paused, and a slow smile spread across her lips, mesmerizing him for a moment. "If it is her, then we've solved the case. If she's innocent, then Davis will step forward?"

"That about sums up the plan." He frowned at how flimsy 'the plan' was. Dad would fall off his chair laughing.

"You want him to confess?" Hux pursed her lips. "We don't have anything pointing to him. Not the memories, not the crime scenes although if he's the mole, we need to double-check those."

"I've checked the drone footage." Gibs raised the venti-mask, allowing it to obscure his eyes for a moment. He popped a pseudo-potato fry into his mouth and shut the mask while savoring each chew.

"I'll check the 'autopsy' reports from Renovare." Huxley turned her plate until the stuffed pigeon breast was in front of her and the salad farthest away. She dipped her head to inhale the delicious aroma steaming off the garlic-infused sauce drenching the poor bird.

"He has to use the Center's servers. I'll stop by Montgomery's office and ask for access," Gibs said, flipping the visor up again. He gathered the burger into his hands, tucked an escaped relish back in with his pinkie finger, and took a bite. Down went the venti-mask. Annoying but necessary, for now.

"So we have a real suspect?" Hux sipped her water then forked in another mouthful of roasted pigeon and salad.

The food was delicious, and he'd ensure he remembered the restaurant. Mom would love the food, too, now that she was over her pigeons-aren't-meat phase. He longed to lick the sauce off a thumb, to enjoy the sharp notes of mayo, mustard, and dill, but he'd taken too many chances already while eating his burger. He studied Hux, hoping she hadn't figured out who he was.

"Something like that. I had one man who works in Renovare's manufacturing department, but the enforcement tracking didn't place him or his wife at all three scenes." Gibs wiped his hands on his napkin. "Oh, and the strangest thing, Lord Fields gave me files showing inkjobs with *real* emotions."

Hux shrugged. "The coding is so complicated nowadays, Wash, they're perfecting fake emotions."

"Huxley, I'm serious." He met her gaze. "I know a real orgasm when I see one." Activating his holo-wrist, he searched for the file. "I made a copy to show you."

She snorted, a mischievous smile twisting her lips as her cheeks flushed a beautiful pink. "I'm not looking at inkporn with you, Wash."

"Just look." He huffed and shuffled his chair closer to her to share his holo screen. The scene played out. He snuck glances between the orgasming inkjob and Hux's face until he couldn't focus on any-thing else.

She gaped, speechless, her plump lips opening. Frack, without his venti-mask on, he could kiss her right here and now. "This is wonderful." A frown slid across her face, dampening her excite-ment. "Why would Lord Fields share this with you?"

"My thoughts, as well. I'll stop by Renovare sometime today." *Like tonight at eight.* She wasn't invited, and whatever the hell the three amigos had planned, he didn't want Hux involved. He grimaced at having to hide things from her. It had started as a way to save his ass, but now, the lies and deceptions were spinning out of control.

"Since you took your venti-mask off, *Gibs*, why don't you tell me what the frack is going on?" She gestured to the waiter and ordered wine, not caring that she'd frozen him to his chair.

"What do you...?" Gibs faltered, stumbling over his words, tying his tongue. What could he say?

"I've kissed those lips, partner. P.S.: try switching your cologne and finding another nickname other than Hux." She narrowed her gorgeous eyes, a pulse ticking at her jaw. "I should be super pissed, and I would be if I didn't find those tattoos so damn sexy."

He released his pent-up breath in a whoosh. "Em insisted you shouldn't know, that you might inadvertently reveal my identity."

"Em?" Hux twisted her lips.

"The Master of Shadows." He winced.

"Frack, Gibs, who else are you in bed with? I mean, I knew about the Master, but I didn't realize you two were as tight as a Twizzler." She slammed her palm on the table, rattling the glasses. Then in slow motion, her sinful mouth formed a smile. "Your mother's performance was amazing."

He chuckled. "She'll be delighted to hear that."

35

7#1|27Y-|=1U3

Date: 2170.18.10

The Holies

Nate's home

NATE DRAPED A BLANKET across Kylie's shoulders as she sipped, with due diligence, the tea he had made her. She curled into herself, her lips pinched and as pale as her cheeks. He'd never seen her this fragile, timid, and broken. She said a few polite words of courtesy, and neither of them mentioned the elephant in the room.

Lissa.

He fidgeted, squeezing and wringing his hands. If he sat, he'd bounce his knee in agitation. If he stood, he hovered or paced, his thoughts and tongue colliding with the things he wanted to say.

Mom and Dad had cleaned up the apartment and left takeout food on the kitchen counter. The way Nate's stomach wrenched meant he couldn't eat right now. He drew in a deep breath, preparing to reveal all. Why the hell not when their relationship was already in shambles?

"I can see people's negative emotions in the form of clouds hanging over their heads. Most days, yours is gray and turbulent. I can't deal with that anymore." He assessed every twitch of emotion from her, trying to read if she thought him insane. "Lissa never has bad mood swings. I guess I found her exuberance attractive."

"That video I smuggled was just confirmation then?" She sipped her tea. "You already knew about the synthetics evolving?"

He nodded. "There are a few inkjobs who visited my parlor. I thought it was a malfunction in their last upgrade."

"You see my emotions? Even now?" Kylie furrowed her brow, not in judgment but with concern.

"Right now, it's so dark, it's almost black." He rose to take her empty cup from her and tugged the blanket tighter around her.

"I'm so sorry, Nate. I should have told you about the E7s, and I shouldn't have monitored your feed." She pinched her lip to smother a sob and shuddered with the effort to restrain her sorrow. "I saw the Lissa ling on the horizon—the way your gaze lowered, lingered. But I couldn't confront you because I wasn't supposed to know."

"I'm sorry, too. I succumbed to temptation when I should've been strong for us." He dropped onto the couch beside her and looped an arm around her shoulders, pulling her into the curve of his body. "I should've put you first. You were changing into this woman I didn't recognize, not the one I fell in love with. I should've asked you why instead of ignoring it, hoping you'd change back to the happy Kylie I married."

Tears streaked her cheeks, but she smiled. "We're idiots, Nate. How did we let this happen?" She rubbed her face on the blanket and chuckled. "Want to start again, if Lissa hasn't claimed your heart, that is?"

"She hasn't, and I would very much love my Kylie back." He snatched a kiss and crushed her against him, so grateful that he couldn't contain the smile splitting his cheeks. He squeezed her tighter and rubbed his chin across her crown.

"I didn't try to kill myself, Nate, I swear." Her mumbled words reached him, and his shoulders slumped with relief.

"Let me make fresh tea, and you can tell me how the evening played out?" He pulled away from her, arching a brow to ask if another cup of tea would please her.

She nodded. "What I can remember of it, at least."

"Hungry?" When he entered the kitchen, the containers on the counter reminded him to at least feed her.

"A little. As a precaution, they pumped my stomach." She followed him and leaned one shoulder against the cupboard. "When you confronted me about the E7s, I went back to watch your footage."

He winced. So, she'd seen the chaser scene with Lissa, but he wouldn't mention it if she didn't. "Rhona was unaware how much she'd shaken my world."

Kylie nodded. "I wish I were there for you, instead of supporting R4S. I thought I was chasing something on your behalf and for all synthetics. And here you are, an example of how real a synthetic can be. After the smuggled video and with Lord Fields's offer, I doubled my efforts. I'm sorry, I committed myself further." She shrugged off the blanket to remove plates from the cupboard. "I should've listened to your warnings, Nate. You were right to be suspicious of Fields's generosity."

The door pinged, interrupting their shared stare.

"Let me guess, Uncle Martin?" Kylie chuckled and opened the door. Instead, the man on the platform had Nate circling Kylie's waist and shuffling her aside.

"Oh, good, you're both home. May I come in?" The man flashed a smile, a forgotten venti-mask shoved to the side.

"Detective Shaw?" Nate gasped and shifted backward, taking Kylie with him. "What the frack happened to you?"

The detective entered with a snort, and the door slid shut behind him. "This is a weak disguise, one not intended to convince, or so it seems."

"Disguise?" Nate returned to the task of making tea. He shook the tea container at the detective, who nodded.

"Someone poisoned my partner with Pure Rage, and your Uncle Martin told me I was the prime suspect." Shaw rested his gaze on Kylie, searching for answers from her.

"And you think one of us did it?" Nate offered the steaming cup of tea, which the detective accepted.

Shaw shook his head. "I came for answers, Nate. I'm searching for the golden thread, and I think Mrs. Dough might be able to help me."

"Me?" Kylie squeaked, placing her cup on the counter.

"What are the odds of two cases of Pure Rage poisoning in the same clinic?" Shaw sipped his tea, cupping it with both hands.

"Since Pure Rage is scarce, I'd say slim to none." Nate gestured to the lounge and led the way. He took a seat next to Kylie, leaning back to appear casual when he was far from it. What had *Uncle Martin* done now, and how did it impact Kylie? The bastard had grilled Nate as if Kylie's poisoning was his fault.

Shaw placed his cup on the coffee table and activated his holo-wrist. "I'll cut the BS and just ask. Mrs. Dough...Kylie, did you deliver anything for Davis? A parcel or a box of chocolates to a home in the Holies?"

"No." She rolled her backside to recline against Nate.

Shaw nodded as if her answer was expected. "When last did you visit the Promenade?"

"Lux?" Kylie twisted her lips in thought. "I haven't been there in years, not since I bought a gift for Nate for our first anniversary."

Shaw scanned her hands. "Where's your wedding ring?"

"I'm sorry, but why does that matter?" Nate stiffened, sat up, and pulled away from Kylie's warm body.

"Please, indulge me." Shaw rested his gaze on Kylie and waited.

"I threw it in a fit of anger. It bounced off the wall. I don't know where it landed." Kylie's red-rimmed eyes shimmered with unshed tears. "I'm sorry, Nate. I was so furious, so hurt, lost... When the Rage kicked in, my thoughts and emotions blurred. I *hated* you then."

He crushed her against his side, kissing her temple. "All's forgiven. A new beginning, right?" When she nodded, he rose to retrieve his tablet. "How did you take the drug, love?"

"A bouquet of hot-house fragrant zinnias arrived, and the card said it was from you." Kylie chewed on a fingernail. "Uncle Martin said he'd retrieved the flowers to test them."

"The Rage must have been on the petals." Shaw tapped on his holo-wrist.

"I still have the design sketches of our wedding rings. Will that do, detective?" Nate offered his tablet to the man, having located the images for him. He dropped beside Kylie and threw an arm around her.

A bold smile split Shaw's face. Nate struggled to align the tatted man in front of him with the clean, almost nondescript Cent who'd first walked into The Skin Canvas.

"It's not the ring. That clears you as a suspect, or at the very least, an accomplice." The detective frowned. "Which might mean Davis isn't the perp." He pinched the bridge of his nose as if he warded off a headache.

"You said you'd explain about the ring." Kylie gripped her hands in her lap but didn't look away from Shaw.

The detective handed Nate his tablet and removed his own from a coat pocket. "Security footage showed a woman casing the second crime scene, and she had a distinctive ring."

Kylie cuddled into Nate's side to look at the image. She gasped, slicing glances between the tablet and the detective. "I know that ring." She enlarged the image. "It's Lissa's."

Cold tingles slithered down Nate's spine at the idea of Lissa mutilating the inkjobs. Bile rose to choke him, and he gagged. He'd fucked her, spent years with the woman, and had never guessed she was capable of such violence.

"Are you sure, Kylie?" Shaw took his tablet, switched it off, and slid it into his pocket.

"Of course. It's a data crystal that clips onto a gold band. When she first bought it, she waved it around at the weekly R4S meetings." Kylie laced her fingers through Nate's, resting their clasped hands on his thigh.

"I've never seen her wear it." Nate frowned, sifting through his memories, trying to remember. But to be fair, he hadn't looked at her hands when her other delights were on display.

"This makes no sense. Why would your receptionist mutilate the Walker's, the mayor's, and Lord Fields's inkjobs? They're from prominent clients, still..." Shaw pursed his lips.

"At an R4S meeting, we did once discuss how to reach the upper echelons, what it would mean if they helped our cause." Kylie shrugged. "No one mentioned anything as complicated as this appears to be."

"How could she control or hurt them? She's such a little thing." Nate squeezed Kylie's hand, hoping she understood that he asked out of curiosity and not the remnants of affection.

"She knows the manufacturing safe word." Kylie's voice was soft, and color stained her cheeks. "Once, I shared a story from my lunch with Shelley and how her husband had to restrain an inkjob that day."

"What story?" Shaw's expectation thickened the air.

"It was about a misbehaving or malfunctioning inkjob, and instead of yelling 'eject,' the manufacturing's kill code, he yelled 'ejaculate.'" She giggled, and the cloud above her head lightened. "I asked why they used only one word as a code, and Shelley said that they change it every three months, so whatever they chose didn't matter."

Shaw chuckled. "When did you tell—?"

"I told Lissa the story about two months ago," Kylie whispered.

"Frack, Kylie." Nate gasped.

"How could I know she'd do this, Nate?" She flashed him a glare.

"None of us could've predicted this." Shaw rose. "I'm seeing Lord Fields tonight at eight. You can choose to attend or not." He smiled. "But my thanks to both of you."

Nate escorted the detective to the door. "Thanks for the invite. I don't like this hovering over our heads without closure."

"If you're not there, I'll make sure you're informed of the outcome. Good day, and thanks for the tea." Shaw stepped onto the platform where his chaser waited.

Lost in his thoughts, Nate stared at the closed door. Could Lissa have done this?

"Hungry?" Kylie placed the takeout in the warmer and chose the time.

Nate nodded, taking cutlery out of the drawer. Tonight would reveal much.

36

7#1|27Y-S1X

Date: 2170.18.10
The Colony
The Center

Tonight would reveal much. Gibs delivered Hux to the Center post-lunch, hoping she'd find the information on Kylie he'd asked for. He headed out to the Doughs. He now had a promising suspect. With a bounce in his step, he returned to the Center to invite Montgomery to attend tonight after explaining what information he had, what his suspicions were, and what his plan was. His captain's lost-in-thought expression didn't bolster Gibs's confidence.

He strode onto the Center's platform, planning to head home for dinner with Mom when two detectives walked past him. By now, everyone in the Center knew he was Shaw and that Wash had been an Internal Affairs exercise to test whether anyone could infiltrate enforcement, or so the captain had claimed.

"She was sprawled like a doll, all artistic and the like. The killer had even taken the time to mold tiny roses with her skin."

Those words pierced Gibs's thoughts, and he froze, spun on his heel, and hurried after the speaker. "What did you say, Parker?"

"What's it got to do with you, Shaw?" His eyes narrowing above his hawk nose implied he thought Gibs a traitor for helping IA. Gibs hadn't fracken cared about their opinion before, and he sure as hell didn't now.

"Sounds like it's my case, Parker. No evidence other than the body, right?" Gibs activated his holo-wrist to share images of the Eve Roes.

Tennyson, Parker's partner, nodded. There was no judgment in his brown eyes, summoning Gibs's smile. That the Center still had decent enforcers meant honor and integrity weren't dying out completely.

"This ain't no inkjob mutilation." Parker smirked.

"It could be the same perp, though." Tennyson enlarged the images of the first Eve Roe. "Our victim had a fresh tatt of roses and daisies."

Parker glared at Tennyson, offered Gibs his back while he ran his hand through his hair, then faced him. "They found her body in the Deadzone beneath a Holies ink parlor." He swiped his wrist over Gibs's, transferring the files. "Looks like you have a legit case now, Shaw. I'll let Montgomery know."

"My thanks, Parker, Tennyson." Gibs opened the file on his holo-wrist and gritted his teeth. The victim's face tumbled his house of clues. "Hux, where are you?" Each second passed at an excruciating crawl as he waited for her to answer his call.

"In the morgue with Davis. He placed trackers on Kylie's files and caught me searching for her history. I'm with him now, filling in the blanks." She turned to show Davis at the coffee station behind her.

"Frack," Gibs grunted. "She isn't the perp."

"I know, but there are interesting titbits." She paused, nibbling on her lip. "Want me to meet you somewhere?"

"No need, I'm here at the Center. I'll see you in five." Gibs jogged to the elevator.

While he waited for it, he read over the new crime scene notes and sifted through the images the drone had taken. Something about victim bothered him. Well, other than her death. Such an innocent, vivacious woman had been murdered without mercy.

"Frack." As he'd expected, the killer had escalated to humans. Montgomery would chew his ass off for this. The press were going to have a field day.

"What is it?" Hux met him at the elevator doors, holding out a coffee.

He took it with a nod of thanks and flipped his mask back to take a long swallow. Nate's tea was good, but nothing compared to coffee and the caffeine kick it would give him. "The perp has moved onto humans. We have our first victim, and she isn't a Jane Doe." He transferred his cup to his left hand, so he could call up the images on his holo-wrist. "Parker and Tennyson just came in with this."

Hux gasped, grabbing his arm. "You know her?"

"Yes, it's Melissa Lorenzo, The Skin Canvas' receptionist." Gibs scowled. After leaving Nate and Kylie, he'd thought he'd known who the killer was. Lorenzo being murdered in the same way as the inkjobs implied otherwise. The precise intricacies of the flowers crafted out of her skin ruled out suicide.

"She's wearing *the* ring." Hux shook his arm, almost spilling his coffee.

He held the cup out of harm's way but blinked at the pearlescent light glinting off the gem. Hux was right. "It's a data crystal. I doubt the murderer realized. There might be incriminating information on it."

"Margo just left to collect a body," Davis called from down the passage. "This isn't good, Gibs. Seems like I'm the target."

Gibs jolted, too late to clip the mask in place. His secret was out. Hux looped her arm through his and ushered him forward. Unable to resist the temptation, he dipped and kissed her temple before sliding into a chair to watch Davis refill the coffee machine.

"Kylie's my niece, Nate's her husband, Lissa was her friend. Huxley and you are my colleagues," he said with his back to them. "I'm the common denominator."

Well, Gibs had figured out most of that; the Lissa-part was new. "You think Em's behind this?" He arched a brow, waiting for Davis to reveal he worked for the woman.

Placing his steaming coffee in front of him, Davis dropped into a chair opposite Hux and Gibs. "I've worked for her for years, Gibs. I was the accountant, channeling millions as required. I queried one unusual transaction, and my sister's inkjob went insane, killing her. That's when I started to have second thoughts about my commitment to the Master. I took a job at the Center to 'supposedly' search for the reason behind my sister's death. The Master approved my request so she could use my position here to her benefit."

"Why target you?" Gibs sipped his coffee, but when Hux gripped his knee, he jerked, almost spilling it. Despite the fire of need shooting up his thigh, he tossed her a warning look but couldn't smother the smile her daring elicited.

"Over the years, I've gathered information on her dealings, and should I die, everyone will receive a copy." Davis smirked, a wicked gleam in his beady eyes. "The mutilated inkjobs were warning shots, Gibs." He picked at a crumb on the table. "At first, I didn't think it was anyone from the Shadows. I blamed Renovare and Lord Fields, so I delved into his dealings. That's how I found out that I'm an E7 inkjob—an experimental child-range Renovare dabbled with. The ironic part is, despite Kylie losing her mom to an inkjob, she went and married one, too."

"You and Nate are E7s?" Gibs gasped. He would've sworn in a court of law that both were human. "I've seen footage on emotional inkjobs, but I hadn't realized it was that old."

Davis gestured to his face. "I had a malfunction, but the living E7s all look like Nate; even the females share similar features." He shrugged as if he'd accepted the bad hand life had dealt him. "Kylie loves him."

"I'd never have guessed, Martin. You're as human as I am." Hux gripped his forearm. "Knowing this doesn't change my opinion of you, just in case you were wondering."

Davis slid his arm from her grip and offered her a weak smile.

"We did think you were the perp, though. Data was leaking from the cloud, and it wasn't one of us..." Gibs jerked again when Hux scrapped her nails up his thigh. He covered her hand with his, pinning it in place. "I can't rule anyone out, and our evidence is circumstantial, for the most part. We have nothing pointing at anyone specifically. Which means forcing the perp to reveal themselves, to confess." He swallowed hard. His father's name rested on this case. "I have to meet with Lord Fields tonight. I want to know how long these mutations have been occurring, and whether the Council is aware of it."

"You said they will all be there, the mayor, and Em, as well." Hux squared her shoulders. "I'm coming, too."

"No, I don't want you targeted." Gibs cupped her cheek, forcing her to meet his gaze. "Montgomery will be there, and Nate might attend. I want as many witnesses as possible because I suspect the perp will reveal themselves, frustrated with our inability to solve these crimes."

"You know who it is." Hux shook her head. "That means a possible arrest. The more enforcement present, the better."

That she thought him so capable as to have identified the killer... Gibs tried not to let that swell his pride. "It's taken care of." He squared his shoulders, prepared to argue with her. "Davis and I will go; you wait here for the data crystal. Message me the moment you've opened it."

"But..." She harrumphed, removing her claws from his thigh.

"Gibs is right, Naomi. It's our duty to ensure you don't die on your first case." This time, Davis reached across the table to pat her forearm.

Gibs smirked—condescension tit for tat. "Here's how I want it to play out." He leaned on his elbows to fill them in on his weak-ass plan and their roles to play.

37

7#1|27Y-S3V3/\/

Date: 2170.18.10
The Colony
Gibs's apartment

"Sorry, I'm late, Mom." Gibs stepped onto his platform, later than he'd expected since he had taken the time to explain to Hux why he needed her safe. He'd wanted to kiss her every time she opened her mouth but had decided that would lead to him never making it home for dinner.

He paused on the platform to water his vines, thankful Mom was there to nurture them. If there was anyone who knew how to cultivate plants, it was his mother.

"Look who I ran into at Bohemian," she said when he strolled inside.

On the couch beside her, in a fuchsia hibiscus-patterned dress, sat Em. She sipped tea with grace, knees crossed and feet tucked in, looking every inch a woman of substance.

"What a surprise." Gibs smiled as the hairs on the back of his neck rose. "It's wonderful to see you, Em."

"Em says she's helping you with your case." Mom pouted. "How come you never ask for my help?" Not waiting for his response, she poured him a cup of tea.

He sighed and took the seat opposite her, accepting the cup. What he wanted was a vodka, a whisky, hell, he'd settle for bad wine. Finding Em in his home didn't sit well with him.

"I stopped by to celebrate. Word has it that you've arrested someone." Em split her ruby lips into a wide grin. "And since we have this pesky meeting with Lord Fields, I thought we could spoil your mother with dinner afterward. Y'know, to celebrate."

"Lord Fields?" Mom gasped, dropping her gaze to her heaving bosom. "I don't have anything to wear."

Em flicked a dismissive wrist. "Nonsense, you look stunning in that ensemble, and you know it, Cassie."

Mom blushed and said no more.

Gibs scowled. He wanted his mother there about as much as he wanted Hux present. All eyes would be on him, and should things turn sour, anyone could be caught in the crossfire.

"I'd prefer to collect you afterward, Mom. It would give you time to dress." He put his cup on the table, unable to take another sip when his throat burned for vodka.

"I insist Cassie come with, Gibs, unless you're expecting it to be a long meeting?" Em arched a brow, patting her dress where it draped onto his couch. There, bulging with definition, was a gun.

He nodded, pasting on a smile. "You're right, Em. I'm being silly." When his gaze rested on his mom, her face had paled. She must have noticed the bulge, but as Em glanced her way, she pinched her cheeks and smiled.

"Then it's settled." Mom pointed at his neck, her tone accusatory. "What's that tatt? I can't quite make it out. I hope it's not anything religious, Gibson Shaw."

"Not that I know of. Em chose them. What is this one?" He peeled his shirt collar back for Em to see. Why his mother wasn't a spy or an actress, he'd never know. He struggled to smother a smile. With their 'guest' distracted, his mother pulled a packet of powder from her cleavage and poured it into Em's tea.

"Tribal markings, I believe," Em said, raising her cup to press her red lips to the rim. "We should be leaving soon." She took a sip, then another.

"Gibs, finish your tea; let's not keep Lord Fields waiting." Mom gestured to Em and him, and he hurried to do so despite his earlier disgust. "I'll powder my nose and be out in a minute." She darted into his room and closed the door behind her.

"What are you doing?" he whispered, fury grating his voice. There was still time for them to leave before Mom came out.

"Giving myself a little insurance, my dear Gibs." Em shrugged a delicate shoulder, her skin shimmering in the lamplight. "Of course, that was before I heard about the arrest. I knew I could trust you to solve this. It almost makes tonight's meeting redundant."

"Then cancel it." He placed his cup on the table with force and rose.

"I didn't organize it, Fields did. I'd love to know why, and if luck goes my way…" She covered her mouth while she giggled. "As it always does…then you'll have a chance to shine."

"Fine, just leave my mother out of this."

"Why do you think you can tell me what to do, Gibs? Of all my servants, you're the least respectful." Em tapped her chin. "At first, I found it entertaining; now, it's becoming irritating." She stood, fluffing the creases from her dress. "If I want, I could have you both killed right now."

"I'm not your servant." Gibs clipped each word.

"Your mother is joining us." Em glared at him.

"I'm ready," Mom sang as she waltzed into the lounge resplendent in a rainbow-colored dress. She'd swept her black hair up and painted her lips a dark pink.

"You look lovely, Mom." Gibs forced his shoulders to relax—the tension building down his spine adding a painful distraction.

"He's right. You look amazing, Cassie. Shall we?" Em headed for the door, and as she did so, Mom patted her bag and made a gun gesture with her fingers.

Gibs grinned at her, gripped her ticklish elbow, and whispered that he loved her.

The chaser ride was made in silence. He'd asked where Schneider was and had received a clipped response. Busy. Mom had kept quiet, as well. Huxley followed through, sending him a summary of the data on Lissa's crystal, confirming his suspicions. When the chaser landed on Renovare's platform, he climbed out first to offer the ladies a hand. If he didn't, his mother would smack him as she had when he'd 'insulted' Hux. A bleeding nose wouldn't help tonight.

He prayed everything ran according to plan. Sure, he had evidence, thanks to Lissa, but he wanted a full confession...for the show of it. Strolling into Renovare and taking the pod up to Lord Fields's office continued in silence. A new Zeta greeted them, ushering them into Fields's office. Along one wall stood four Sec2s, their hands clasped in front of their groins, tightening their suits across their bulky Titanium shoulders.

Gibs released Mom's elbow and fell back to talk to Em. "Why all the security? Do you think Fields is guilty of something?"

Em's chuckle was feminine and rich with victory. "Reggie has many secrets, and the unknown factors of this investigation might have him on the defensive."

Gibs nodded, hurrying ahead to introduce his mother to Lord Fields and Captain Montgomery, again. Mom giggled, apologizing for her earlier abuse, and Montgomery shrugged it off like a gentleman. Tamara had found a better man. Montgomery's support of Gibs's venture proved that.

"Is it true, Captain Montgomery, that you had a man arrested for the crimes against Renovare's synthetics?" Em batted her eyelashes and pouted her lips, acting like the hostess rather than a guest.

"It is, indeed, ma'am. We arrested Officer Martin Davis, both for the mutilations and the murder of Melissa Lorenzo." Montgomery grinned, puffing out his chest.

"Martin did it?" Mom gaped, her cheeks paling. "But he's such a nice man."

"Nice people do commit crimes, Cassie." Em patted her forearm then glanced at her holo-wrist. "Where is Schneider? I asked him to deliver a crate of champagne."

The door opened for Mayor DuPont—a tall man carrying his experience around his middle. On his arm was Hux. Gibs smothered a growl as fire traveled the length of him. Trembling with anger, he pinned a glare on her, conveying how dearly she would pay for defying him. He hadn't wanted her in harm's way. Behind him trailed two more Sec2s, DuPont's guards.

"Detective Shaw, I'd like to introduce you to Mayor DuPont." Hux wrapped her arms around Gibs as if he wasn't furious with her. She tugged on his coat pocket and snuck something there. He sighed, letting the fury seep from him. There'd been a purpose to her defiance.

"Crystal copies, just in case," she whispered as she kissed his cheek. "Uncle Charlie, this is Cassiopeia, Gibs's mother."

Charles DuPont shook Gibs's hand and kissed Mom's knuckles before glaring at Em. "I hope this was worth my time, Master."

Mom frowned at Em, mouthing the word "Master." Gibs gave her a slight shake of his head, and she nodded, splashing on a fake smile. Her gaze darted around the room, revealing her discomfort.

"I didn't request this meeting, mayor," Em snapped, her cheeks pale. A grimaced contorted her lips. In obvious discomfort, she pressed a hand to her belly.

"May we begin?" Fields addressed the room. "Who else are we waiting for?"

"Lord Fields, but if you don't mind, I'd like to speak?" Gibs arched a brow at him, waiting for his nod before assuming center stage. "Thank you all for coming." The door opened, and in strolled Schneider. A Sec2 behind him carried a crate. "I don't doubt that the news has reached you already. This afternoon, Captain Montgomery arrested Officer Martin Davis. The decision wasn't taken lightly, and if you'll allow it, I'll explain how this came about."

"Please continue." Fields folded his arms across his chest and rested a hip against his desk. The Zetas had summoned chairs for this meeting, but everyone remained standing.

"Thank you." Gibs shared a polite smile. "Let's start with you, Lord Fields. Initially, you were a prime suspect since you had both opportunity and motive."

Fields laughed. "What motive could I have to mutilate my own creations?"

Gibs activated his holo-wrist and flicked a video onto the screens behind the desk. An inkjob cried, surprised by the tears spilling down her cheeks. "Your creations were becoming sentient beings, violating the Pancras Treaty. Do you deny this?"

Zeta escorted Nate into the room, and he bowed his head at Gibs. As he found a place to stand, others shifted on their feet or cleared their throats.

"I do not." Fields's shoulders slumped, his gaze lingering on Nate. "With the E7s, we knew we had mastered human-like emotions and could build a synthetic that was born out of a test tube but raised as a child. When the Council of Ethics shut that project down, we accepted their decision, yet, one by one we received reports of...malfunctions." Sadness darkened his features. "We encountered a dilemma neither I nor the Council had considered. We couldn't terminate a creature that had a soul, and this malfunction had done just that...created souls where I had failed."

Fields flicked his holo-wrist, and a grainy image appeared of a woman working a domed apple farm on Ganymede. "Tessa was the first malfunction. She's happily married and has given birth to her third child. At first, we thought she and a few others were an anomaly, and with an amendment of the treaty allowing Renovare and the Council to monitor all synthetics, we discovered that the coding had evolved...and with it, so had my creations."

The screen flickered to the crying inkjob.

Fields rested his hip on his desk once more. "It looks like I have motive, but I can have any inkjob terminated or replaced without going to the extent of mutilating them. Besides, I never leave this building. My security feeds and tracking will prove it."

"But you could've commanded your *creations* to commit the deeds, and your advanced tech team could've tampered with the feeds. How else could the Walker's inkjob leave the premises without any security footage? Which brings me to Mayor Charles DuPont." Gibs turned on his heels to face the man.

The mayor gasped, and his cheeks mottled red. "Why the hell would I kill inkjobs?"

"Yours knew too much, and you did have your niece conveniently placed on the investigation team." Gibs glanced at Hux and frowned. Pain reflected in her eyes for a moment before she dipped her head. He tried not to sigh. This was one of the reasons he hadn't wanted her present. Not that he thought her a bad detective, just that he needed to use her to twist the knife in her uncle.

"Now see here, Shaw, I don't have the motive or the opportunity, and I certainly don't have the time." The mayor scowled. "Didn't you just say you arrested a man?"

"We did, but I'm explaining the hell I went through in the last week or so. Your inkjob was the second mutilated. You see, your niece is my partner, and you have your inkjobs tattooed at the same parlor as the first victim." He waved Nate closer. "This is Jonathan Dough. He owns a tattoo parlor called The Skin Canvas, and he placed the marks of ownership on both victims. I investigated him for that coincidence.

I considered someone close to him might be the killer, especially when his lovely receptionist was tortured to death."

Gibs flicked an image of a smiling Lissa onto the screen. "We found her this morning killed in the same manner as the inkjobs."

Nate cried out, his cheeks shuddering. He swung out a hand to catch the closest chair and slumped onto it. "Why? How? Who would do such a thing?"

"Which brings me to the Master of Shadows." This announcement wiped the smirk off Em's face. The woman had done nothing to hide her enjoyment at hearing Gibs bare Fields's secrets. "Martin Davis is a mole for the Master, yet despite his diligent service, she targeted him, allegedly having his sister killed in an inkjob accident. When Detective Huxley and Mrs. Kylie Dough suffered from poisonings using rare Pure Rage, that led me down the deliberately crumbed trail to a culpable Martin Davis."

"Very funny, Gibs; why would I bother with any of this?" Em laughed. "It's beneath me."

"Davis has a detailed file on you as life insurance. That didn't protect his loved ones, and someone as spiteful as you would stoop to murder to get your way." Gibs held up his hand when Em opened her mouth to speak. "Not Davis's death because that would release the file to every press and political source. But getting him arrested would remove the thorn in your side, your one weakness, as you saw it. Killing off his loved ones was to prove to him you were fearless, when you were, in fact, running scared."

With a ladylike snort, Em flicked a dismissive hand.

Gibs ignored her. "Especially since access to Pure Rage is easy for you. Lissa was your servant and used Nate to befriend Kylie and infiltrate the R4S. With Kylie's unknowing help, Lissa bypassed the inkjobs' safe codes. She failed to kill Kylie and Huxley, though, and we all know, the Master of Shadows doesn't tolerate failure..." Gibs ran a disapproving glance down Em's body. "...Or rejection."

She pursed her lips, glaring at him. "This is all supposition."

Her attitude was starting to grate, so Gibs whipped out a name he'd skim-read from Davis's file. "Is it, Alessandra Mastrantonio?" He grinned when she twitched, surprise twisting her features. Withdrawing the crystals from his pocket, he handed them to Fields, the mayor, and Montgomery. "These carry the data found on Lissa's body and a copy of Davis's file."

Em spluttered, then lunged forward to snatch the crystal out of the mayor's hand. "You're bluffing." With a confident sashay, she strolled across the room and placed the crystal on the data reader on Field's desk.

Images and folders appeared on the screens, and as Em flicked through them one by one, her face hardened. Her laugh was cold, almost maniacal. Lissa had been as diligent in recording Em's instructions as Davis had been in assembling his file.

"So, Lissa failed me again." Em threw the crystal on the floor, stomping on it with a steel-tipped stiletto and missing. "You're right. The poisoned chocolates were meant to kill your *precious* Hux." The audience gasped. "But your desperation brought you to me. I took great delight in having you shot. You were a means to an end but a loose tie. Your job was to convict Davis for Huxley's death—failing that, the attempt on her life." Em snatched an opened bottle of champagne from Schneider and drank deeply.

Mom stepped forward, stretching out a hand as if to warn Em, then shook her head and returned to Hux's side.

"Lissa failed to kill Davis's niece, too." Em pointed at Nate. "When the three of them walked out of that clinic, Lissa had to go." Em giggled. "The web I spun was ingenious, a sure-fire way to rid myself of 'bugs.' Davis's family dead and the idiot arrested. Old Charlie DuPont's political career in ruins after his own inkjob was victimized. If he can't take care of his property, how can he serve the people, or so the rumors will say. Reggie's precious babies will be the talk of the world, what with the poor dears discovering emotion as if *that* makes them human and worthy of love. His shares will plummet, his name will be worth shit. And these stupid inkjobs will die out like the toasters of old."

Em took another long draw from the bottle. "You're collateral damage, Gibs, unable to shine under your father's shadow, relying on luck rather than skill to solve your cases. You're my pawn, my ace in the hole, but even you failed me." She swung out her arm, sloshing champagne. "You'll all be dead by tomorrow, so I might as well give you my villainous monologue. Yes, I had Abigail Davis killed, *and* Kylie and Naomi poisoned. That was to torture Martin Davis, the little weasel and to put Gibs on his ass for Huxley's 'death.' As to the mutilated inkjobs, I arranged those to showcase my reach—that none of you, from the Walkers, the mayor, and even Field's Zetas are safe. The revelation of Renovare's treaty violation will be my *coup de grâce.*" Em's nod was so vigorous that she teetered on her feet. Mom's concoction was kicking in.

"Yes, I have motive, opportunity, and damn it, the balls none of you have." Em grabbed her crotch with a lewd chuckle. "Schneider, kill them." She stumbled back and landed on her ass, gasping at finding herself on the floor.

At the same time, Mom hurried forward to hand Gibs her handbag, concern twisting her features. The familiar weight of his spare Glock made him grin. He withdrew it and slid it into the back of his pants, dropping her bag onto a nearby chair.

Six Sec2s circled Em, their arms at their sides in preparation.

Schneider turned on his heel, gestured to his Sec2, and left, taking the crate of champagne with him. He saluted Gibs on the way out, a small smile playing across his lips. Em's arrest would birth a new Master of Shadows, and so the cycle continued.

"Alessandra Mastrantonio, you are under arrest for...everything you just said." Davis stepped through a hidden door, satisfaction and peace illuminating his features.

"Davis? You're supposed to be in jail." Em gagged, then vomited tea, champagne, and the contents of Mom's packet onto the polished stone floor. "What's wrong with me?" Her ruby lips trembled, and she sobbed, dribbling bile and champagne onto her sundress.

"A powerful diuretic." Mom giggled. "A teaspoon of it is good for you, but the entire packet? Not so much. Then you added alcohol, you silly woman."

Two Sec2s carried a blubbering Em out. Davis and Montgomery trailed them.

Nate stumbled forward, his eyes red and his cheeks wet. Pain pinched his lips white. "Thank you, Detective. I'll head home now and let Kylie know."

Gibs frowned, guilt eating at the relief and the sense of accomplishment warming his chest. He shouldn't have revealed Lissa's death like that, but he'd needed Nate's reaction to eliminate him as a suspect, once and for all. In case anyone queried the thoroughness of his investigation.

Hux squealed and darted across the room to throw herself in Gibs's arms. "You did it," she said, burying her face in his neck.

Gibs crushed her against him. "*We* did it, Hux."

38

7#1|27Y-319#7

"As requested, I'll send over the recordings of Master's confession. A job well done, Gibs." Fields patted his shoulder on the way out. Four Sec2s turned as one and marched after him.

"I need a drink," Mayor DuPont said, facing Mom. "Care to join me, Mrs. Shaw?"

Mom arched a brow, ran a knowing gaze over Gibs and Hux, then flashed the mayor her most charming smile. "Call me Cassie."

They left, taking the mayor's Sec2s with them.

"I told you to stay away." Gibs nuzzled Hux's hair away from her ear to nip her.

"I know." Those two words and the kiss she pressed to his neck deflated any remnants of his anger. He was such a sucker for this woman.

Lacing his fingers through hers, he raised their clasped hands to kiss her fingertips. "Shall we, Hux?" He studied her face, trailing his gaze over every detail. Em had been right about that. She was his precious Hux.

She nodded, and he tugged her toward the pod, snatching small kisses while they waited.

"My place or yours?" She curled against his chest and rested her palm over his heart.

"Mine is closest." Gibs grimaced. His mother and his bed weren't a romantic combination. "Let's go to yours."

"Will your voice return to normal?" Hux stepped into the pod first.

"Yes, the chip will dissolve over time." He tugged her against him, looping an arm around her waist, needing to feel her warmth and softness.

"Okay, but keep the tatts," she said, brushing kisses along his jaw.

He smirked. "Wait until you see them all."

At her soft moan, tingles traveled from his chest to his groin, hardening him...again. *Frack*. He tightened his hold on her, dipping to inhale her rose perfume. If he pinned her to the pod's wall and kissed her, then what? He could restrain himself for a ten-minute chaser ride, couldn't he?

They didn't stroll across Renovare's foyer but ran to the platform like eager teenagers. A chaser waited, and he opened the door, watching as she clambered in, all ass and limbs. He closed his eyes, fighting for control. *Soon*. He repeated the word like a calming mantra.

"We'll need to inform Montgomery," he said after she instructed the chaser to take them to her home. "We can't be partners if we're...together."

"I don't see why not." She cuddled against him, scraping her nails along his thigh. She came so close to touching an aching part of him that he struggled to keep his hips from rising to meet her fingers. "I thought we could form a team of three?"

He nodded, so aroused he couldn't string thoughts together. Team of three? The name 'Davis' penetrated his lust-fogged mind. "Let

Montgomery decide." He shuddered, arching his back when she nipped his neck. Frack, she was going to kill him.

At last, the chaser pulled up alongside her platform, and he bolted out, tugging her behind him. As soon as she opened her door, he lifted her inside, spun, and pinned her to the wall. He gripped her wrists in one hand and yanked them above her head, then with a slow, torturous caress down her spine, palmed one backside cheek, pulling her into his groin.

"I should punish you for misbehaving." He bit her neck in retaliation for her torturing him in the chaser, snatched a quick kiss, then swatted her backside. She moaned, arching and grinding against him. "But I believe I owe you a kiss?"

She nodded, her breathing ragged.

He released her ass to run his fingers from her collarbone and down her cleavage, tugging at the magnets. Her shirt parted to reveal a white bra. "Frack."

He slashed his mouth over hers, tasting her like he'd dreamed. Her tongue dueled with his, and it was all as he remembered, snatching his breath, skittering his heart, and pooling heated desire in his loins. His cock throbbed and twitched with eagerness.

Moaning, she shoved him back, breaking their kiss. She tugged on his Questa uniform, tossing his Glock onto the couch, followed by his coat and shirt. With his chest bare, she stilled, trailing a feathering touch over each tatt.

"You're keeping these." She leaned in to press her lips to the leopard over his left nipple.

He lifted Hux into his arms, crushing her against him, one arm around her waist, another under her ass. She wrapped her legs around his hips, and he carried her to the bedroom.

"Yes, ma'am." He chuckled. "I'll call Nate in the morning."

Date: 2170.19.10
The Colony
Gibs's apartment

GIBS STROLLED IN TO find his mom sprawled on a leather couch that wasn't his. Someone had transformed his home into Master's office. Screens lined one wall. The desk was to the rear, closer to his refitted kitchen, now sporting a deluxe coffee machine he wasn't friends with.

The soft susurration of waves and the hum of the pump told him what awaited him in his bedroom. What the frack?

"Mom?" He pulled his blaster from its holster and worked the apartment, checking for intruders. She still hadn't stirred by the time he returned to the lounge, a large snoring lump on the couch. He sighed and started on the coffee. Might as well use it. In the frosted glass of his new cabinets, packets upon packets of imported coffee beans had excitement exploding in his chest. This was insane. Why would Schneider do this?

On his desk rested a stack of data tablets, and he flicked through them. Cases Schneider wanted solved? Alongside them were digital business cards featuring Gibs as a private eye. He frowned. What if Montgomery heard about this? Moonlighting wasn't tolerated in any industry.

"Captain Montgomery." He addressed the screens, taking a long draw from his coffee as he wanted for the call to connect.

Mom mumbled from beneath the blankets. He grinned, imagining her standing in the middle of his call to the captain, hopefully not naked.

"Shaw, I'm glad you called." Montgomery grinned. "I wanted to ask you for Tamara's hand in marriage."

Gibs choked on a sip of coffee. "Me?"

"I'm old school that way, and if I marry my top detective's ex-wife, I sure as hell don't want it impacting our work lives." Montgomery fidgeted with his collar, his fingers trembling.

Top detective? One high-priority case solved, and he was Montgomery's favorite? "If she agrees to your proposal, then I can say, without any doubt, she got the better man, sir."

Montgomery's smile was slow to form, but when it did, it dominated his face. Gibs had never seen him this happy.

"Is that a yes?" Montgomery shoved his face into his holo-wrist.

Gibs nodded. "Congratulations, Captain."

His roar disturbed Mom who rolled over. The image on the screen went wild as the captain danced around his desk.

Gibs cleared his throat, trying to draw his attention. "The reason for my call is my apartment."

The jerking stopped, and the screen filled with a red-faced Montgomery. "What about it?"

"Schneider...the new Master of Shadows, has set it up...and set *me* up as a private eye. If you hear anything, it isn't me moonlighting. I'll take care of it."

Montgomery frowned. "Why would he do this?"

"There's a stack of unsolved cases on my new desk. I suspect he wants closure."

"Mm." Montgomery paced, his back-and-forth motion churning Gibs's stomach. "This might be a way to leverage your success. See it as undercover work, Gibs. Solve the cases and any others sent your way, but keep the Center in the loop."

"But...Huxley and I...with Davis..." He bit his lip, stilling his rambling.

"You can't have a partner you're dating, Gibs. You know the rules, and besides, she'll be available should you need her." Montgomery beamed, too joyful to contain it. "The Center's resources are at your disposal. I'll notify payroll to adjust your salary in accordance with undercover work." He ended the call.

Frack. Gibs texted Huxley to come over; perhaps they could decide if he should or shouldn't accept this change in his circumstances. Look at him, consulting the love of his life? Heat radiated from his heart outward. Soon, he'd tell her how he felt about her.

"You should take it," Mom said, sitting up. Her hair was everywhere as if she'd taken to tazing herself before bedtime. She still wore the dress from last night, the rumpled garment preferable to her prancing around naked. Ah, the childhood memories that couldn't be removed, not without extensive therapy or a lobotomy.

"And owe the new Master of Shadows?" Gibs waved his cup at her.

"Please. So, iron out the contract before accepting." She folded the blankets and draped them over the back of the couch. "It's time I left." She accepted the offered coffee and sat on the edge of the couch, cradling the cup in her hands.

"You can stay as long as you want, Mom." Somehow, her leaving had an ache squeezing his lungs. It had been wonderful to see her. "You could be my receptionist, or we can—"

"Oh, Gibson, you've always had the biggest heart." She raised shimmering eyes to the ceiling as she sucked in a shuddering breath. "But I'll be bored to tears, and you know it."

He did know it, but without her, arresting Mastrantonio might have gone another direction. She'd saved lives, and she didn't realize it.

"I'll take the off-world shuttle at six; oh, and invite me to your wedding," she said, placing her coffee on the table and disappearing into his room.

Gibs slumped into his chair behind the desk, testing its swivel and tilt. Once he ran it past Hux, it looked like he'd be in business for himself, with double the paycheck and three times the freedom.

Tapping the closest tablet with a fingertip, he slid it across the desk, then activated it. Tingles skittered down his neck as he read the details. A child-kidnapping syndicate in Nova? With ties to Dad's last case?

He was in.

About the Author

Sevannah Storm is a fiction writer who immerses herself in fantastical worlds both magical and science fiction. She has a flare for the creative, having studied art and interior architecture, and spends her time drawing, oil painting, and writing. An avid reader from an early age, Sevannah finds her inspiration from various sources: games, novels, music, and the land of make-believe. The unique versus the practical has brought on numerous debates.

In her spare time, she does Pilates and rereads novels that snatch her breath away. Having embraced the social media world, you can find her on most platforms.

Her home is a land south of Wakanda, where animals roam free. Born in Zimbabwe, she grew up in South Africa. The crisp blue skies with cotton-candy sunsets expand her heart and soul, encapsulating a sense of freedom.

Words she lives by: "Know your pothole and dodge it. Don't work in a pencil factory if you're a vampire."

Sevannah loves to hear from her readers. You can find and connect with her at the links below.

Website/Newsletter:

https://www.sevannahstorm.com/

Facebook:

https://www.facebook.com/sevannah.storm

Instagram:

https://www.instagram.com/sevannah.storm/

Twitter:

https://twitter.com/sevannah_storm

Thank you for taking the time to read *Inkoded*. If you enjoyed the story, please tell your friends and leave a review. Reviews support authors and ensure they continue to bring readers books to love and enjoy.

www.ingramcontent.com/pod-product-compliance
Lightning Source LLC
Chambersburg PA
CBHW070546120726
47909CB00007B/2252